Changing Teams

Changing Teams, Book One

Jennifer Allis Provost

Changing Teams

First Print Edition: November 2015

Limitless Publishing, LLC
Kailua, HI 96734
www.limitlesspublishing.com

Formatting: Limitless Publishing

ISBN-13: 978-1-68058-353-3
ISBN-10: 1-68058-353-0

Dedication

For anyone who has felt trapped by their past.
Life is how you change it.

Chapter One

Britt

"So, how much cleavage?"

I blinked. "Um, what are you talking about?"

"Cleavage. Boobage. The girls." Sam nodded toward my breasts. "How much are you comfortable showing?"

The question was a valid one, being that I'd been hired as the cover model for a romance novel and was standing in costume at said novel's photo shoot. Since the story was set in the eighteenth century, my costume consisted of miles and miles of rich ochre silk and frothy white lace; as gowns went, it weighed a ton. It came equipped with a set of underpinnings that resembled torture devices more than garments, including a corset that pushed my breasts almost up to my chin.

Since I couldn't resist flirting with the cute boy, I gave Sam my slyest grin. "Well, it is a bodice ripper, isn't it?"

Sam threw back his head and laughed. He was

the superhot assistant to Nash Williams, currently the hottest photographer in New York City, and we'd been teasing each other with abandon since we'd met earlier that day. "That it is, darlin'."

I glanced down at my already overflowing cleavage. "Aren't I showing enough already?"

"C'mere, darlin'," Sam said. "Let me, the master of fluffers, fluff your breasts to perfection." I stepped closer, letting Sam straighten the side seams of my bodice, then he tugged at the lace edging. "We have a few options here, darlin', and it all depends on how daring you'd like to be."

I could do daring. "And those options are?"

"We can keep the lace edging right here," Sam said, running his index finger along the top edge of the silk but below the lacy ruffles. "It's a good, sexy look. Or, we could place this seam right below your nips."

"Below?" I repeated. "What is this, porn?"

He waved my concern away. "Please, a nipple or two hardly constitutes porn. Turn around and face the mirror, and let me show you what I mean."

Eyeing him dubiously, I turned toward the full-length mirror. Sam stood behind me and began his demonstration by pushing my breasts together to deepen my cleavage. Since I'd been modeling for years I was no stranger to nudity, or having my body and clothing adjusted rather intimately by someone I'd just met, but I'd never had someone that looked like Sam doing the adjusting. He was well over six feet tall, with broad shoulders and thick quads that bespoke a muscular frame, and had this sexy accent that I couldn't quite place;

Southern, maybe? His dark hair was boyishly tousled, his blue eyes were piercing, and that devilish, lopsided smile of his completed a rather attractive package.

Too bad he was gay. Also of note: that gay man was lowering my bodice way past my nipples.

"Hey," I said, trying to squirm away.

Sam clamped a strong hand on my hip, and nodded toward the mirror, "Have a look, darlin'."

I did, and saw that while the gown's upper edge was indeed resting just below my nipples, the lacy ruffles still covered most of my breast. I'd worried such a low neckline would make me look sleazy, but this was more like decadent elegance.

"Wow," I said. "That does take it to the next level."

"Sure does." Sam grinned. "Best of all, anyone looking straight at you won't even see your cute little nips."

I smirked at his reflection. "But anyone standing over me, like you, gets a show." Seriously, anyone taller than me would be treated to a full view of my naked breasts. It was like they were sitting out on a platter.

Sam nestled my hips against his, cupping my breasts as he adjusted them further. "Don't worry about me, darlin'. You don't have the equipment I'm after."

"Then why do you keep touching me?"

"Hey now, it's my job to make you look good. Not that you weren't gorgeous to begin with," he added. Sam's hands left my breasts as he focused his attention on my hair, which had been looped and curled into a rather fussy up-do. "Now, if you're being ravished by our hero, I imagine a few of these pins would have come loose," he said, freeing a few tendrils to float around my shoulders. "That's better, softens up your look a bit."

"Who's this hero going to be?" I asked, meaning the other model for the shoot. As if on cue a door opened behind us, and Sam and I watched in the mirror as a fortyish man entered the studio. My counterpart for the shoot was almost as tall as Sam, but he had shoulder length blond hair and wasn't half as muscular. He was wearing a gentleman's version of formal eighteenth century dress, complete with frilled cuffs and a frock coat. He strode directly to the cyc wall, with three assistants—who needs *three* assistants? The queen of frickin' England?—following close behind. Then, he unbuttoned his coat and shirt and one of the assistants started rubbing something on his chest.

"Are they oiling him?" I looked up at Sam. "Really, *oiling*? Is he pretending to be a romance novel sex god or something?"

Sam snorted. "Giovanni wishes he was a sex god. I've seen him naked at more than one shoot, and I happen to know that his cock bears an uncanny resemblance to an uncooked French fry."

I laughed out loud, the force of which sent my left boob popping free of my corset. "Maybe we should keep my nipples covered."

"Nah, let's give ol' Gio a run for his money." Sam turned me around, then he set to work on my bodice. "I mean it, you really do have great breasts," he said as he wrestled my breast back inside my gown, pinching my nipple in the process. I wondered if that was accidental. "Nash has this ongoing harem girl series; you should audition for it."

I stared at Sam, unsure how I felt about the hot gay guy telling me I should sign up for a bunch of topless photos, not to mention all the fondling. "If you keep it up with the cupping and pinching, I'm going to cup and pinch something of my own," I warned.

"I love it when you tease me, baby." Sam extended his arm and I tucked my hand into his elbow. As we crossed the set toward Giovanni, Sam whispered in my ear, "Now darlin', you need to keep your nips up," he advised. "If you let them go flat, your dress will slip and it'll ruin the look."

"I can't exactly control my nipples," I said, wondering if men were capable of exerting some sort of influence over their mammary glands that women just couldn't mimic.

"Don't worry, darlin', if they go down I'll just come after you with an ice cube." When my eyes widened at his threat, Sam laughed and gave me a gentle push toward the cyc wall. "Now, don't you fret over a bit of ice. Just get over there and be beautiful."

I tried glaring at Sam, but his infectious grin won me over. "You come after me with ice and I'll retaliate in kind."

"I've no doubt you will, darlin'."

***

The photo shoot hadn't exactly gone as planned, and it was only partially the fault of my breasts. Since Giovanni was taller and therefore looking down at me, he was treated to the full view of my cleavage. As it turned out Giovanni was a breast man, and decided to enhance his already extensive view of my assets by dipping me backward until my breasts popped all the way out of my gown. Ever the gentleman, Giovanni then sought to conceal my wardrobe malfunction by hauling me upright and pressing my breasts against his oily chest.

A world of yuck.

Chivalry notwithstanding, that move left my skin and the bodice of my gown covered with greasy stains. What the hell had he spread across his chest, rendered bear fat? Since the only available period gown was now ruined, the photographer, Nash, ended up positioning me so that my back was to the camera, my face in profile as Giovanni speared me with his sultry gaze; Giovanni's description, not mine. Of course, Giovanni's oily chest remained in full view.

Despite the mishaps we had, the final images were breathtaking. For all my griping, Giovanni really could turn on the smolder, and the uber-tight gown showcased my waist and back. All in all, Giovanni and I could pull off a cover.

"You've got a great look," Nash said as he signed some paperwork so I could collect my fee. "I'd like to use you in a few other projects—if you're free, that is."

For the three hundred dollar fee he offered, boy was I ever. "Sam mentioned you had a harem-themed series going?"

Nash smiled. "Did he, now? Yes, I do have that series in the works. Do you have a comp card?"

"I do," I replied, grabbing one from my bag. It featured a rather sexy shot of me on the front, with the reverse listing my measurements, eye color, shoe size, and other fascinating things about me.

"I'll call."

With that, Nash gave me a courtly nod and went off to deal with whatever photographers deal with after a shoot wraps up. As for me, I handed in my paperwork to the accountant, then I headed home to my studio apartment, intent on washing off Giovanni's oily residue. I hoped it wouldn't make my chest break out. That, I did not need.

Chapter Two

Sam

After the cover shoot wrapped and most everyone else had gone home, I puttered around the studio seeing to things that both were and were not part of my job description. While Nash employed several individuals who were perfectly capable of making sure that models were booked and sets and costumes were available, I didn't mind handling those tasks myself. What I did mind was the chance that one of those tasks wouldn't be completed, and the subsequent delays we'd suffer.

There was also the fact that I was soaking up information like a sponge, and fully planned to use every last detail when I opened up my own studio. I'd come to New York intent on being a photographer, not some other photographer's assistant, and my pride had taken a hefty blow when I accepted Nash's offer of employment. The common sense portion of my brain had recognized the opportunity for what it was, so I shelved my dreams for a time and made myself indispensable to the fashion scene's current favorite photographer. In another year or so, I would open my own studio and take the city by storm, not to mention take Nash's place.

As I made my final circuit of the studio proper, I spied a woman's denim jacket flung across the back of a chair. Since I didn't recognize the jacket as belonging to one of our employees, and that we'd only had a few for-hire individuals on site, I deduced that the garment was owned by one Britt Sullivan, the lovely young thing who'd stood for the cover.

No, calling Britt lovely was an understatement. When she'd shown up at the shoot wearing skinny jeans, black cowboy boots, and a slouchy gray and black off the shoulder tee, I couldn't help but notice her. She had long, light brown hair with just enough wave, clear honey brown eyes, and curvy hips that I wanted to grab hold of and never let go. If we'd been back home in Iowa, all the local jocks would have been vying for her, enticing her with pop and cotton candy, and winning her musty stuffed animals at the local fair. Thank God we weren't in Iowa.

I managed to play it cool when Nash introduced me to Britt, and I'd even flirted a bit with the new model. Then Britt put on her costume for the shoot, an eighteenth century gown made of a tawny silk that paled next to her rich, almost golden hair, and I nearly lost it. I'd been an artist and photographer for years, and worked with many models garbed in sumptuous costumes as well as nude, but none of them had ever taken my breath away.

What the hell was wrong with me, getting all worked up over a woman?

I shook my head, clearing all those unsuitable thoughts from my mind, and picked up the jacket. It wasn't remarkable in any way, just a generic cotton garment from a department store chain, but it held my attention nonetheless. After I stared at it for a few seconds, I went to my laptop and looked up Britt's number. I was punching it into my phone less than a minute later.

"Hello?"

"Is this Britt Sullivan?" I asked.

"It is," she replied. "Who am I talking to?"

"This is Sam MacKellar, Nash's assistant," I explained. "I believe you left your jacket at my studio."

"Oh! I'm so glad you found it. I'm sorry, I don't usually leave things behind."

"No worries," I said. "I can deliver it to you, if you'd like. Are you near the studio?"

"I'm a few blocks away."

I glanced at the time on my laptop; it was just before six. "Want to meet up at Catalonia at seven?" I asked. "It's that new tapas place."

"Is that the one with the raw bar?"

"I believe so."

"All right, Sam MacKellar, it's a date."

With that Britt ended the call, and I stared at the phone in my hand. Had I really just asked a girl out on a date? Well, the lady was mistaken because this event was not a date. This was a jacket-returning, nothing more.

I left the studio and swung by my apartment to change my shirt; just because I was going out on a not-date didn't mean I couldn't look good. After I'd exchanged my black tee for a dark purple one and swapped my black Chucks for my favorite Doc Martins, I headed on over to Catalonia.

I found Britt seated at the bar, sipping a glass of red wine. She was wearing the same slouchy gray and black striped tee and skinny jeans from earlier, her long hair pulled forward over her shoulder. Since she wasn't wearing her jacket I saw that the back of her shirt had a low neckline, exposing her to below her shoulder blades. I'd never known that a woman's back could be so beguiling.

"Your jacket, darlin'," I said, presenting her the garment as I claimed the chair next to her.

"Thank you," she said, draping the jacket across the back of her chair. "I hope you don't mind, but I ordered for you."

"Ordered what for me?" I asked, then the bartender set a pint of beer before me. He glanced at Britt and winked at me before wandering back down the bar; wow, did he ever have the wrong idea. Seemed like everyone did except me. "No wine for me?"

"You strike me as more of a beer guy." Britt eyed my shirt. "I see you changed. Sort of."

"Sort of?" I shot back, then that nosy bartender returned with a plate of raw oysters and another set of winks. He deposited a rack of various sauces and lemon wedges before us a moment later. "Did you order us half the place?"

"You have to get oysters at happy hour," Britt

you showing up for a shoot with puffy eyes."

"Oh, I'm not modeling tomorrow," she said. "But you probably have work."

"That I do."

The bartender took my card and the check, and Britt frowned. "Did you just pay for the whole thing?"

"Seems that way," I replied. Since Britt had arrived with the intention of eating dollar oysters and sipping four dollar glasses of Merlot, I couldn't expect her to foot the bill for the culinary adventure I'd taken her on. "Take care of the tip, if you like."

She scowled at me, then she fished in her purse and dropped a twenty on the bar. "You really didn't have to do that."

"Where I come from, a gentleman pays the bill."

She laughed shortly. "Yeah, well, it's not like we're on a date."

Okay, that comment stung. I knew Britt wasn't trying to be hurtful, and she was right, this was not a date. However, when she said it out loud it made me realize how much I wanted to be on a date with her. I wanted it a lot.

God, why did I want this woman so much? Had I taken a blow to the head?

The bartender brought me my receipt, and I scrawled my name on the dotted line. I also added an extra twenty to the tip. Yeah, maybe we'd gotten a bit too extravagant with all that seafood. The bill thus settled, I stood and Britt followed suit.

"Which way to your place?" I asked once we were outside the restaurant.

"Seeing me home?" she asked, batting her

eyelashes at me. "You really are a gentleman, aren't you?"

"My momma raised me right," I said. "If she, or my gran, had the slightest notion I hadn't walked a lady home, they'd tan my hide but good."

"Even now?"

"Especially now, since I'm old enough to know better."

Britt looped her arm with mine, and we headed down the sidewalk. "Well, I'd hate for you to get in trouble on my account. Come on, it's this way."

A block and a half later found us standing in front of an apartment building. "This is it," Britt said, then she stood on her toes and kissed my cheek.

"What was that for?" I asked.

"For bringing me my jacket, for buying dinner," she replied. "And for hanging out with me. I know you must be busy."

"I'm not that busy," I said, "but you're very welcome."

Britt smiled, then she petted my cheek. "And let your beard grow in, will you? This stubble's all scratchy."

"Yeah, we wouldn't want you getting beard burn on your lips."

"That would be awful."

We stood there grinning at each other, only stopping when a passing pedestrian sneered that we should get a room. "Well, upstairs with you," I said, jerking my chin toward the door. "Get some rest, young lady."

"Yes, sir," Britt said. "Night, Sam."

full of friendly people, and some of them let me keep the clothing I'd modeled. I was particularly excited about a catalog shoot booked for the upcoming week that would feature winter gear; in addition to my sitting fee, I hoped I would score a sweater or two.

Maybe it was because I had winter on the brain, but my painting that day turned out icy blue, like the heart of a glacier. Blue like the eyes of a certain photographer's assistant, along with some dark slashes that matched his scruffy, scratchy beard…

I shoved those thoughts away. I was in the midst of a dry spell of epic proportions, that much was true, but fantasizing about a gay man was just lame. Wicked lame, as my mom would say. Then again, she'd married my stepfather, which made her opinion of the opposite sex questionable at best.

My phone squawked, so I wiped off my hands and picked it up. I checked the display and found a text from my best friend and fellow model, Astrid:

Astrid: Free tonight? I thought I'd treat NYC to one of my legendary Thursday night parties.

I laughed; the only thing legendary about Astrid's parties was that she kept having them. After I replied that I'd be there around nine, I set my painting aside to dry, laced up my sneakers, and went for a walk.

Later on, after I'd showered and dressed myself in skinny jeans, a dark chiffon peasant blouse, and a pair of strappy flat sandals I'd scored from a recent shoot, I headed over to Astrid's party. She only lived a block away from me, but her place was about four times the size of mine. Astrid was a sought-after model, and didn't have to work as the occasional life subject at one of the local art museums to make rent like I did. Hopefully, if Nash called me for a few more sessions, I'd have some more images to add to my portfolio, and be well on my way to scoring gigs that paid as well as Astrid's. Who was I kidding? I'd settle for more gigs that let me take the props home.

I walked up the three flights to Astrid's, then I knocked on the reinforced steel door. The small town girl inside my New Yorker shell was amazed at the amount of money people would pay to live in a repurposed slaughter house.

"Well, hello there," Astrid greeted, looking me up and down as she opened her door. "Aren't you a sexy thing?"

"You know it," I said. Astrid, an expert at channeling the sixties, was wearing a floor length caftan in a knockoff Pucci print. At least I assumed it was a knockoff; if that was the real deal Astrid was wearing the equivalent of a month's rent—rent on her place, that is. She'd teased and then smoothed her dark hair into a perfect bump, and her green eyes sparkled. Completing her look was a wide white headband and platform espadrilles.

"Really, Britt, you have got to play up your hair," Astrid said as I stepped inside her apartment. "You have length and waves other girls would die for, and you just let it hang off your head."

"Maybe I'm going for the peasant vibe." I looked around her apartment; there were at least twenty

I figured out how to make a living via my art, modeling was paying the bills, and the good jobs never went to wallflowers.

What no one mentioned about socializing was that all that smiling and being polite was hard work. About an hour after midnight I wandered over to Astrid's couch and flopped down, exhausted. Despite my best efforts at looking unapproachable, I wasn't alone for long.

Sam strode up to me, hiding both of his hands behind his back. "Brought you a present," he said, swaying a bit.

"Oh? What sort of present?"

Sam brought his hands forward, revealing a glass of red wine in each. He offered one to me and said, "You looked thirsty."

"How did you know I only drink red?" I wondered aloud.

"All the pretty girls drink red," Sam demurred. "And you only drank red at Catalonia."

"Aren't you the detective," I said as I accepted the glass. It was my fourth glass of wine, but hey, it was a party. Drinking too much was something of a requirement, especially at Astrid's soirees. "Thank you. Want to sit?" I asked, indicating the cushion next to me.

"Surely." Sam plopped down beside me and drank from his own glass. "I meant what I said earlier. I really didn't think I'd get to see you again so soon."

"Yeah, all that shellfish definitely got to you."

"Tease," he said. "I mean, I thought about calling you. I was thinking about calling you as soon as you were inside your place last night. I was actually going to call this afternoon and ask if you'd come to this party with me, but I chickened out."

I laughed, mostly to overcome the awkwardness of the drunk gay man saying he wanted me to be his party date. Was I exuding desperate pheromones or something? If that was the case I was on track to win Ms. Pathetic Girl of NYC, Manhattan Borough. "Well, I'm here and you're here, so the universe worked it out for us. " I eyed his near-empty wineglass and asked, "How many of those have you had?"

"Wine? This is the first." He drained his glass. "However, there were the beers back at Michael's, and the tequila shots we did earlier—"

"What? How many beers did you have? No, tell me how many shots?"

At least he had the decency to look ashamed. "Five, maybe six. Seven? Were they all tequila?" Sam thought for a moment. "Yep, just tequila. And I'm pretty sure there were just six. Or seven."

He'd had enough booze to knock out a Clydesdale. "How are you still conscious?"

Sam gave me a sly gaze. "I have an indomitable will, darlin'," he slurred, slumping toward me.

"That's it, I'm getting you out of here." I set our glasses on the coffee table and hauled Sam to his feet, which wasn't easy being that he was half a foot taller than me and a great deal heavier.

"But the party," Sam protested, swaying in the alcoholic breeze only he could feel.

"Is over." I slid my arm around his waist and guided him toward the door. "At least, it is for you."

"Where are you two going?" Astrid asked as Sam and I hobbled toward the door like the world's lamest three-legged racers.

"Sam's wasted," I explained. "I'm going to get him downstairs, put him in a cab."

With that, I steered Sam out of Astrid's apartment and toward the elevator; in his current state stairs were a bit beyond his drunk ass. After we stood on the curb for about twenty minutes with no cabs in sight, I changed plans.

"Stupid nonexistent cabs," I muttered. "Come on, you can sleep it off on my couch," I said, grabbing his arm and dragging him toward my building. "My place is just down the street."

"Taking me back to your place?" Sam inquired with that grin of his. "Trying to get me to change teams, darlin'?"

"You wish," I snapped.

I endured more of Sam's teasing, and his hand in the back pocket of my jeans, for the rest of our walk. Once we were inside my apartment, I gave him a tour of the important features.

"There's the couch, bathroom, and refrigerator," I said, pointing at each in turn. "Need anything? Water, aspirin, perhaps a lecture on temperance?"

"I'm good," Sam replied, then he flopped face first onto the couch.

Having seen to my guest, I grabbed a tank top and fresh panties from my dresser, then went to the bathroom to wash up and change. Not five minutes later, I was snuggled up in bed. Not a minute after that a drunk man slipped under the blankets beside me.

"Hope you don't mind sharing space with me, darlin'," Sam murmured. "I was cold."

"I would have gotten you a blanket." He put his cold toes on my calf and I yelped, kicking him away.

"Aww, baby, am I not welcome?" Before I could reply, Sam slipped his hands around my waist, bringing my back flat against his chest. "You're so warm and soft," he said, and I felt his hard cock pressing against my butt.

"I-I thought you were gay," I said, wondering who I'd let into my apartment.

"I thought so too," he said thoughtfully. Sam slid his hand up from my waist, cupping my breast and rolling my nipple between his thumb and forefinger. "Must be your cute nips."

"Must be all the booze you had," I retorted, noting how my voice wavered. I'd had more than my fair share of alcohol as well, and man did he feel good in my bed. More than that, Sam was funny and easy to talk to, and I'd enjoyed his company both at the party and last night at the tapas bar. And there was the not so small fact that he was gorgeous.

And gay. Let's not forget the gay part.

I rolled over and looked him in the eye. "So, what's all this about? Are you telling me you want to mess around?"

Sam smiled an evil smile that turned my insides to jelly. "I do believe some messing around is in order," he replied, settling his hands on my hips.

"Don't you think you'll regret this?"

"What? This?" he asked, sliding his hands down to my butt.

"Yeah. That."

He squeezed. "Only if you will."

I looked at him, taking in his strong jaw and piercing blue eyes, and figured a little fun wouldn't hurt. "I guess we can always blame whatever happens on the booze."

"Mmm. Booze." Sam slid his hand underneath my panties, his fingertips drawing tiny circles on my skin.

"Ever kiss a girl?" I asked, pressing my hand against his chest; his heart was pounding, just like mine was.

Sam snorted—wicked sexy—then he closed his mouth over mine. His mouth was hot and demanding, his tongue moving expertly against mine. And yeah, he tasted faintly of tequila.

That kiss was like nothing I'd ever experienced. Sam lit me up from the roots of my hair to the tips of my toes, set every nerve in my body on fire. Sam's hands were all over me, caressing me from my back to my thighs, and his bare feet stroked my calves. It was a full body kiss in every sense of the term. I have no idea how long that kiss lasted, whether it was a second or a minute or an hour. All I knew was that I wanted more.

"Do all gay men kiss like you?" I gasped when we parted.

"Not hardly," he said, his hand traveling from my butt up to my breasts. "No more than all breasts are as beautiful as yours."

He started in with the fondling again, so I thought it was time to set some ground rules. "Let me explain something about the female anatomy to you," I said, ruffling my fingers through the dark hair at the nape of his neck. "When you touch a woman's breasts, especially her nipples, it tends to arouse her a great deal."

"Really," he said, arching a dark brow. "What about yesterday, at the shoot?"

"After your fluffing I was so horny Giovanni almost looked good."

Sam laughed, pressing his forehead against mine. "And now?"

"Maybe I'm a little excited," I said, fluttering my lashes. We laughed together, then Sam kissed me again while his fingers caressed their way down my abdomen. When he paused to circle my navel I grabbed his wrist and warned, "Go any lower and I'm going for your cock."

"Promises, promises. Just remember, I get to grab you wherever you grab me."

"And vice versa?"

"Vice versa." He slid his fingertips under the top edge my panties, stroking me almost to my clit. "You're really smooth. Silky, almost. Shave?"

"Wax," I replied. Only a gay man would interrupt making out for a discussion on depilation techniques. "Keeps you smoother longer." I undid the top button on Sam's jeans, then I pulled down his zipper. We stared at each other for a moment, each daring the other, then I finally had enough and shoved my hand inside his boxers. His cock was hot in my hand, so wide at the base I almost couldn't get my fingers around it.

"You're frickin' huge," I said, shoving aside the blankets for a better look. The gay man in my bed had the most perfect cock I'd ever seen in real life. "Are your balls big too?"

Sam got himself out of his jeans, then he pulled the waistband of his boxers down below his balls. Yeah, they were nice too.

"Great package," I said, palming the heavy weight of his balls. "I bet all the boys like it."

Sam ignored my teasing. "I believe I'm owed something."

I shivered, deliciously aware of what he was owed as Sam nudged me onto my back. I kept hold of his cock, rubbing my thumb against the base of his shaft as he slid his hand inside the front of my panties. He brushed his fingers up and down the front of me a few times before venturing lower. The way he tentatively rubbed my most intimate place was enough to melt me.

"Am I being too rough?" he asked when I gasped.

"No," I replied, pressing my hips against his hand. "Perfect."

Sam chuckled, his deep voice rumbling across me. "Good," he said, his mouth moving across my jaw. "May I look at you?" he asked.

"Yes," I breathed.

Sam rose up on his knees and peeled off my panties, leaving me in nothing but my thin tank top. Sam looked at me for a moment, then he stripped off his boxers, dropping them on the floor as he straddled my thighs.

"Sorry about yesterday," he said, one of his hands massaging my pussy while the other fisted his cock. "Making you all horny like that."

"It's okay," I said, rotating my hips under his hand. "Felt kind of good, you know?"

"I do." He stroked me for another moment, then said, "Well, show me how you work one of these."

I blinked. "What?"

"You're horny, I'm horny," Sam said, rubbing his cock with long, slow strokes. "Let's get off." He leaned closer and said, "Show me how you get off."

The boozy voice in my head drowned out the rational part of my brain as it pointed out what a bad idea this was. "Are you going to get off with me?"

He pointed his cock at me. "Race you to the finish line."

"It's on."

Sam grinned, then he straightened his back, hand motionless on his shaft. What a gentleman, he was waiting for me. I licked my fingertips, then I pressed my middle and ring fingers against my clit and rubbed, slowly at first, but my pace quickened as Sam stroked himself faster and faster. Masturbating while Sam jerked off over me was the hottest thing I'd ever done, hotter than anything I could have ever imagined, and it wasn't long before my back arched and the world shattered around me. A moment later, something hot splashed onto my belly.

"Oh, darlin', I'm sorry!"

I opened my eyes and saw Sam pulling his shirt up and over his head. Just so you know, the top half of him was just as gorgeous as the bottom half. "Let me clean you up, baby."

I stared down my body as Sam cleaned off the

evidence of his orgasm, taking a moment to dab between my thighs. Once he was done he dropped his shirt on the floor by his jeans, then he knelt and took me in his arms.

"Crap, it's on your shirt too," he said, then he whipped my tank top right over my head. It was only after he tossed it aside he asked, "Oh, do you mind being naked with me?"

As if me not wearing a shirt really mattered at that point. "Come here," I said, holding out my arms. Sam let me wrap myself around him, and we held each other as we drifted off to sleep.

Chapter Four

Sam

Before I opened my eyes, I knew that two things were wrong. For one, I was in a bed that wasn't mine. Too soft, too comfortable, and the sheets and blankets smelled like lavender. I adored the scent of lavender, but I'd never once rubbed tiny purple flowers on my bedding. I'm just not that gay.

That scent of lavender brought me to my second problem: the woman who owned the bed I was currently lying in was snuggled up against me, naked as a jaybird, and damn it all if I didn't like being in that bed with her. I had no idea what sort of insanity had come over me. I had a nice life here in New York, with cool friends and a budding career, as far removed from my past as I could get. The last thing on my mind had been lolling about in bed with one of Nash's models, male or female. Then two days ago, I met Britt Sullivan.

I hadn't been kidding when I told her I'd wanted to call her after the tapas bar and spend the night talking to her, or about wanting to bring her to Astrid's party. Then, in the ultimate act of serendipity, Britt had strutted right into the party looking like the sexy Bohemian goddess she was. After introducing Britt to the boys, I downed shot after shot of liquid courage while I tried to get up the nerve to talk to her. By the time I found her alone I was out of my mind drunk, but Britt didn't mind me sloppy. She hadn't minded when I crawled into bed beside her, either.

And there was what happened afterward. If I hadn't been so embarrassed over coming on Britt's stomach, I'd have called last night the best sexual experience of my life. Maybe I could get myself a replay that didn't involve so much mopping up.

Since Britt was still asleep, I took a minute to look around her apartment. It was a small studio—cluttered, but it was a good sort of clutter. One corner held the kitchen, two others the couch and the bed we were nestled in. What interested me the most was the wall between the bed and couch, which contained a table heaped high with canvases and brushes and tubes of paint.

Good God, Britt was an artist. And if the canvases propped up against the wall were her work, she was a damn good one. All that magnificent art multiplied the desire I'd already felt for her by ten. No, a thousand. A million, maybe.

I kissed Britt's hair, and realized that for all that was good in that room a third thing was wrong: while I'd slept in Britt's bed, I hadn't had any nightmares. Some pretty terrible stuff had happened to me when I was a kid, and I had the misfortune of reliving those events whenever I closed my eyes. It made intimacy hard for me. I'd hardly ever been close with a man, much less a woman. Not only had my nightmares forgotten to pay me their nightly visit, lying there in bed with Britt felt more right than anything I'd ever known.

Britt stirred to wakefulness, shifting her hips against me in a way that reinforced the rightness of the situation, then she raised her head and kissed me full on the mouth. "You suck at being gay," she said against my lips.

I grinned, because it was true. "I thought we were blaming last night on the booze."

"Mmm. Booze." Britt stretched next to me, then wrapped her arms and legs around me like an octopus. Maybe that's why she won't eat them, because they're her kin. "You were pretty drunk, and we didn't really do anything."

With my forefinger, I tilted her chin up so she faced me. "Excuse me, darlin'? I may have been drunk, but I recall many, many things that were done."

"Not really. We made out a bit, then we got ourselves off. Without penetration, it was just drunk groping." She leaned forward and kissed my nose. "Don't worry, Sam, your virtue's safe with me."

If I had any more virtue, my balls would be cadmium blue. "Britt," I murmured, my hand coming to rest on the curve of her bottom. "Short for Britney?"

"Not hardly." When I kept looking at her, she elaborated, "I'll tell you, but you have to promise not to laugh."

watched her for a moment, wetting her hair, reaching for the shampoo, and it was like the last thirteen years hadn't happened. I was just a man, Britt was just a woman…

My cock twitched, reminding what a bad idea all of this was.

"Get down," I hissed, turning my back to the shower. I wanted to step under that spray with Britt more than anything, but going in at half-mast would just spell disaster.

"Sam?" Britt called. "Everything okay?"

"Yeah," I said. "Just looking around, poking through your stuff."

She laughed. "Stop being a creep and get under the water while it's still hot. I swear, this building has a water heater the size of a can of Coke."

I grinned—had I ever grinned so much?—and stepped into the tub just as Britt was rinsing the shampoo from her hair. She blindly reached for the conditioner, but I snatched the bottle from her hand.

"You put this garbage on your hair?" I demanded. It was generic drugstore conditioner, nowhere near worthy of Britt's silky waves. "What, are you *trying* to go bald?"

"Cheap conditioner has never made anyone lose their hair," she said. "It works just fine."

"I know what I'm getting you for Christmas," I muttered as I opened the bottle and poured a palmful into my hand. With stuff this terrible, the standard quarter-sized application just wouldn't do. I massaged the creamy liquid into Britt's hair, drawing the long strands through my fingers. If I could concentrate on her hair, maybe I could forget about the rest of her.

Just as I had that thought, Britt turned around and faced me. "Now, I know you're gay," she said, pouting.

"Proper hair care is what designates one as gay?"

"No, the fact that I'm standing here naked and you're more interested in my brand of conditioner than me."

I glanced down at Britt's face, worried that I'd upset her, but found her wearing a shit-eating grin. "Don't you worry, darlin', you're still the second hottest girl here," I said, then I gave her breast a tweak with my slippery fingers. Before I did anything stupid—well, more stupid than what I'd already done—I backed her under the spray and rinsed her hair.

"Listen," I said, pressing my face against the top of her head as the warm water cascaded over us, "I'm sorry about last night. Real sorry. I was drunk, and I shouldn't have gotten in bed with you, and I'm sorry for—"

"Hey." Britt touched her fingers to my mouth. "It's okay. I mean, we mostly just kissed, and I like kissing."

"Do you now?" I tilted her chin upward and rubbed my thumb across her lower lip. "There's something about you, Britannica Lynn."

"My middle name isn't Lynn."

"Oh? What is it, then?"

"Janet."

"Britannica Janet doesn't exactly roll off the tongue." I draped my arms around her waist, and added, "When you're with me, you're my

Britannica Lynn."

"Am I?" she asked, arching a single brow.

"You surely are," I said, and then I kissed her. I mean, she just said how much she liked kissing, so I was doing her a favor. A kindness, really. The fact that I'd been trying to figure out how to kiss her again since she'd kissed me awake had nothing to do with it. The fact that my cock was standing up straight as a flagpole, well, that was relevant. So relevant it was scaring the shit out of me.

All at once, the hot water we'd been standing under turned Arctic. We shrieked as we broke apart, Britt fumbling at the faucet handles while I jumped out of the tub and grabbed some towels. Once Britt had the water off she fled the tub as well, and I wrapped a towel around her.

"That was fucking cold," I said through chattering teeth. At least the icy water made my cock go down.

"Like I said, hot water heater the size of a Coke can." Britt wrapped her arms around my waist and pressed her body against mine, warming us both.

"At least you got all of that vile slop out of your hair," I said, rubbing her back dry with the towel.

Britt stood on her toes and kissed my nose, the tips of her breasts brushing my chest. "Product snob." With that she freed herself, twisted her hair up in a towel and left the bathroom. I followed, and found Britt rooting around in a dresser drawer. She found what she was after and pulled on a pair of black panties. Figuring naked time was over, I picked up the heap of my clothes.

"Aww, shit," I said when I touched something

damp. I'd forgotten how I had cleaned up Britt and myself with my shirt. "It's on my frickin' boxers too."

Then Britt was standing in front of me, holding out a faded NYU shirt. "This will probably fit you," she said. "I'd offer you a pair of panties, but I don't think that would work out too well."

"Probably not." I pulled the shirt over my head; it was snug, but it would do. When my head emerged from the collar I saw Britt standing before me, her topless and me bottomless.

"Guess I'll be going commando," I said, then I pulled on my jeans. Britt scooped up my shirt and boxers and dropped them into her laundry basket. I'd have just burned the things. Once I found my shoes and socks, which were in a heap by the couch, I turned toward Britt.

"I was going to offer to buy breakfast, but you are decidedly indecent," I said. She hadn't added a single article of clothing to herself, not even a sock or an earring.

"Sorry, I'm used to being nude for work," she said. "Are you working today?"

"Yeah." I grabbed my phone from my back pocket, and swore when I saw the time. "Work starts in ten minutes. Rain check on breakfast?"

"Deal."

Britt walked me to her door, rather graciously for a girl clad in just her underwear. Once we reached it, I hesitated before opening it.

"Last night was…well, it was a lot of things," I said in a rush. "No matter what else, I hope we can be friends."

Britt stood on her toes and pressed her lips to mine. "Friends to the end," she murmured.

"I'll call you," I promised.

"You better."

Chapter Five

Sam

After leaving Britt's, I hailed a cab and headed straight to Nash's studio. I was late for work, but I'd been late plenty of times before and Nash had always been cool. Hopefully, this wouldn't be the time he blew a gasket on me.

You see, that's how it was with Nash: you were his favorite, until suddenly you weren't. Anything could be the cause of your demise, from wearing the wrong shoes to being seen with the wrong person at the wrong party, or the wrong person at the right party for that matter. The only reason Giovanni had been modeling for Nash for so long was that the lunk was so dense he didn't understand when Nash was angry with him, and he just kept coming back for more abuse.

In addition to Gio's thick skull, there was the fact that Nash had made a ton of money off of those cheesy romance covers. Nash might be vain and spiteful, but he wasn't one to look a gift horse in the mouth.

I arrived at the studio at exactly ten forty-three; late enough to cause concern, but not job termination. I hoped. When the elevator door slid open, I realized that my whereabouts was the last thing on Nash's mind.

Nash had dragged out the harem set, and two girls were draped across it wearing those glorified genie outfits he liked, incredibly tacky numbers that were nothing more than golden belts and sheer pink skirts. Only, these girls weren't any models we'd hired recently. In fact, they didn't look that far out of high school, and their vacant gazes made me wonder if they'd had vodka for breakfast.

"Sam," Nash called, striding toward me. "I didn't know you were coming in today."

"Schedule said we had a shoot this morning," I said. Nash was shirtless, and instead of his usual still camera he was recording video. Interesting. "What do you need me for?"

"Actually, this is a closed shoot," Nash said. "Why don't you take the day off, with pay?"

I glanced at the girls, then remembered something my gran had always said: not my circus, not my monkeys. "You're the boss," I said. "Call if you need me."

With that I stepped back onto the elevator, studiously not thinking about what was going on in the studio. When I stepped out onto the sidewalk I turned my face toward the sun, and wondered what I'd do with myself all day. Before I knew what my hands were doing, I grabbed my phone and sent Britt a text.

Chapter Six

Britt

As soon as Sam shut the door behind him, I went to my kitchen and started throwing together breakfast. I wish we'd been able to have breakfast together, but Sam had work and work was important. Speaking as the poorest girl on the block, I knew just how important work was.

Which is why when my phone beeped with an email alerting me to an opening for a life model at the museum's eleven o'clock art class, I immediately accepted the assignment. Putting my breakfast fixings back in the fridge, I threw on some clothes, grabbed a granola bar and bottle of water, and ran out the door. The gig only paid fifty dollars, but that was a heck of a lot better than no dollars.

I got to the museum with ten minutes to spare, and went straight to the glorified broom closet that served as my dressing room. After I'd taken off my clothes, I donned my black velour robe, took a seat, and tried to meditate. Sitting naked in front of

Yeah, but maybe I won't be alone right now.

Eventually the forty-five minute session ended, and I slipped my robe over my shoulders and fastened the sash. While the students packed up their supplies, Sam met me at the base of the dais.

"Good show, darlin'," he greeted. Lower, he added, "You do a lot of these?"

"A girl needs to pay the bills," I replied.

"Exactly how much are they paying you?" Sam demanded.

"Fifty," I replied. Sam's brow furrowed, but I ignored him as Ben approached.

"Lovely as always, Miss Sullivan," Ben said as he handed over the envelope with my sitting fee.

"Thank you," I said, stashing the envelope inside my robe pocket. "I'm surprised you let Sam join us."

"You know I wouldn't normally let a non-student attend," Ben said. "However, I could hardly say no to your boyfriend."

"Boyfriend," I repeated, giving Sam a look. "Yeah, we wouldn't want to keep my *boyfriend* waiting outside."

"Come on, darlin'," Sam drawled, "let's get you dressed. We've got that lunch date to keep."

Sam guided me out of the studio with his hand on the small of my back, then I grabbed his wrist and dragged him inside my dressing room. Once the door was shut behind us, he hissed, "Don't you know the first rule about these gigs?"

"Always demand payment in cash?" I quipped.

"No, always bring a friend." He looked at me, his brow furrowed and lips smushed into a crooked line. "Anything can happen at these places, Britt. Best have a friend nearby in case anything goes south."

"I know, but…"

Sam stepped forward, grasping my elbows. "But what?"

"I don't really have anyone to come with me," I confessed. "I mean, I'm sure Astrid would, but she has real, paying work to do. Ben's always been real chill, and the museum is close to my apartment, so whenever they need a life model I sit in if I can."

"For a measly fifty bucks?"

"That fifty bucks will buy me a week's worth of groceries," I said. "Not everyone pays as well as Nash."

Sam's frown transformed into a smile. "Then I'll just see about getting you more gigs with Nash," he said. "In the meantime, I'm coming with you to these sessions."

"Don't you have your own work with Nash?"

"I'll make time." He released me and made a twirling gesture with his hand. "Get your clothes on. Lunch is waiting."

"Why are you buying me lunch?" I asked as I turned my back and dropped my robe. "Not that I don't appreciate the offer."

"A gentleman always buys a lady lunch after spending the night with her," Sam replied. "Breakfast would have been better."

"About that," I said as I stepped into my jeans. "I thought you had work today."

"I have learned that today's shoot is a private session," Sam said, "Nash has no need of me."

It might have been my imagination, but Sam's voice seemed a bit strained. I pulled my shirt over my head, then I sat and slipped on my boots. Sam had his back to me, arms folded across his chest while he stared at the door. His butt looked pretty good in those jeans, and I remembered something from earlier that morning. "Hey, boyfriend," I said with a smirk, "still going commando?"

He glared at me over his shoulder, eyes narrowed. "Fresh," he admonished. "Come on, I'm starving. Are you in the mood for Thai?"

***

Lunch was all kinds of terrible. Thai isn't really my favorite sort of food, what with all the weird spices and abundance of fried dishes. However, it was what Sam wanted, and since he was paying I went along with it. I made the best of things and ordered a bowl of miso soup and a green salad, while Sam went for some kind of hundred-course midday feast.

"Hungry?" I asked Sam as the waiter deposited the first few plates before him.

"I haven't eaten since breakfast yesterday," Sam replied. "I was busy with the shoot, then I went straight to Michael's and on to Astrid's."

"You had all that booze on an empty stomach?" I asked. "No wonder you were crawling into a strange woman's bed."

"Hush," Sam admonished. "You were the one who decided to bring me home with you."

"Someone had to look after you." I started on my

soup, which was the hot salty goodness one would expect from a cup of miso. When my salad arrived, Sam expressed his displeasure over my selections.

"Are you really eating nothing but broth and leaves?" he demanded.

"This is what I usually eat for lunch," I replied. "I need to watch my weight, you know."

"What you need, darlin', is a healthy dose of protein." With that, Sam carved off a portion from one of the dishes before him and plopped it onto my salad. "Try that."

"What is this?" I asked, poking it dubiously.

"Fried duck, and it's amazing."

I sliced off the smallest sliver, and hesitantly placed it on my tongue. The skin was crisp perfection, while the meat was moist and succulent, almost decadent. No, it was definitely decadent. "It's okay."

"Okay?" he repeated. "No one thinks roast duck is just okay."

"I don't really like meat," I demurred.

"You'll eat a thousand kinds of shellfish, but unfamiliar poultry skeeves you out?"

I shrugged. "What can I say, I'm a pescetarian." I ate some more soup, then asked, "So tell me, Sam MacKellar, do they eat a lot of duck where you're from?"

"I'm from Iowa," Sam replied. "You know what Iowa's got? Pigs and corn."

"Pigs means there's bacon."

Sam gave me a look that made me shiver in all the places I liked to shiver. "I thought you didn't care for meat."

"Bacon is in a class of its own." I finished the duck, all the while ignoring Sam's smug grin, and asked, "What made a nice boy like you leave Iowa for the big bad city?"

"I came because the city *is* big and bad," he replied. "Everything in Iowa was so…safe. Boring." He chewed for a moment. "I knew that if I wanted to make it as an artist, I needed to get the hell out of there."

"So you came here," I said. "Why New York? Why not Chicago, or Los Angeles, or Europe?"

"Because, New York is where everything happens," he replied. "Isn't that why you're here?"

"I've always been here, or nearby at least. I'm from New Rochelle." I chewed a slice of cucumber, and amended, "Well, I'm really from this nowhere town in Massachusetts. But after my mom married my stepfather, he moved us to New Rochelle."

"Was New Rochelle nice?"

"I'd have preferred staying in Massachusetts." I took another bite of my salad, and added, "I would have preferred keeping my original last name too, but my stepfather went and adopted me. Something about making me feel like part of the family, yadda yadda yadda."

"Seems like a nice thing to do," Sam said. Oh, yeah, my stepfather was always doing nice things for others while secretly plotting out people's lives for them. "At least you ended up with a nice Irish name."

I laughed. "I've always been Irish. My last name used to be Cavanaugh."

"Your father's name?"

"No, my mother's. My father's surname is O'Rourke. Irish all around, you see."

"That I do." Sam's brow furrowed. "Forgive me for asking, darlin', but is he still around?"

"My father?" I asked, and Sam nodded. "Yeah. I talk to him all the time. Why?"

"Just wondering why a man would allow his daughter to take her stepfather's name."

Since that was a complex situation, I gave Sam the simple version. The full version would take approximately one year to tell, and only if I skimmed over most of the details. "My father agreed because it was what my mother wanted. He's always done everything he could to make her happy."

"Sounds like a good man."

"He is," I said. "Best man there is."

We ate in silence for a time, then Sam asked, "Tell me, Britannica Lynn, are you one of those jaded New Yorkers? The seen everything, done everything type?"

I laughed through my nose. "Hardly. My stepfather was so strict I wasn't allowed to come to the city except with him or my mother. I couldn't even attend school trips to Rockefeller Center."

"Maybe he was concerned for your safety."

"No, he just didn't want me to do anything that might embarrass him. I spent years plotting how I'd escape from him."

"Escape?" Sam repeated. "Was he really that bad?"

"You have no idea." I finished my salad. "My opportunity came after I got accepted to a college in the city. Stepdaddy didn't want me going to school there, but my mom put her foot down. Told him he had no right interfering in my education."

"Do you really call him stepdaddy?" Sam asked.

"I'd stick a fork in my eye before I said that to his face," I replied. "Anyway, once I hit twenty-one and my trust fund matured, I dropped out of college to concentrate on my art."

"Those canvases in your apartment are your work?"

I hadn't realized he'd seen them. "Yeah. They are."

"They're great. You've got a great sense for color and composition."

People had complimented my work before, but it had never made me blush. Now, my face was so hot I could have fried an egg on my forehead. "Um. Thank you."

Sam looked at his food, giving me time to get my face under control. "What's a fine artist like you doing modeling for romance novels?" he asked.

"Modeling wasn't really part of the plan," I admitted. "Since the term starving artist is around for a valid reason, I picked up some modeling work. I'd modeled a bit when I was younger, and my agent is an old family friend. My mother's family," I amended.

"What did your mother and stepdaddy think of your career change?"

"Mom was cool, but according to stepdaddy, artists are too lazy to find real jobs," I replied, remembering his red face as he screamed about me throwing away a perfectly good future as an accountant or legal assistant. “As for modeling, he says it’s a scandalous way to make a living.”

“That’s my Britannica Lynn—scandalous,” Sam said. “If you don’t mind my asking, if you’re a trust fund girl, why do you sit for art classes?”

I gave him a wry smile. “That trust fund was just north of fifty thousand. It got me my down payment on my current apartment, a year’s rent, and held me over while I built up my portfolio. My paying modeling gigs picked up just as the money ran out.”

Sam nodded. “It would seem that in your mad scramble to thwart your stepfather’s plans for you, you might have missed out on some of the best, cheesiest parts of New York City.”

“What, like the tourist traps?” I asked. “I’ve been to Times Square, just like everybody else.”

“Not Times Square.” Sam signaled for the check. “Finish up, darlin’. I’m taking you to the Mecca of tourist traps.”

***

It turned out that Sam’s idea of the ultimate New York tourist destination was the Statue of Liberty. However, Sam didn’t take me to Battery Park and to the boat chartered to Liberty Island. Instead, Sam and I boarded the Staten Island Ferry.

“It’s a nice, relaxing ride,” Sam explained when I asked why we were getting on the wrong boat. “Besides, it’s free.”

In addition to being free, since it wasn’t rush hour the ferry was nearly empty. We found a spot against the railing, and after the ferry launched we watched the Manhattan skyline move off in the distance.

“Tell me whose shirt I’m wearing,” Sam said, gesturing at the NYU logo across his chest.

“It’s my shirt,” I said. “My two years in college were at NYU.” When Sam’s brow furrowed, I asked, “Worried you were wearing my boyfriend’s shirt?”

A panicked look skated across Sam’s face. “Do you have a boyfriend?”

I laughed. “No, Sam, there isn’t any boyfriend.” I didn’t add that I’d been single for so long I could hardly remember what it was like to be in a relationship. “You’re the only man in my life right now.”

Sam draped his arm around my shoulders. “I like that,” he said.

“Do *you* have a boyfriend?” I asked.

“I do not,” he replied. “Looks like we’re two single girls in the city.”

Since we were just two single girls, I thought it might be fun to tease him a bit. I reached across his body to where his hand rested on the railing and stroked his long fingers. “Maybe we can make out from time to time, to take the edge off.”

I don’t know what I’d expected Sam to do, maybe huff that despite last night he was only interested in boys, or even storm off and leave me standing all alone at the railing. Instead, he glanced around the ferry. When he confirmed that we were relatively alone, he tilted up my chin and kissed me. I moaned against his lips, my knees turning to water.

There was no reason for me to react that way; I mean, it wasn't the first time we'd kissed, or even the most passionate. But there was something about Sam's hesitant nature, how he gently touched his mouth to mine, that made me feel like one of those heroines in the romance novels that bore Giovanni's image. I was the damsel with her bodice ripped open, and Sam was my hero. No, he wasn't my hero; he was my kryptonite.

"That take any edges off?" he asked when we parted.

"I think it added a few," I mumbled, burrowing into his arms. "You're really bi, aren't you?"

"What's your criteria for bi?" he asked. When I looked up at him, he elaborated, "You have all these rules as to whether making out counts or not. What are your rules for someone to be bisexual?"

"I never really thought about it. Kissing both genders the same amount of times?"

Sam nestled me closer, resting his chin on the top of my head. "Then I am definitely not bi. The only other woman I've kissed is my mother, and my grandmother before her."

"Oh," I mumbled as my heart fell. Sam's admission meant that there really wasn't any hope for us, and stupid me had fallen for New York's most eligible gay man.

"Hey," he said, tilting my face upward. "Doesn't mean I like kissing you any less."

"I like kissing you too," I said, then I stood on my toes and showed him just how much I liked it. Maybe I didn't have to have a real relationship with Sam. Maybe we could be friends with benefits.

Hopefully lots of benefits.

Once we parted, Sam pointed out toward the harbor. “Look, there’s our girl,” he said as the ferry chugged by the Statue of Liberty. “Wave, darlin’.”

I did, then I wrapped my arms around Sam’s waist, ignoring the voice in the back of my mind as I laid my head on his shoulder. Maybe Sam and I could make this work. Maybe love didn’t have to make sense.

Chapter Seven

Sam

Since Nash didn't work Saturdays, Sundays, bank holidays, or any of the Catholic high feast days, Saturday morning found me bored and lonely, two states I have never enjoyed. I contemplated calling Britt, but every time I tried to dial her number, I chickened out, just like after that night at the tapas bar, and before Astrid's party. What was wrong with me that I couldn't call this one particular girl?

Shoving all thoughts of Britt aside, I texted Michael. We'd broken up over a year ago, but somehow had managed to remain friends. Scratch that; Michael wasn't just a friend, he was my best friend, one of those rare souls that I knew had my back no matter what, just like I had his.

Sam: What are you doing?

Michael: Sculpting. Show next week,

remember?

Sam: How could I forget?

Michael: Let me guess, the prince is bored.

Sam: Little bit.

Michael: Come on by, cowboy.

My invitation thus secured, I shoved my phone in my back pocket, hopped in a cab, and made my way to Soho. While Michael's living quarters were near his cousin Astrid's, he also kept a one thousand square foot studio space funded by his various daytime pursuits. Since I'd met Michael he'd worked as a waiter, doorman, escort, actor, messenger…and those were just the jobs I knew about. Who knew what other nefarious pursuits he'd engaged in to fund his work?

"Hey, buddy," I greeted as I stepped inside the studio. Courtesy of our past relationship, I had a key. "What's the good word?"

"Samuel, your expressions are so old they qualify for Medicare," Michael replied from behind his work in progress. "What kind of old fogeys raised you back in Iowa?"

"The usual sort."

Michael wandered out from behind his creation. In its present state it was nothing more than a wood and wire armature, though it was shaping up to be a water buffalo or some other behemoth. The artist himself was stripped to the waist, a pair of red gym shorts hanging precariously from his hip bones. "What brings you by, Sam my man?"

"Wanted to see how the water buffalo was doing." Michael had been having a hard time bringing this one to life, which meant that I teased him about it whenever I could. I walked up to the sculpture and patted it on the nose. "How ya been, Walt?"

Michael's nostrils flared. "That is a horse, and his name is not Walt."

I grinned. "Not Walt is an awful unusual name. All the other water buffalos will tease him. Gonna give him a complex."

Michael rolled his eyes. "You're hopeless." I followed him as he walked to the back of the studio. Michael had a little crash pad in the rear, complete with a futon and mini fridge. He grabbed two bottles of water and tossed one to me. "Are you planning on explaining your little disappearing act after Astrid's party?"

"The explanation is I was so drunk I could hardly walk," I replied. "You remember Britt, the model I introduced you to?" He nodded. "I slept it off at her place."

Michael raised an eyebrow. "You got yourself plastered and went home with *a girl*? Lord, Sam, I am signing you up for AA."

"Come on, man, it's not like that," I said, though it was actually a lot like that. "Britt's real cool. You'd like her."

"Would she call my horse a water buffalo?"

"Only if it looked like one."

Michael threw back his head and laughed.

"Okay, maybe Not Walt turned out a little stockier than I intended. Why don't you take off that fancy jacket and help me with the armature?"

I tossed my leather jacket onto the futon and strode toward the mess of wood and chicken wire. I rubbed my chin as I studied it, then I said, "Now then, Not Walt, I am putting you on a diet."

Chapter Eight

Britt

Sunday afternoon found me lazing around my apartment—bored, lonely, and accomplishing a whole lot of nothing.

Earlier, I'd gone out for brunch with Astrid and stuffed myself with eggs Benedict and home fries, then gone window shopping while she went actual shopping. I didn't mind—much—that Astrid's financial situation was so much better than mine. What I did mind was when she dropped an extra hundred or so on something just because of the label sewn into the back. But it was her money to waste as she saw fit, so I held my tongue.

Once Astrid was laden down with elegant paper shopping bags—hmm, I wonder why those boutiques charge such high prices?—we both retreated to our respective apartments. I played on my laptop for a while, then I doodled at my art table. The fourth time I sighed I threw down my pencil and stretched.

I could always call Sam. I picked up my phone and stared at it, wondering what Sam was doing. Probably working, or on a date with some guy. Some guy who was a much better fit for Sam than I'd ever be.

My phone vibrated with an incoming call, startling me so much I dropped it. I picked it up and checked the display, smiling when I read the name.

"Hi, Daddy," I greeted. No matter how old I got, I'd always be a daddy's girl.

"Hey, pumpkin," he replied. "How's my big girl?"

"Oh, you know," I replied. "Just waiting for my art to be discovered and become a millionaire. Or maybe a billionaire."

"Only a matter of time." He cleared his throat. "Listen, the twins' birthday is in a few weeks. Emily and I would really like it if you came up."

And the real reason for the call was revealed. Emily was my father's girlfriend, though I knew he'd rather she wasn't. Let me give you some backstory.

That incident in the school library that had resulted in my existence happened when my parents were only fifteen. Apparently Dad offered to marry Mom as soon as he'd heard the good news, but both sets of grandparents decided that my parents were too young for such a lifelong commitment. Not too young to bring a child in the world, but definitely too young for marriage. Whatever.

Anyway, Mom and Dad had stayed single. After I was born, Mom and I lived with her parents, but Dad was always a big part of my life. He was his high school's star baseball pitcher and was always taking me to practice, and me and Mom cheered him on at every game. As far back as I can remember Dad always said that he'd earn a college scholarship, make a ton of money, and finally marry Mom. I wanted that nearly as much as he did.

After they graduated high school, my parents got an apartment and the three of us lived together as a family. Mom always said that money was tight, but all I knew was that I finally got to be with my two favorite people all the time. Well, all the time when I wasn't in school. Then Dad went and won the lottery and ruined everything.

Mom had wanted Dad to buy us a house with his winnings, but he invested in a comic book store instead. He invested in a few other things as well, namely that trust fund for me, but Mom freaked and walked out. Then Mom got that job at the law firm, and ended up meeting and marrying my stepfather. The only shouting match I've ever heard between my parents was when she told him she'd met someone; the only time I've ever seen my father cry was at Mom's wedding.

After Mom married my stepfather, Dad was so heartbroken he stopped dating altogether, then a few years ago he met Emily. She was nice, I guess, though her blonde hair and blue eyes reminded me an awful lot of my mother. Emily was about eight years younger than Dad, and turned out to be one of those women that thought getting pregnant was a great way to keep a man. Only this time around, Dad didn't offer marriage to the woman carrying his child. That was about the time Emily decided I was her competition.

I'd been invited to Emily's baby shower, and had dutifully picked up a set of pink blankets and a package of diapers for my soon to be siblings; yep, Emily had gotten herself knocked up with twins. When I arrived, all of Emily's relations assumed I was Dad's sister, partly because of our strong resemblance, partly because how could thirty-five year old Sean possibly have a twenty year old daughter?

"Your daughter is ruining everything," I'd overheard Emily say. "Can't you just pretend you're her brother?"

"Why would I do that?" Dad shot back. "You knew we had Britt young. You never had a problem with it before."

"Yeah, well, now my parents are asking me questions," Emily said. "They're wondering if you've got some string of illegitimate children out there." She sniffed. "They're wondering if you'll be here for the twins, or if you'll just run off and get some other girl pregnant."

"First of all, you told me you were on the pill," Dad said, his calm tone doing little to hide his anger. "Second of all, I do not abandon my children. I was always there for Britt, even when I was a stupid kid up to my eyeballs with algebra homework. Britt is the most important person in my life, and that will never change."

"But what about our babies?" Emily wailed.

"I will always be there for them too. I will love them just as much as I love Britt." Dad cleared his throat. "But don't you ever try to push Britt away.

She's my daughter, whether you like it or not."

"Hey," I said, stepping into view. "If it's a problem, I can leave."

"How much did you hear?" Dad asked.

"Enough." I looked at Emily, and wanted to give her a speech about how awesome my father was, the best father in the history of fathers. Instead I said, "Sorry I'm too old to be the twins' sister."

Emily frowned and stomped away. Dad shook his head and rubbed his eyes. "I swear to you, Britt, I don't know how this happened."

"She's just cranky. Hormones or something." I leaned my head on Dad's shoulder. "I really don't want to upset the pregnant woman. It's no big deal if I have to leave."

Dad smiled, then he wrapped his arms around me. "Greatest daughter ever," he declared. "Such a big heart, just like your mother."

I left the shower shortly afterward, and since then I'd only seen my father once, right after the twins were born. Emily had conveniently been out when I arrived, which was fine with me. I wasn't there to see her, anyway.

"Are you sure Emily wants me to come?" I asked. "Or is she going to tell everyone I'm Auntie Britt?"

"I really don't care what she says," Dad replied. "Come on, you know you want to play with your sisters."

I sighed. I did want to know my baby sisters, that much was true. I just didn't want me or my father ridiculed by Emily's stupid family. "Will Grandma be there?"

"Of course."

Hmm, sisters *and* Grandma were just enough to sway me. Before I could say as much, my phone beeped. "Hang on, Dad, I have a message. Might be my agent." I swiped to my text messages, and smiled when I saw the sender.

Sam: How are you, baby?

Sam called me baby. Those four letters made me grin literally from ear to ear, maybe even around to the back of my head.

Britt: Home, bored. My dad invited me to a birthday party.

Sam: Today?

Britt: No, it would be around October 1. It's for my sisters.

Sam: Sisters? Thought you were an only like me.

Britt: Twins, Penelope and Veronica. Dad's kids. They're going to be two. Hang on, talking to Dad.

I put the phone back to my ear. "Sorry, Dad. I got a few texts."

"You're smiling," Dad observed.

"How would you know that?" I demanded. "It's not like you can see me."

"I can hear it in your voice." When I neither confirmed nor denied, he said, "Okay, tell me his name."

"What makes you think I'm smiling because of a boy? Maybe I just got a gig, or sold some art?"

"You sound exactly how I sounded when I was with your mother."

How he sounded before Mom had married my evil stepfather, that is. "Dad—"

"I know, I know," he said. "Listen, I'll make you a deal: I won't question you about the boy as long as you say yes to the birthday party. You can even bring the boy."

"You sure about that?"

"Sure. His presence will give Emily something new to complain about. You know how she loves complaining."

We laughed, and I wondered for the millionth time why my mother had chosen my stepfather over my real father. "I accept your offer, and I'll ask Sam about the party."

"Sam," Dad repeated. "Nice name, sounds like Sean. Good choice."

I laughed again. "Email me the party information. I'll talk to you later."

"Bye, pumpkin."

I ended the call and went back to my text messages.

Britt: You like kids?

Sam: You expecting?

Britt: No! Want to go to my sisters' birthday party?

Britt: It will be in Oct, up in Western Mass.

Sam: Sure. I'll make balloon animals.

Britt: You know how?

Sam: No, but I have almost a month to learn. How hard can it be?

Britt: Thank you. You're the best.

Sam: No, we're the best.

Britt: ☺

Chapter Nine

Britt

Like most other people in the city, Monday morning found me waking up in a foul mood. However, I wasn't in a bad mood because my weekend had ended and I had to trudge off to work. My gray mood was because my weekend had ended and there was no work to go to.

Sure, I had stuff booked for later in the week, but it bothered me that I still hadn't scored any regular gigs. My plan had been to work my butt off modeling for a six to nine months, save up enough to pay my bills for the next few months, and take some time off from modeling to concentrate on my art. However, that first part of my plan hinged on people not only hiring me, but hiring me for regularly scheduled, well-paying gigs.

And that's how I'd ended up sitting naked before a room full of art students.

So I spent the morning trolling websites looking for gigs that seemed legitimate; there weren't many.

I did see a few open casting calls, but I hated those. All the respondents were herded around like cattle, clutching head shots and batting their eyelashes at who they hoped were the right people. Okay, most models didn't behave that way, but it only took one to irritate me, and no one wants to hire an irritated Britt.

After checking my email for the bazillionth time and finding nothing from my agent, I sent Astrid a text.

Britt: Lunch?

Her reply came a few minutes later:

Astrid: Sure. Café near my place in 30?

Britt: Sounds good.

The café in question was Café Luna, a bistro situated almost exactly between my apartment and Astrid's. Geography alone hadn't made the café our go-to hangout; the proprietors had the decency to serve their breakfast menu until two in the afternoon on weekdays. Really, all restaurants should be so civilized.

I got to the café before Astrid, which was no great surprise. Early on in our friendship I'd learned to add fifteen minutes onto Astrid's estimated times of arrival. Just after I'd chosen one of the outdoor tables and ordered a beer, I got a call from my mother.

"Hey, Mom," I greeted. "What's up?"

"You are aware that Melody's wedding is Saturday?" she said, forgoing a proper greeting to her only child. "Why haven't you sent in your RSVP?"

"Um." Truth be told, I was hoping that if I laid low for a few weeks, everyone would forget about me and I could avoid the event altogether. Melody was my cousin on my stepfather Patrick's side, the eldest child of his dearly departed sister. While Melody and I had gotten along well when we were younger, once we graduated high school our lives took very different paths. I went on to college with the intent of becoming an artist, while Melody concentrated on honing her gold digger skills.

"Would you believe me if I said I forgot?" I asked.

"No," was Mom's frosty reply. "Let me help you out. I'll check off your response for you. Will you and your guest be having chicken, fish, or beef?"

"Guest?" I repeated. "I have to subject a poor innocent to all of this?"

Mom was silent for a moment; I could picture her pinching the bridge of her nose. "The invitation was for you and a guest. Did you even read it?"

"I read most of it." Mom made a soft, strangled sound, and I knew I was getting off easy. I can only imagine the tongue lashing she'd gotten from Patrick about my failure to respond. "What kind of fish will it be?"

"Salmon, your favorite," Mom replied. "Will your plus one be having salmon as well?"

"Better put down chicken," I said, since I really had no idea who I was going to ask to go with me. I liked my friends, which was why I kept them as far away from all Sullivan-centered events as possible.

"Thank you, sweetie," Mom said. "See you Saturday?"

"Saturday it is."

I ended the call and held my head in my hands, thinking of all the wonderful things I could be doing with my weekend instead of spending it at Melody's wedding. I could do some laundry, scrub the grout in my shower, or volunteer to scrape gum off playground equipment…

"Why the long face?" Astrid asked as she sat opposite me.

"I have to go to my cousin's wedding on Saturday," I whined. "They're all going to be staring at me, judging me for not being a poor little rich girl like she is. It makes my skin crawl just thinking about it. And I have to bring a date."

"You *have* to?" Astrid asked, raising a perfectly plucked eyebrow. "Or what, they'll doubt you're a real girl or something?"

"Or something." I peeked at Astrid through my fingers. "Hey, you want to go with me? It's open bar."

"With the glowing endorsement you just gave? A world of no."

"Some friend," I grumbled. I opened the contacts folder on my phone, trying to decide who I liked enough to spend the day with, but not so much that I'd feel guilty about taking them to the wedding. Pickings were slim, indeed.

Astrid tapped her chin, then asked, "Why don't you ask Sam MacKellar to be your date?"

I glanced up from my phone at Astrid. "Date? You want me to take a gay man to my cousin's *wedding*? As my *date*?"

"Can you think of better arm candy than him?" Astrid countered.

Well no, I couldn't. I flipped to Sam's number and dialed. Astrid, the bitch, grabbed my phone, set it between us on the table, and put it on speaker.

"Hey darlin'," Sam drawled when he answered.

"Hey yourself."

A pause. "Am I on speaker?"

"Unfortunately so," I replied, while Astrid trilled, "Sammy, baby, it's Astrid!"

Sam chuckled. "What can I do for my two best girls?"

"Britt needs a date," Astrid said. "Will you be her date?"

"Date for what, exactly?" Sam asked.

Astrid looked pointedly from me to the phone. Great, I got to talk about the awkward parts. "It's for a wedding. Specifically, my annoying cousin's wedding."

"When is it?" Sam asked.

"This Saturday."

"I'm all yours, darlin'," Sam declared. "Where are you now?"

"Café Luna, the bistro by Astrid's place," I replied. "Why?"

"Stay there," Sam said. "I'm picking you up."

"Sam, the wedding isn't until this weekend."

"Yeah, I figured as much when you said it was Saturday," Sam said. "Today, I'm taking you dress shopping."

"Um, why?"

"If I'm gonna be stepping out with you, you'll need to look good."

"Sam—"

"Gotta go, hailing a cab," Sam said in a rush, then the line went dead.

I stared at my phone for a moment, then I looked up at Astrid. "Shopping? Sam is seriously taking me shopping?"

"You never know what will happen where Sam's concerned," Astrid said. "From the day he showed up in this town, that man has been an enigma."

"Really." I didn't add that I'd found Sam more than an enigma. Ever since that night in my apartment I'd been assuming he was a closeted bisexual, though outed homosexual, but Astrid's comment made me wonder if there wasn't a bit more to Sam's story. Based on Sam's past relationship with her cousin, I bet there was a lot more.

Fifteen minutes later a cab pulled up and Sam exited in all his glory. He was wearing dark washed jeans, a dark blue tee shirt, and Doc Martins, with his black leather jacket slung over his shoulder; basically, this outfit was a variation on the jeans and tees he always wore, but damn did he wear them well. He looked like sex on a stick and I was about to place an order.

"Pick up your chin," Astrid whispered. I scowled at her, but before I could snap that my chin needed no such maintenance I felt Sam's hand on my shoulder.

"Darlin'," he greeted, giving my shoulder a

squeeze. "Astrid." Sam grabbed a chair and spun it around, straddling the back.

"Nash let you just take off?" I asked.

"No shoot today," he replied. "Nash hates working on Mondays. And before ten a.m., after five p.m., with children, or animals; he really hates animals, especially parrots."

"I bet the parrot community is devastated," I observed. "Such pretty feathers and no one to immortalize them in pixels."

"Of that I have no doubt," Sam replied. "Tell me about this wedding."

"It's for my cousin, Melody," I whined. "She's on my stepfather's side, and they all hate me."

"Then why are you going?" Sam asked.

"I kind of have to," I said. "They've all looked down on my mom for the longest time, all because of me—mostly because I dropped out of college, wanted to be an artist instead of a slimy lawyer, and all that. If I don't show up they'll just harass my mom, saying I'm ungrateful, a brat…the list goes on."

"So, she figures if she shows up looking like a million bucks with a hot guy on her arm, it will at least take the heat off her mother," Astrid said, swirling her drink.

Sam looked at me and cocked a dark eyebrow. "You think I'm hot?"

I looked him up and down. "You're okay."

Astrid snorted. "Come on, Sam, it's common knowledge that every woman in the borough wishes you were straight. Just be Britt's safe little date so she can shove her bitch cousin's nose in it."

Sam looked at me expectantly, so I said, "Well, yeah, that's the gist of it."

"All right, then, I need details," Sam said. "Time of wedding, requested attire, wedding party colors?"

I blinked. "You'll seriously do this?"

Sam smiled. "I'll seriously do it." Wow, did that mean he'd really go to my sisters' birthday party too? He really was the best. We grinned at each other until Astrid cleared her throat. "About those details," Sam said.

"Three o'clock wedding, formal but not black tie, no wedding party, and therefore no official colors," I rattled off.

"No wedding party?" Sam repeated. "What kind of bride doesn't at least have a maid of honor?"

"Melody isn't what you'd call friendly," I said. "Besides, she's concerned someone will upstage her."

Sam grinned that devilish grin of his. "Darlin', you are just the girl to put this Melody in her place." He stood, then he grabbed my hand and hauled me upright. "I'm taking you to Jorge's."

"Jorge's?" I asked, Astrid echoing me.

"You'll like him. He makes the costumes for Nash's shoots." Sam reached for his wallet. "How much do you owe?"

"Why would you pay for my lunch?" I countered. "Besides, I already took care of it."

Sam ducked his head, then he walked to the curb and hailed a cab. "Astrid, you want to come with?" I asked.

"Nah," she replied. "You two are like an old married couple. I'll let you have your marital discord together."

Normally I would have fired off a snappy comeback, but Sam had a cab waiting. I jumped into the cab, and held on for dear life as it lurched into traffic.

"Want to make out?" Sam asked, wiggling his eyebrows.

"I've never made out in a cab," I said, sliding closer. "You?"

The cabbie made a hard left, and I slid away from Sam. "Guess that ends that," Sam muttered.

I patted his hand. "We can always find time later."

The cab deposited us at a store front in Greenwich; the sign over the door read ***'Tienda del Sastre.'*** "This is Jorge's? And he's a…" I searched my memory; I'd been good in Spanish class, but that was years ago. "Seamstress?"

"I believe Jorge refers to himself as a tailor," Sam replied. "Come on, I'll introduce you to the diva himself."

The shop evoked every sample sale I'd ever patronized, what with its white walls and selection of timeless neutrals displayed on lacquered wood hangars. Sam led me through the shop and through a door at the rear, beyond which everything changed. This room, which was obviously Jorge's design studio, was a riot of color. Bolts of fabric were heaped upon tables and stacked against the walls, and a shelving unit was full to bursting with all sorts of trim. There had to be a hundred kinds of lace, and thousands of ribbons in every color of the rainbow packed in every available crevice. The finery didn't end there, for against the back wall there were shelves of shoes and racks of jewelry. To top it off, the desk near the door, the only semi-clear surface in view, boasted a bowl of glittering rhinestones in lieu of candy.

"Jorge," Sam barked. "I need a dress."

"Whatever for?"

I turned toward the voice, and saw a slight Hispanic man wending his way among the racks of clothing. He wore a checkered button down shirt, khakis, and tan leather loafers. A pair of wire rimmed glasses were perched on his nose. Basically, he looked like the complete opposite of a hip New York City fashion designer.

"For a wedding, actually," Sam replied. "Jorge, meet Britannica Lynn. She wore your frilly orange gown at one of Nash's shoots the other day."

"Did you?" Jorge said, his face lighting up. "How did everything go? Was the lighting good? I chose that silk to reflect well under both natural and artificial light."

"It was beautiful," I said. "Probably the most perfect gown I've ever worn."

Jorge clasped his hands together. "Good, good. I can't wait to see the images."

Sam whipped his phone out from his back pocket, and thumbed open a folder. "As a matter of fact, I've got 'em right here."

Jorge looked at Sam's phone, while I wondered why Sam had a phone full of pictures of me. Figuring it was part of his job as Nash's assistant, I peeked over Sam's shoulder. He tipped the phone toward me as he swiped to the next image, which was taken mere moments after Giovanni had liberated my breasts and ruined my gown.

"What happened to the bodice?" Jorge demanded.

"You know how Gio likes to oil himself up?" Sam asked. "His Greasiness got a little too close to Britt."

"Way too close," I added.

"That bastard got grease stains on my gown," Jorge muttered, then he let loose of a string of Spanish expletives I definitely hadn't learned in Mrs. Garza's class. "Next time Giovanni orders something from me, I'm sewing a pouch of itching powder into the crotch."

"Does Nash use Giovanni often?" I asked.

"Mostly for romance novels," Sam replied. "Gio's got a good look for that. He's even got his own fan clubs." Sam shoved his phone in his back pocket and said to Jorge, "Here's the deal: Britt needs to attend her snooty cousin's wedding, and she needs to look better than the bride."

"I don't need to look better than her," I said.

"Too bad, you're gonna." Sam turned back to Jorge. "Can you help us out?"

"Of course," Jorge replied, looking me up and down. "Take off your jacket." I did, and handed it to Sam. "Your boots too. I need to see how tall you really are."

The answer to that was I am really tall for a girl; if modeling or art doesn't work out for me I could definitely have a career in basketball. Well, except for my whole lack of athletic prowess. I slipped off my boots, but even in my stocking feet I towered over Jorge. Sam, however, still topped me by a few inches.

Jorge nodded. "Good, good. I can work with this." With that he went to the racks at the back of the room, furiously sliding hangers back and forth. Once he found what he was looking for, he returned with a length of sky blue fabric draped over his arm. "Before I let you try this on, I need to know if you sweat."

"Doesn't everyone?" I countered.

"This fabric is quite delicate, and sweat stains will ruin it," Jorge explained.

"She didn't sweat when Gio plastered his greasy self all over her," Sam said.

Jorge nodded, then he handed over the dress. "You can change there," he said, indicating a curtained alcove.

I stepped into the alcove and pulled the curtain shut, then I hung up the dress and took a good look at it. It was pale blue satin, floor length with a halter back and plunging neck line. I sighed, then I removed everything but my panties and stepped into the dress. The fabric skimmed over my body, so soft I could hardly feel it. As I fastened the single button at the back of my neck I felt like a princess.

I hiked up the skirt before I drew back the curtain; the dress was a bit long, but that would be fixed once I put on some heels. Since there was no mirror in the alcove, I had no idea what I looked like. When I saw Sam's face, complete with glazed eyes and open mouth, I had my answer.

"Beautiful," Sam murmured. "Jorge, you've done it again." Jorge, however, did not share in

Sam's opinion.

"It's all wrong," Jorge wailed. "It's too plain, too soft, and that color does nothing for her." Jorge stomped toward the back of his workshop, muttering, "*Dios*, Sam, do you even have eyes? How can you think that dress is anything but terrible for Britt? Did you want her to look terrible?"

"So, this is not the dress?" I asked, watching Jorge as he delved into the back of his shop.

"Evidently not," Sam replied. He glanced sidelong at me. "For all that it's the wrong dress, you do look great, darlin'."

"Thanks, cowboy," I said. Sam cocked a dark eyebrow, but before he could question his new nickname Jorge returned, bearing a measuring tape, a mouthful of pins, and more fabric draped over his shoulders.

"When is this event?" Jorge asked around the pins.

"Saturday," I replied.

"Arms straight out," he ordered. I complied, and Jorge commenced measuring every part of my anatomy. He didn't write anything down, instead muttering furiously in Spanish around all the pins. After a few minutes of this he dropped the tape, grabbed one of the lengths of fabric, and draped it around my neck. It was a sheer tulle, the color reflecting blue or gold, depending on the angle.

"You are comfortable forgoing a bra, yes?" Jorge asked as he pinned a second swathe around my torso.

"Not wearing one now, am I?" I countered.

"Good. This dress will have a low neckline."

"Wait." Jorge halted, mid-pin. "You're *making* me a dress?" I asked.

"I will customize a dress for you, yes," he said, straightening up. "You cannot outshine a bride on her wedding day in something off the rack."

"I can't afford a custom dress," I said. Hell, I could barely afford groceries.

"No charge," Jorge said, resuming his pinning. "You are Sam's friend, therefore you are my friend. I do not charge friends. However," he added, "should I need a model of your height and coloring, I do hope you will return the favor."

"Of course I will," I said. "Thank you, Jorge."

He waved away my gratitude. "Now, about the skirt. Will there be dancing?"

"Honestly, I have no idea," I said. Melody hadn't exactly involved me in the wedding plans.

"If you're going with me, we're going to dance," Sam declared. "I always show my dates a good time."

"Sam will be your date?" Jorge asked, and I affirmed that he would be. "I assume you will want me to dress him, as well."

"Couldn't hurt," I said. "All he owns are jeans and tee shirts."

"I have an excellent and extensive wardrobe." Sam huffed.

"And you're keeping all these items hidden, because?"

Jorge poked me with a pin and I yelped; I was pretty sure he did that on purpose. I guess Sam's and my bickering got on his delicate nerves. "I will construct the skirt for ease of movement," Jorge said. "It will take me a few days to complete, then I will have it delivered to Sam's apartment." Jorge stood and waved me toward the changing alcove. "You may dress now. Be careful not to disturb the pins."

"I'll be careful."

After extricating myself from the fabric while keeping each and every pin in place, I exited the alcove and reentered the studio proper. I found Jorge and Sam discussing a gallery opening. "What opening is this?" I asked, reverently handing the pinned fabric over to Jorge.

"Michael's," Sam replied. "You met him at Astrid's party, remember?"

Of course I remembered the beautiful black man with the killer sense of humor. "What sort of artist is he again?"

"Sculptor," Sam replied. "This showing will be his first."

"Sam, why don't you take the lovely Britt as your date?" Jorge called as he secreted the pinned fabric away in the back of the room. "It can be a rehearsal for your wedding adventures."

Red dusted Sam's cheeks, but he didn't miss a beat. "You free Wednesday night, darlin'?"

"Sure am," I said. I wondered if Astrid would be there. Based on how much Astrid had always supported me, I imagined she'd be there for her cousin.

Sam grinned. "Good. I'll pick you up at eight."

"And I have just the dress for Britt to be seen in," Jorge announced, emerging from the racks. It was styled after the mod dresses of the sixties, with a short skirt, long sleeves, and an A-line silhouette. The dress itself had a white background and was patterned with abstract vines and deep green leaves. Astrid would freak if she saw something that so perfectly captured her favorite decade.

"It's gorgeous," I breathed. "You'll let me wear this?"

"No, I will let you have it," Jorge clarified. "It was part of my retro line a few years ago. Styles have since moved on, and I've been searching for the perfect person to bequeath it to. You, Britt, have the height and bone structure needed to carry off this dress."

"Thank you," I said, hugging the dress to my chest. "What kind of shoes should I wear?"

"Size?"

"Eight and a half."

Jorge darted back into his store room, returning a moment later with a pair of square toed white leather boots with chunky heels. "These will be perfect," he said. "I will also have shoes sent over with your dress for Saturday."

Figures; the designer didn't trust little ol' me to choose proper footwear for one of his creations. Based on the gorgeous clothes he made, that was fine with me.

"Now, out with you both," Jorge said, shooing us toward the door. "I have work to do. Britt, it was a pleasure meeting you."

"Thank you again," I said as Jorge slammed the workshop door in our faces.

"Jorge is Jorge," Sam said with a shrug.

"Artsy types can be cranky," I said. "Sam, thanks again for going with me to the wedding, and for bringing me here. I really appreciate it."

Sam graced me with that lopsided smile of his, and my heart melted a bit more. Okay, a lot more. "Anything for my Britannica Lynn."

Chapter Ten

Sam

Thank God the Tuesday shoot at Nash's was a standard one, because I was barely going through the motions. Instead of paying attention to my work, all I could think about was Britt. Specifically, Britt in that sky blue dress that enhanced the honey tones in her hair and eyes, and all that soft satin skimming across her curves. Jorge hadn't been kidding about the delicate fabric; the weave was so fine it clung to Britt's body, defining her firm hips and perfect little breasts. I had berated myself at least a thousand times for not having had the presence of mind to take a picture of her in that dress, so I consoled myself by shuffling through the images of her in the ochre gown whenever Nash wasn't looking.

Eventually the shoot wrapped up, and I attended to all the boring details that made up the bulk of my job. While I was shelving a few binders, Nash approached me.

"Remember the brunette from the romance cover

shoot last week?" he asked.

"Britt Sullivan?" I asked without turning around. The last thing I needed was for Nash to see the dumb smile I wore whenever I thought about her.

"That's the one," he affirmed. "She said you mentioned the harem series to her. When are we shooting one of those again?"

I went to the computer and brought up the scheduling software. "Not until the month after next."

Nash frowned. "See if you can squeeze one in earlier. I'd like to do a few test shots with Britt in the costumes."

"Will do." I grabbed a sticky note, scrawled '*BLS-harem soon*' on it, and stuck it to the white board. While my system lacked finesse, I always got the job done.

"BLS?" Nash asked.

"Britt Sullivan's middle name is Lynn," I explained, omitting how that was the middle name I'd chosen for her. "Therefore, BLS."

My phone vibrated on the desk; when I grabbed it I saw it was a text from Britannica Lynn herself. "Excuse me," I mumbled, walking to the far corner of the office. When I was sure Nash couldn't see my screen, I opened the text.

Britt: Want to see me naked?

Sam: Always. When & where?

Britt: Life drawing class, six p.m.

I opened the museum door for her. “After you, my lady.”

Britt giggled, then we entered the museum proper and walked toward her dressing room. Once we were alone in the room, Britt dropped the act.

“Thanks for coming here,” she said. “I didn’t want to say anything out there, but Ben does have a thing for me. I usually downplay it, but when he starts calling me a couple times a week it freaks me out.”

“How is he freaking you out?” I demanded. “Does he know where you live?”

“It’s just the things he says, the way he looks at me,” she mumbled. “I never gave him my address or anything, so I don’t think he knows where I live. I guess he could have followed me home.”

Suddenly, art class geek Ben reminded me of every asshole jock I’d gone to high school with. “That’s it, you’re coming home with me tonight,” I declared.

“What? No,” Britt said. “My building’s safe, and—”

“And if you really felt safe you wouldn’t have called me,” I said over her. Britt worried her lower lip, letting me know I was right. “Come on, darlin’, get naked. There’s a class out there waiting for their subject.”

I turned my back, listening to the soft rustles of fabric that resulted from Britt shedding her clothes. I didn’t look back until she cleared her throat. I found her clad in the same black velour robe she’d worn during the last class, her hands shaking like a leaf.

"What is it?" I asked, taking her hands.

She smiled tightly. "Nerves. Usually, I meditate for a few minutes before I go out there. It's weird being the only one naked in a room full of clothed people."

"I thought nudity didn't bother you," I said, recalling the confident girl strutting around her apartment in nothing but her panties.

"Depends on who's looking at me, you know?"

I sure did know, and I made a mental note to tell Nash that Britt was unavailable for the harem shoot. "What you need to remember, darlin'," I said, drawing her close to my chest, "is that you'll be the most beautiful girl in that room. Don't be nervous, be proud."

Her lower lip quivered. "But—"

"But nothing." I turned her toward the mirror, and smoothed down the robe's lapels. "You are the one they're here to see, Britannica Lynn. You are the woman of the hour." When she smiled, I put my mouth next to her ear and whispered, "And don't forget, I'm here for you. You need anything, I'm here."

She looked at my reflection, then over her shoulder at me and back to my reflection. "Thank you."

"Any time, baby." I slid my arms around her waist and kissed her temple. "Any time." We smiled at each other in the mirror for a moment, then Ben pounded on the door and barked Britt's name. "I guess it's show time."

"I guess so," Britt muttered. We left the dressing room hand in hand, and strode into the classroom.

Unlike the last class I'd attended, this one was packed with at least thirty students set up before easels. When Britt hesitated just inside the studio doors, I squeezed her hand.

"You got this, baby."

Britt flashed me a quick smile, then she walked up the dais toward a wooden chair. "Pose?" she asked Ben.

"On the wooden chair, back straight and legs and arms crossed," he replied. Britt dropped her robe and assumed the pose, as instructed. As the class wore on he had her adjust her pose a few times, but not into anything too scandalous. Too bad; I was dying for a reason to yell at him.

One thing I did notice about Ben was that whenever Britt changed positions, so did he. After the third time she'd altered her pose I figured it out: the bastard was repositioning himself so he could get a full frontal view of her. No wonder Britt had to meditate before each class.

After Britt endured a full sixty minutes of being stared at, Ben announced that the class was over. While the students packed up their charcoals and pastels, I met a robed Britt at the bottom of the steps.

"Another good show, darlin'," I said. Before she could reply, Ben appeared at her side and shoved an envelope at her.

"There's seventy five inside, instead of the usual fifty," he said.

"Did I get a raise?" Britt asked.

"The increase is because the class ran over," Ben replied. He looked from Britt to me, but before he could spit out whatever was eating at him a student called him over. I walked Britt back to the dressing room, keeping my hand on the small of her back the entire way.

Was that proprietary? Yes, it was. I wanted anyone looking our way to know that they needed to go through me to get to Britt.

"Ben has more than a thing for you," I said once we were alone in the dressing room. "He's paying you to sit naked for him. And giving you extra money? What is that all about?"

"The class did go over," Britt said.

"Only because he didn't call time," I said. "I don't want you doing this again."

"Who are you to tell me what I can and can't do?" Britt snapped. "Listen, I'm sorry I asked you to come here. I know Ben's a little weird, but I do need the money. Until I start selling some of my work or hit the lottery, I'll probably keep doing a few sessions a week. And I don't buy lottery tickets."

We stared at each other for a moment, then I said, "Britt, I didn't mean to order you around."

She nodded. "I'd like to get dressed. Could you please wait outside?"

I almost made mention of her kicking me out, but then I remembered that I really had no right being anywhere Britt was dressing. Or undressing, for that matter. Without another word I went out to the hallway, and sat on a bench a little ways down the corridor. I debated leaving the museum altogether, since Britt didn't want to listen to me or common sense in general, and just get her little naïve self into all sorts of bad situations.

I sighed, leaning forward with my elbows on my knees and supporting my head in my hands. A girl like her didn't need a mess like me, and Britt would be much better off without me and all of my baggage mucking up her life.

Just as I decided to move on from this fantasy I'd been living, I heard a rattling sound. I glanced toward Britt's dressing room door, and saw Ben shaking the handle. The door opened, then I heard Britt say, "Sam, I—"

She shut her mouth with a clack when she saw Ben standing there, and took a step back. "Ben. I'm sorry, I thought you were Sam. Why were you trying to get into my dressing room?"

"I came to thank you," Ben replied. "You've been sitting in on a lot of classes recently, and we really appreciate it here. Maybe we can get you a regular position."

"That would be nice," Britt said. "Would that make me a museum employee, with a regular paycheck and everything?"

"We can get some coffee and talk about it," Ben said, ignoring her question. "We can go now, if you like."

"I have plans now," Britt mumbled, her panicked gaze searching the hall. When she saw me sitting on the bench, her relief was palpable.

"Sam," she said, slipping around Ben and walking toward me, "I thought you'd left."

"Leave my Britannica Lynn? Never." I stood and held out my arms, kissing the top of her head as I gathered her close. As I pressed my face against her hair I decided that she really was my Britannica Lynn, and I never wanted to let her go. How I was going to work that out, I had no idea. "We off to my place?"

"Your place." Britt glanced at Ben. "Bye, Ben. Thanks again for calling me."

We left the museum with my arm draped across Britt's shoulders. I'm pretty positive I heard Ben swearing a blue streak under his breath as we walked away, but I ignored him. My only concern was getting Britt as far away from that guy as possible.

Since it was a warm night, we walked to my apartment. We stopped at a bodega on the way and got some dinner fixings, and were at my building before nine. Britt was unusually quiet during our journey, but I figured she was beat after a long day. When we finally stepped inside my apartment, I learned that wasn't quite the case.

"You must think I'm an idiot," she rasped. "Or some kind of a whore."

"Hey, baby," I said, pulling Britt into my arms, "I don't think either of those things." I held her for a moment, my face pressed against her hair. She smelled great, in spite of that cheap conditioner she used. "Get comfy on the couch, watch some television. I'll make us some dinner."

"I'm not hungry."

"Well, I am."

With that I released her and hauled the bags into the kitchen. I managed to create something not entirely awful with the ingredients I'd bought, and not fifteen minutes later I presented my culinary masterpiece to Britt.

"It's a quesadilla," I explained, when she looked at the plate like it was an alien with nine heads and wavy tentacles. "I'm certain you've encountered one of these before."

"Of course I have," she admitted, "but they were never so…charred."

It was a little black around the edges, but my momma had always told me that whenever you burnt food to call that adding a bit of Cajun mystique. "Well, you're in luck, because this one's cooked to perfection. Just cheese, since you don't really like meat."

Britt nodded, though she made no move to take the plate. I set it and a beer before her, then I returned to the kitchen to get my own dinner, balancing a jar of salsa and a tub of sour cream along with it. When I returned to the couch, I saw that Britt hadn't touched her food. I set my plate and condiments beside hers, and took her hands in mine.

"Talk to me, darlin'," I implored.

"I'm just freaked out," she said. "I've been modeling for those art classes for months, and Ben has always been cool. A little awkward, but cool. He sees you with me, and he turns into a psycho stalker."

I refrained from mentioning that Ben had probably always been a psycho stalker, with Britt just too kind to call him out on his bad behavior. "You're a pretty girl. Sometimes, men just can't handle it."

"That's stupid." Britt sniffed. "If you can't

handle yourself in public, get therapy. That's what therapy's there for."

"I agree," I said, not that I'd ever gotten one ounce of therapy for my many issues. I was dealing with them all supremely well, as evidenced by the sad girl in my apartment that I wanted more than air or water or sunlight, despite the fact that I'd lived as a gay man for the past thirteen years. Bringing her here wasn't complicating my life at all.

"I mean, it's an art class," she continued. "An art class! His students are there to learn design and composition, not to watch him ogle the models. Teachers have a duty to their students. What he's doing…it's just sick."

I extended my arm, and Britt tucked herself against me. "I'm sorry, baby," I said, kissing the top of her head. "You're right, a teacher has a moral and ethical obligation to his students. But creeps are everywhere, no matter what field you're in. Our job is to identify them, get them out of our lives, and move on."

"I'm sick of moving on," she declared. "I just want to make my own life free of these assholes."

"What kind of life?" I asked, all the while wondering what she'd moved on from.

"I want to make a living as an artist. A real living." She fingered the hem of her shirt. "I don't want to model any more. My dream is to draw comic books."

"Really?" I asked, downplaying that my heart had just swollen to three times its normal size. "Then why don't you make the change?"

"Well, for one thing modeling is what's paying

me right now," she replied. "It's not that I don't enjoy it, I just don't want to do it long term."

"I get that," I said. "So what are you doing about your art?"

"Honestly? Nothing. Nothing at all." Britt traced small circles on the back of my hand. "I'm so busy going to these stupid shoots and casting calls and sitting for life drawing classes I hardly have time to draw or paint anymore."

"Maybe you should make time," I said. "What about having a gallery opening of your own? I'm sure Michael would help you arrange one."

Britt smiled tightly, then she kissed my cheek. "Thanks, Sam." She hugged me a bit tighter. "Okay, I'm done being a downer. Where's the remote?"

"Um…" Since the remote wasn't in its usual place on the coffee table, I searched around my apartment and ended up finding it in the bathroom closet, of all places. I clicked on the television, and asked, "Tell me, my lady, what shall we be watching tonight? Romantic comedy?" I queued up the latest movie adaptation from that romance author everyone was obsessed with. Personally, I thought he told the same story in every book.

"Ack, not in a million, billion years." Britt snatched the remote from my hands, and flipped through the channels. "I hate romances, really. I want to watch something fun, with monsters and explosions and maybe an axe murderer. Ah, this is perfect."

I glanced at the screen, and saw that we were about to watch *Evil Dead,* the original version with Bruce Campbell. God, just when I thought I couldn't love Britt any more she went and outed herself as a geek.

"You do like horror movies, don't you?" Britt asked. The look in her eye told me that if I claimed preference for the romantic comedy, she would severely reevaluate our relationship and possibly kick my ass.

"I sure do, darlin'," I said as I sat beside her. Once she fit herself against my side we clinked beers. "And I'll have you know that *Evil Dead* is my second favorite movie."

"What's the first?"

"I'm warning you, it's not a horror movie."

"Tell me, already."

"*Empire Strikes Back.*"

Britt nestled closer, then she admitted, "That's my favorite too."

***

"Yeah, that's it. You're getting it. Finally! Took you long enough, you little shit. Now just move a little faster—"

I woke with a start, shaking as if I'd run a marathon as sweat poured off me like rain on asphalt. A quick glance assured me that I was safe in my apartment, and that my nightmares had only been in my head. Thank fucking God for that. As my breathing slowed and my heartbeat returned to normal, I realized I was sleeping on the couch instead of in my bed. Britt was sleeping with me.

Thank fucking God for that too.

I took a moment to look at Britt, her honey brown hair mussed with sleep, her cheek pressed against my chest right above my heart. Why weren't all of my mornings like this? Why couldn't I just be myself around her? Then again, who knew if Britt would even want the real me? Maybe all she saw in me was her safe gay friend, the one she could take with her when she modeled nude without fear of him hitting on her. Maybe Britt only wanted to be my fag hag.

No, that wasn't it. Ever since we'd first met, Britt had seen through all the false layers I'd built up over the years to the real me, the Sam I hadn't been sure still existed. And damn it all if the real me didn't want to come out and introduce himself to her.

I tried stroking Britt's hair, but my hand shook so much I worried I'd wake her. Knowing that I needed to burn off some of the leftover adrenaline from my nightmare, I slid away from her and entered my bedroom. After throwing on my running gear, I grabbed the blanket from my bed, carried it to the living room and tucked it around Britt.

"Sam?" she mumbled.

"Mornin', baby," I said. "I'm going for a run."

"You're running now?" she asked, cracking an eyelid and looking toward the darkness outside my windows. "It's like, the middle of the night."

"It is *not* the middle of the night," I said. Three a.m. was way past the middle. "Gotta clear my head. You stay cozy, okay?"

"Okay," she murmured as she burrowed underneath the blanket.

I ran for about half an hour, the scenery whizzing past me as I thought about nothing at all. That was what I loved best about running; it absorbed all of my attention, leaving me unable to think about anything but placing one foot in front of the other. I'd started running when I was a kid, back when both of my parents had been deployed to Afghanistan at the same time. Running had comforted me when I was a scared, confused kid; now it comforted a scared and utterly befuddled man.

I got back to my apartment just before four a.m. and was greeted by the heavenly scent of coffee, not that I'd put any coffee on before I left. Deciding to investigate the situation, I entered my kitchen and found my coffeemaker working away, and my fridge door flung wide open.

"I thought you said you were from Iowa," Britt said from the other side of the refrigerator door.

"Sioux City, born and bred," I informed. "Why?"

"You said Iowa was all about the pigs, but you don't have any bacon."

"I thought you didn't care for meat."

"I told you, bacon is in a class by itself."

I chuckled, then I reached above the fridge door and opened the freezer. "Bacon's in here."

"You froze your bacon?" Britt gasped as she straightened, as if I'd committed a most grievous sin.

"If I don't freeze it, I'll eat it all in one sitting," I said, handing Britt the package. While Britt muttered on about the sacrilege I'd committed, I took in her appearance. She'd showered and had twisted her wet hair into a knot on the top of her head. Instead of putting her clothes back on, she was wearing one of my tee shirts. It was navy blue, and fell to just below her thighs. While she was decent, the sight of Britt in my shirt was nearly more than I could take that early in the day.

"I hope you don't mind," Britt said, misinterpreting why I was staring at her. "I was going to put on my NYU shirt, but I didn't want to go through all of your stuff to find it. This was the first shirt I found that was, um, long enough."

From that last statement, I inferred that she was only wearing my shirt. "No worries, darlin'," I said. "May I ask why you were looking for bacon?"

"To make you breakfast," she said as if it was obvious. "Cooking is one of my many talents."

"Is it, now?"

"Sure is." Britt put the package of bacon in the microwave and set it to defrost. "After my stepfather moved us to the house in New Rochelle, he hired a full-time chef. Since she—the chef, that is—was the only person in the house I liked besides my mom, I spent a lot of time in the kitchen. Chef Aggie taught me everything she knew."

Beauty, brains, and she cooks. I watched Britt turn toward the counter and retrieve a few plates from the cabinets. "What's on the menu?" I asked.

Britt glanced over her shoulder and fluttered her eyelashes at me. "It's going to be a surprise. Well, except for the bacon. You already know about that."

"Can I help?"

"You can help by showering."

"Was my quesadilla really that bad?"

Another glance over her shoulder, another eyelash flutter. "Oh, you mean your Cajun masterpiece?"

"It wasn't that burnt."

"Mm hm."

When I still didn't move, Britt turned around and shooed me out of my own kitchen. "Go on, relax. I've got this."

I took Britt's advice and headed to the bathroom, where I spent the next twenty minutes standing under the hottest water I could stand. After I toweled off, I pulled on a pair of gym shorts and a tee shirt, then I followed the mouthwatering smells back to the kitchen. When I stepped into the room, my mouth watered for reasons other than the food.

Britt was bustling about the kitchen table, setting out plates and pouring coffee. She was still wearing my shirt, but she'd loosened her hair and it cascaded down her back in perfect bed head waves. At the sight of Britt barefoot as she set breakfast on the table, I finally understood all those adages about keeping women in the kitchen.

"Nice spread, darlin'," I said. "Isn't it a little early for such a big breakfast?"

"If it's not too early for you to run, then it's not too early for me to cook." Britt looked from me to the plates and back to me. "Seriously, Sam, food is better hot. Eat."

I smiled at her mother hen attitude and took a seat. On my plate was an omelet stuffed with spinach and cheese, toast, and Britt's centerpiece, bacon. "This all looks amazing. Thank you."

"I'm the one thanking you," Britt said. "Now,

eat."

"Yes, ma'am." I tucked into my plate, starting with the omelet. "This is probably the best omelet I've ever eaten."

"Told you I can cook," Britt said. "Try the coffee."

I did, and was amazed at the black silk that washed over my tongue. "Did you go out for new coffee?" I asked. "I don't have anything that tastes this good."

"Actually, you do," Britt said, then she leaned forward and whispered, "I fixed your coffee."

"You surely did." I took another sip. "You going to share your secret with me?"

"Only after you've cleaned your plate."

I followed her orders, not that it was a hardship to eat such an excellent meal. Once we were both done, I took our plates to the sink, then I glanced at the clock. It wasn't even five a.m. "You know, I usually don't wake up for another two hours," I said.

"That just means we can have second breakfast later on," Britt said. She rose and poured another cup of coffee; while her back was to me, she said, "I'm sorry for doing all of this so early. I just wanted to thank you, for, you know, earlier."

"I know."

"I mean it's hard—so frickin' hard—being alone in the city, and I don't have a lot of people I can lean on, but then I met you and you've just been so awesome—"

She spun to face me, spilling coffee on herself in the process. Britt yelped and I leapt into action, grabbing a towel and soaking it in cold water before pressing it to her thigh.

"Hold that," I said, putting her hand on top of the wet towel. I dashed into the bathroom and grabbed my first aid kit, rifling through it until I found the burn cream. I rushed back to the kitchen and knelt before Britt, flinging the towel aside as I spread the burn cream across her pink flesh.

"Sam."

I looked up and saw her smiling at me. "What?"

"It was just coffee," she said, working her fingers into my hair.

"Well, I don't want it to scar," I muttered, then resumed applying the burn cream. "Could impact the modeling gigs you're offered."

"Mmm."

I glanced up at Britt and her wry smile, and realized that I'd shoved her thighs apart and had wedged myself between them. And that burn was awful close to an area of hers I had no business visiting. I stood, coughing to cover my embarrassment. "Sorry."

"S'okay. I like that you're concerned."

"Are you, now?" I glanced at the clock; it still wasn't five. "Sorry I got you up so early. You have a lot planned for today?"

"Actually, I have nothing today except for Michael's opening. You?"

"I have to be at the studio by nine."

"Oh, you should probably catch some sleep," Britt said. "I can go—"

I grabbed her wrist. "You're right about us getting some rest, and you can stay." Truth be told I was bushed, and my bed was calling me in a profound way. "Want to take a nap together?"

"Sam, you just drank half a pot of coffee," Britt protested.

"After a run," I clarified. "I should probably recharge before work."

Britt nodded, then she dropped her gaze. "I don't want to impose."

"Darlin', I made you come here with me. There is no imposition, except on my part." I moved closer and took her hands in mine. "What do you say, darlin'? Feel like taking a nap with me?"

Britt looked at me from beneath her lashes. "I can do that."

I smiled, then tugged Britt out of the kitchen. I tried bringing her to the bedroom, but my nightmares wouldn't allow that just yet; I wondered if they ever would. Since collapsing in a weepy mess would likely ruin our morning, I led Britt back to the living room couch instead of my bed. I laid down first, then she fit herself against me while I yanked the blanket up to our chins.

"You're like an octopus," I said, shifting as she wound her limbs around me. Made me wonder if the girl had bones.

"Hush. You like octopuses. Octopi?" She thought for a minute. "No, I think it's octopuses."

I did like it, her wound around me that is, and I kissed the top of her head to prove it. After a few moments of silence, Britt asked, "Whatever this is between us, it's weird, isn't it?"

I kissed her hair again. "It surely is. Can something weird be something good too?"

She leaned up and kissed me on the lips, and didn't protest when I deepened the kiss. God, I just wanted all of her. "I think this can be very good," she murmured when we parted, then she laid her cheek against my chest. As for me, I gathered Britt against me and smiled. Without a doubt, weird could be good.

Chapter Eleven

Britt

After our early morning nap, Sam and I shared a cab so I could get home, and he could get to his job. When the cab pulled up in front of my building, Sam had grabbed my hand and said, "You need me today, you call. I mean it, darlin'. Otherwise, I'll pick you up at eight."

"Eight it is," I'd said, then I kissed him goodbye and climbed the three flights to my apartment. Once I was inside I took my phone out of my pocket, and had a good look at what I'd been hiding from Sam all morning: Ben had called and texted me over a dozen times. So yeah, I was officially freaked out.

All these months—five, to be exact—that I'd been modeling for the art classes I'd known that Ben had a thing for me, even though I hadn't admitted it out loud before Sam called me on it. Part of why I was in denial was that Ben had never been anything other than professional with me—well, not until he saw me with Sam. It made me wonder if

Ben hadn't made up some sort of fantasy about me sitting for the classes just to see him.

Oy. Boys and their ideas.

I thought back to when I met Ben; it had been at that same museum, though instead of modeling I'd taken a class in watercolor painting. Ben had been the instructor, and during one of the lessons I'd told him that I did some modeling on the side. He asked me if I'd like to sit for the life drawing class, and just like that I became his go to model. He never had me fill out any paperwork, or sign any forms. No, Ben had just showed me to a room to change in and handed me an envelope full of cash after I sat around naked for three quarters of an hour.

"Crap," I muttered, having come to a rather scandalous conclusion. I powered up my laptop in the hopes of disproving it. Once I found the museum's contact information, I gave the art department a call. After I navigated through the automated menu, I connected with a real live secretary.

"May I help you?" asked a female voice.

"Yeah, do you have life drawing classes?"

"We do. Would you like to sign up?"

"Actually, I was wondering how much you paid the models."

"Oh, we don't pay them in cash. They are given either a free museum membership, or are allowed to attend a class of their choice for free. Are you interested in modeling for us?"

"No, thank you," I mumbled as I hung up.

God. I really am an idiot.

After I stared at the museum's webpage for a few

minutes, I considered my options. I suppose I could have called the cops, but what case did I really have against him? Ben had never laid a finger on me, and he had paid me for each sitting. Really, this was just a case of a poor girl not asking too many questions so she could keep getting paid. Ben's actions were certainly unethical, but I guessed that they weren't criminal.

It wasn't like I could report him to the museum, either. Since Ben had always paid me in cash—his own cash, it seemed—there wasn't a paper trail and therefore no way to prove I'd ever really modeled there. Mind you, the fact that I'd never signed any forms like a standard issue W-9 really should have been a red flag, or at least provoked me to ask a few questions. It seemed that my only recourse was blocking Ben's number and never setting foot in the museum ever again.

I shut my laptop, shoving all thoughts of shady art teachers to the side as I wondered what I'd do with myself all day. After wandering around my apartment for a bit, I sat at my art table and started sketching. Probably since I was feeling a bit frustrated, what with sleeping against Sam's hard, muscular body last night but not doing a thing with it, I'd drawn a nude man. He turned out to be smoothly muscled, with dark hair that fell rakishly across his eyes, a scruff of a beard darkening his chin.

Sam's hair was always falling in his eyes. On the one hand I wondered why he didn't cut it, but he sure was cute peeking out from under that dark fringe. And that body of his…Sam must do more than just run. He must belong to a gym or something, or have a personal trainer instructing him on how to keep those muscles plump and healthy.

Actually, I bet his building had a gym, probably on the first floor or thereabouts. I bet Sam took regular classes there, lifting weights, doing a bit of cardio…

I blinked, snapping myself out of my daydreams about Sam's body and all the ways I could play with it. When I looked down at my sketch I laughed out loud; I'd drawn Sam naked.

"Wow, I really am a mess," I said to the sketch. "I didn't even notice that the art teacher was obsessed with me, and now I'm obsessed with a gay man." I added a few more lines to the sketch, and mumbled, "Please be bi, Sam. It would really make me happy if you turned out to be bi."

At seven forty-five on the dot there was a knock at my door. I looked through the peephole and saw Sam standing in the hallway, wearing his typical uniform of tee shirt, jeans, and boots; he'd also thrown on his battered black leather jacket for the occasion. My mouth practically watered at the sight.

"You're early," I said as I opened the door. "Miss me?"

"Always." Sam looked me up and down, his appreciative gaze telling me how much he liked Jorge's dress on me. In keeping with the hippy vibe of the dress, I'd straightened my hair and parted it down the middle, and created a cat eye look with some black liquid liner. After adding some clear gloss and the white boots, I was the perfect sixties siren.

"Around," Sam said, making a twirling motion with his hand. I spun around, letting the dress's hem bell out. When I faced him again, he pulled me into his arms. "You look great."

"You too," I said, stroking my hand over the flat plane of his chest. "Burgundy shirt tonight? You really do have one of these in every color, don't you?"

"I match the colors to my moods," he replied. Before I could ask what mood burgundy signified, Sam slid his hands down my back, underneath my skirt, and squeezed my butt.

"Hey," I said. I tried squirming away, but I had no chance against those muscles of his. "What gives?"

"Just making sure you're wearing something appropriate underneath this very short dress."

"And if I hadn't been?" I asked, winding my arms around his neck.

"You would have gotten a stern talking to, young lady." His blue eyes bored into mine for a moment, then he said, "Come home with me tonight."

"Why, Mr. MacKellar, whatever for?" I asked, fluttering my lashes.

"I want to shoot you in this dress. I'm a photographer too, remember?"

"You're suggesting that I let you take pictures of me at night, in your apartment?" I asked with a raised brow. "Sounds like you're an evil mastermind, luring me to your lair so you can have your way with me."

Sam gave me a crooked smile. "That a yes?"

"It's a maybe." I kissed his chin, then I wiggled out of his arms and grabbed my purse. "I'm ready if you are."

"Then let's go, darlin'," he said, offering me his arm.

After a short cab ride we arrived at the gallery, which was one of those impossibly hip places in Soho that didn't deign to advertise, but all the cool kids knew about anyway. Michael's colorful sculptures were arranged against the stark white walls, like little pockets of rainbows. The man of the hour was standing in the center of the room, wringing his hands.

"Oh, Sam, thank God you're here," Michael said when he caught sight of us.

"Like I'd miss this," Sam said. "Michael, you remember Britt?"

"You talk about her so much, how could I forget?" Michael grabbed my hand, holding my arm to the side while he checked out my dress. "Thank you for attending my showing, sugar."

"Of course," I said. "Is Astrid here?"

Michael dropped my hand. "No, my own flesh and blood had something better to do than watch me succeed. Her loss." He raked his gaze over my dress. "You look great, sugar. Maybe you can be my wingman while we troll for hotties."

"Hey now, Britt's here with me," Sam said, slipping his arm around my waist.

Michael looked down his nose at Sam. "Like she'll ever get any from you. Oh, hey!" Michael called, as he went off to greet more people, leaving me standing there in Sam's arms.

"What was that supposed to mean?" I asked Sam. When he gave me that innocent face, I added, "About me not getting any?"

"I have a reputation of not going all the way," Sam replied. "Michael and I used to date, but we never…um…" Sam's cheeks darkened as he rubbed the back of his neck. "You know."

"I'm not sure I understand. Please explain it to me, using small words whenever possible."

Sam put his mouth next to my ear, and whispered, "I never fucked him."

I shivered, every hair on my body standing on end. "Maybe if you stopped talking about girls all the time, you'd do better with the boys," I suggested.

"Maybe so." Sam released me and grabbed two champagne flutes from a passing waiter. "Drink?"

"Please." I sipped the cool liquid, wishing it would cool down more than my mouth.

We drifted about the gallery, and Sam introduced me to a few of his friends. Jorge was there with his wife, a curvy blonde named Matilda who towered over her husband by at least a foot. While Sam and Jorge discussed wardrobes for an upcoming shoot at Nash's, Matilda and I wandered around the gallery, taking in Michael's work.

"He certainly is talented," I said. Michael's preferred medium was papier-mâché, and I was looking at a sculpture of a piñata hanging from the ceiling revolving above the partygoers.

"Oh, yes, Michael always has been," Matilda said. "If he wasn't sculpting, he was painting or sketching. No matter what he did, it was always something creative."

"Have you known Michael long?"

"He and Jorge have been friends since they were children," she replied. "I met Jorge just after high school, about a year before Michael met Sam."

At the mention of Sam's name my gaze flew across the room. I saw the object of my desire deep in conversation with Jorge. "Sam said he and Michael used to date?"

Matilda nodded. "That was a lost cause from the start," she replied. "Michael was head over heels for Sam, but Sam just didn't love him back."

"Aww," I said, feeling a certain camaraderie with Michael; I was all too familiar with unrequited love directed at Sam. "Maybe Michael just wasn't his type."

"Seems that maybe you're Sam's type," Matilda said with a sidelong glance. Before I could stress that in spite if my wildest dreams that wasn't the case, the last person I wanted to see stepped in front of me.

"Hey, Britt," said Ben, the creepy art class instructor. "I didn't know you liked sculpture."

"What are you doing here?" I demanded, taking a step back.

"I'm friends with Michael," he explained. "Is something wrong?"

"I called the museum," I said. "You know what they told me? They don't pay models. All of their models are volunteers. You're sick, Ben."

Ben frowned, but it was gone in an instant. "You must have called the wrong department," he said. "I hire models all the time."

"Britt, do you work for this man?" Matilda demanded.

"I don't work for him. Ben here just took advantage of stupid, inexperienced me," I replied. "Excuse me." I turned to walk away, but Ben grabbed my elbow.

"Britt, wait," he said. "I can explain."

"I understand things pretty well," I snapped. "Let go of me."

"You heard the lady."

I looked up and saw Sam, my knight in a leather jacket, standing behind Ben. "Sam," I breathed, yanking my arm free from Ben's hold and moving to stand next to Sam.

"Britt and I were having a conversation," Ben snapped.

"It seems that your conversation has ended," Sam said. "Now, Michael is a very dear friend of mine, and I don't want to disrupt his show. However, if you put your hands on Britt again, rest assured I will."

With that, Sam turned and led me to the back of the gallery, keeping his hand on the small of my back the entire way. There was a stucco half wall at the back of the room, and beyond it was a secluded area with a few benches scattered about, a quiet place for patrons to get away from the bustling gallery for a few moments. I sat on one of the benches, Sam crouching before me.

"What happened back there, darlin'?" he asked, taking my hands in his.

"You were so right about Ben," I began, then I told him everything I'd learned when I called the museum.

"And now he's here," I concluded. "I asked him why he's here, and he said he's a friend of Michael's. I feel like he followed me here tonight."

Sam frowned, then he stood, hauling me up with him. "I'm going to have Michael throw that bastard out," he declared.

"Sam, no," I said. "You were right, this is Michael's big night. Don't let an asshole like Ben ruin it."

Sam stroked his thumb across my cheek. "I want you to feel safe."

"I am safe as long as I'm with you," I said, then I stood on my toes and kissed him. Why, I couldn't say; okay, that's a lie. I kissed him because I'd never felt safer in my life than when I was in Sam's arms.

Sam didn't waste any time deepening the kiss, pressing my hips against his as his hands found their way to my butt. Sam's lips against mine somehow removed all the anxiety I'd felt over Ben's presence, somehow it made everything right. I wrapped my arms around Sam's neck and the world fell away around us. I could have gone on kissing him forever.

Before we could get too inappropriate for a public place, a bright light distracted us.

"What the—" Sam said, blinking. "Someone just take our picture?"

"Guess so." I stepped back from Sam and tugged down my dress. "Want to go back out there?"

"Only if you're ready."

I slipped my hand inside his. "Let's do it."

In the short time we'd been in the alcove, the gallery had filled with patrons. Michael waved at us from across the room, surrounded by admirers and purchasers alike.

"I'm so glad this is going well for Michael," Sam said. "He's worked toward this for a long time."

"Thinking about getting back together with him?" I teased. "He is awful handsome."

"No checking out other guys when you're with me," Sam admonished. "And no, Michael and I won't be getting back together."

"Too bad. I bet you two were a cute couple."

Sam speared me with one of those devilish looks of his. "We were damn hot, thank you very much."

I giggled, but before I could tease Sam further, a man carrying a voice recorder stepped in front of us. "Leonard Hughes, covering this opening for the *Soho Arts Weekly*," the man said, referencing the neighborhood paper. "Can I get some quotes from the two of you?"

"Um, sure," I said, glancing at Sam. It was then that I noticed the man with the video camera standing behind Leonard. "Why does a paper need video?"

"It's for the website," Leonard replied. "Names?"

"Britt Sullivan, Sam MacKellar," I said.

"Thoughts on the opening?"

"It's wonderful," I said. "Michael is a very talented man."

Leonard stuck the recorder under Sam's nose. "Yes, Michael is one of the best young artists in New York. The city is lucky to have him," Sam said.

"Great! Thanks, you two." Leonard and the man with the camera went off in search of their next victims, while Sam just shook his head.

"That was surreal," he said.

"I can't believe we were interviewed," I said. "Well, sort of."

"All sorts of interesting things happen when Michael's involved," Sam said. "Come on, darlin', let's get some more champagne."

The crowd thinned out as the night wore on, but that didn't dampen Michael's spirits in the slightest. He was sailing about on cloud nine, and I could hardly blame him. Someday, maybe I'd have a gallery opening of my own, with a packed room fawning over my creations. I thought about what Sam had said, that I just needed to make time for my art, and I decided he was right.

Sometime close to midnight I slipped away from the crowd and visited the restroom. When I emerged, Ben grabbed my shoulders and thrust me against the wall.

"Why won't you talk to me?" he demanded. "I thought we were friends."

"Why did you lie to me?" I shot back. "Why did you trick me into sitting there naked for you? You treated me like some kind of prostitute!"

"Yeah, well, you kept coming back for more," he said, dragging his fingers down the side of my neck. "Admit it, you liked having all those people watch you. You liked getting naked for money. For me."

I gasped, so mad I was speechless. Then Ben was yanked away from me, and I saw Sam holding him by the back of his shirt.

"I told you to stay away from her," Sam growled. "The lady does not want your attention."

"Lady?" Ben spat. "You call a slut like her a lady?"

That was when Sam hit Ben, and Ben's nose spurted a fountain of red as he went down on the hardwood floor.

"You fucking bastard," Ben yelled. "What the fuck is your problem?"

"I'd like the answer to that as well," Michael said, striding over. "What the hell is going on here, Sam?"

"He had Britt up against the wall, wouldn't let her get away," Sam said. "He's been following her."

"He was bothering her earlier too," Matilda said as she and Jorge came to stand next to Sam. I silently sent her my thanks. "Britt was not happy to see him."

Michael looked from Matilda to Sam to Ben, then at me. His lips were pursed so tightly white lines of tension marred his dark complexion. "Well, Britt? What's your version of this mess?"

"Ben's sick," I whispered. "He's been following me, calling, and texting me. I'm thinking about getting a restraining order."

"Restraining order?" Ben screeched. "You kept coming back for more, you—"

"Enough, both of you," Michael barked as Sam wound up for another hit. I grabbed Sam's arm while Michael looked down at Ben, shaking his head. "Well, Benny boy, you'd best go quietly so I don't have to call on New York's finest. On second thought, I do love a man in uniform."

Ben got to his feet, all the while glaring daggers at Sam and me. "You're really taking their side?" Ben demanded. "I'm the one bleeding here!"

"You also seem to be the asshole here," Michael countered, then he made a shooing motion with his hands. "Go on, get. Oh, and if you bleed on any of my work I'll be sending you a bill," Michael added.

Ben turned and shoved his way through the crowd of onlookers. Once he was out of the gallery, I turned to Michael. "I'm so sorry," I said. "I wish none of that had happened."

"Me too, sugar." Michael's frown dissipated, and he patted my shoulder. "Ben's always been a bit, shall we say, socially awkward. Luckily you had Cowboy Sam here riding to your rescue."

"I call him a cowboy too," I said, enjoying Sam's embarrassed frown.

"He is one for the damsels in distress," Michael said. "Keep an eye on your cowboy, sugar. I need to see to my guests."

Michael melted into the crowd, followed by Matilda and Jorge, then Sam pulled me into his arms. "I wish you hadn't hit him," I said against his neck.

"You're not the only one. My knuckles are killing me." We burst out laughing at that, and Sam hugged me a bit tighter. "Want to get out of here?"

"Thought you'd never ask."

***

Sam and I ended up going to his place, just like he'd asked me to earlier. After what had happened at the gallery there was no way I was spending the night alone in my apartment, not until I was positive that Ben had no idea of where I lived. And there was the fact that Sam's apartment was pretty awesome. It was a two bedroom, with a tile-topped half wall separating the living room from the kitchen. The walls of the living room were painted a warm cocoa brown, and Sam's furniture was all buttery soft leather and dark wood. The rich colors coupled with the stark white trim and light blue throw pillows made the place look like a design catalog. Then again, Sam probably had one of his interior decorator friends set everything up for him.

The awesomeness of his apartment didn't end with the living room. The kitchen sported sunny yellow walls, light wood cabinets, and a big window over the sink that let in plenty of light. All of the appliances were stainless steel, and the granite countertops would have made materialistic people like my cousin Melody drool. Okay, maybe I'd drooled a bit when I first saw them. There was also the fact that the kitchen and living room alone were as big as my entire apartment, and Sam still had two entire bedrooms and full bathroom.

The spare bedroom was mostly full of junk, with things like props and costumes from photo shoots past stacked against the walls, along with a few bookcases. I'd investigated the shelves, and found a respectable collection of horror and science fiction movies. He could seriously use some more reading material, though.

As for Sam's bedroom…well, I hadn't been in there yet, except for that quick trip to find a tee shirt after I'd showered. I decided that gaining entry to his bedroom was my mission for the evening. A girl had to have goals, right?

Once we were inside the apartment, Sam and I stood there staring, as if we didn't quite know what to do with each other. I wondered if his thoughts were in his bedroom too. Eventually, I said, "You reminded me earlier that you're a photographer."

"That I did."

"Show me some of your work?"

He offered me one of those crooked smiles that went straight to my heart. "Have a seat. I'll get my laptop."

I sat on the couch, and Sam joined me a moment later carrying his laptop in one hand, two bottles of beer in the other. After he powered up the laptop and opened a few folders, he angled the screen toward me. "Here are some landscapes," he said.

"These are great," I said, scrolling through the images. My favorites were a series of shots featuring a small, oddly-shaped castle. "Was this taken in Europe?" I asked, indicating an image of the castle at sunset.

"Nope, right here in the city at Central Park," he explained. "That's Belvedere Castle."

"Oh," I mumbled, noticing the American flag waving from the castle's turret.

Sam clicked around his desktop, and called up another set of images. "These are of the abandoned hospital on North Brother Island. Typhoid Mary used to be a patient there."

I shuddered. "Isn't that place condemned? How did you even get clearance to shoot there?"

"Clearance?" he scoffed. "Art needs no clearance. I thought your horror movie-loving self would be into that sort of thing."

I smiled and clicked through a few more images. "Do you only do landscapes?" I asked.

"Not hardly." Sam opened a different folder, which was a series of nudes featuring a black man and white woman, the man's dark skin a sharp contrast to the woman's milky flesh. One of the images showed the man's face in profile, and I recognized him.

"Is that Michael?" I asked.

"Sure is," he affirmed. "You're not the only artist that picks up modeling gigs to make ends meet."

"He really is beautiful," I said, taking in the next image. "Who's the girl?"

"Her name is Starla. She used to be Michael's neighbor, but she moved out to Colorado a year or so ago."

"Oh," I said, wondering why anyone in their right mind would leave the city for a godforsaken place like Colorado. I advanced to the next image, only to squeal and hide my eyes. "Sam, he's naked!"

"Michael and Starla are naked in all of them," Sam said with a wry smile.

"Well, I couldn't see Michael's penis in the other shots," I said. I peeked around my fingers so I could appreciate the image. Michael was lying on his back, his arms crossed and propping up his head as he stared into the lens, his sly smile telling the viewer he was unashamed. Starla was pressed against his side with her hand splayed across his abdomen, fingers tense and threatening to grab him. "I can't believe you broke up with someone that gorgeous."

Sam shrugged. "What can I say, he wasn't my type."

Sam and his ever elusive type. I clicked through the rest of the images, all of them showcasing Michael and Starla's distinct complexions and near-perfect forms. "You did a great job with these," I said. "They're so sensual and erotic, but tasteful at the same time. Well, except for the cock shot."

There was the wry grin again. "Hey now, that cock shot's my favorite."

I dropped my gaze, and stared at my fingers. "Do you still want to shoot me?"

"If you'll allow it."

"I will."

Sam's hand was on the nape of my neck, then he touched his mouth to mine in one of his soft kisses that went through me like a hot knife through butter. "Thank you, darlin'," he said against my lips. Then he closed the laptop and retreated into the bedroom, presumably to gather his equipment.

"You kiss all your models?" I called after him.

"I never kissed Starla," he said, returning with camera in hand. Despite my current profession I don't know that much about cameras or other photographic equipment, but that one looked awful expensive. "Now, where to pose you," he murmured, looking around the apartment. "Ah."

Sam beckoned me into the kitchen, then he had me lean against the wooden table where we'd eaten breakfast that morning. "You have legs for days, baby," he said, the camera clicking away. "Move to your left, and cross your ankles?"

I did, and Sam smiled. After a few more shots, he searched in his cabinets and emerged with a brandy snifter. After pouring in a finger's worth of cranberry juice, he handed it to me. "Hold it in your left hand, and stretch your right arm straight across your waist. Let the glass dangle. Yeah, just like that. God, you are so gorgeous."

I was used to photographers instructing me to turn this way and that, but when Sam said I was gorgeous it caught me off guard and I slipped. "Bet you say that to all the models," I quipped, trying to recover.

"I only say it to the gorgeous ones." He grabbed one of the kitchen chairs and set it before me. "Sit backwards on the chair."

I did, my arms extended over the back and crossed at the wrists, aware that the position pushed my dress up to my waist and put the white hot pants I wore underneath on full display. I tossed my hair to the side, giving Sam my best sultry gaze as he snapped away. After he'd captured me from a few angles, he lowered the camera.

"Do you trust me?" he asked.

"I do," I replied. Right then, I trusted Sam more than anyone else in my life.

He nodded, formulating what he'd say next. "Will you pose for me without the dress?"

The request intrigued more than shocked me.

"I'm not wearing a bra."

He swallowed. "Is that a no?"

"No, it's not." I stood, and turned my back to him. "Unzip me?"

I heard him set his camera down on the counter, then I felt his hands trembling as he pulled down my zipper. Once I had stepped out of the dress and set it on the counter, I asked, "What about the boots?"

"Leave them on for now."

I did, and resumed straddling the wooden chair. Sam looked at me for a moment, then he darted into his bathroom, emerging with a brush. He went to work on my hair, carefully smoothing down any flyaway strands. Having Sam tend to my hair was pure luxury, so much so I closed my eyes. Once he'd arranged my hair so it was hanging down either side of my neck and hiding my breasts, he grabbed his camera and sat on the floor in front of me.

"Give me sexy, baby," he said as he snapped away. "You're the sexiest woman in the world. Show me. Show everyone."

Sam stood and moved back from me, presumably so he could fit the boots into the shot. I tossed my hair over my shoulders, baring my breasts. Behind the camera, Sam grinned. "That's it, baby. Show me how hot you are." After a few more clicks, he asked, "How do you feel about losing the boots and getting up on the table?"

I unzipped one boot and then the other, and extended my legs toward Sam. He reached forward and liberated my feet from first the right, then the left boot. Once that was done I hopped up on the table. "Lay on your belly," Sam instructed. I did, and arranged my hair so it was falling past the edge of the table like a pale brown waterfall. He took a few shots, then said, "Hands and knees."

I did as instructed, rising up on my knees with my breasts in full view of the lens. After a few shots I rolled over and leaned back on my hands and stretched out the plane of my belly, my hair pooling on the table behind me. Sam took a final shot, then he put down his camera and stood between my legs.

"I'm taking you to bed," he rasped, his hands under my butt as he lifted me. I wrapped my legs around his waist and my arms around his neck, and let him take me.

"Gonna take my picture there?" I whispered, my mouth against his ear. I felt his face stretch into a smile, then his hands were at my lower back as he unzipped my hot pants. Sam dropped me on his bed, then he retrieved his camera from the kitchen.

"You know, I think I will take a few pictures."

Sam got on the bed and stood over me, a foot on either side of my hips as he immortalized the moment. I arched my back for him, enjoying the sight of the bulge in his jeans. I worked my hot pants lower, exposing the lacy pink thong I wore beneath.

"Off," Sam grunted. I slipped off the hot pants and tossed them into a corner. "That too," he said, jerking his chin toward my thong.

I wiggled out of my thong, then Sam grabbed it and flung it aside. Sam took one last picture of me lying naked in his bed, then he set his camera on his dresser and pulled his shirt over his head as he kicked off his boots. When he shoved down his jeans his cock sprang out; if anything, it seemed bigger than it had that night in my apartment. Then Sam was kneeling above me, taking me in his arms.

"Tell me if you want me to stop," he said.

"I don't want you to stop," I said, then I pulled him down and kissed him. He nibbled my lower lip before delving into my mouth, stroking his tongue against mine while his hand massaged my breast. I slid my hands down his back, feeling his smooth skin and hard muscles, my hands coming to rest on his butt. God, my hands on that butt was probably the closest I'd ever get to touching perfection.

Eventually Sam broke our kiss, wending his way down my neck and to my breasts with his mouth. I cried out when he took one in his mouth, his callused hand kneading the other. He bit down on my nipple, then rolled the nub between his tongue and lips. I nearly died from pleasure.

"Is this going to be like the last time?" I asked. "Just making out?"

Sam kissed me between my breasts, then he moved back up my body until his face was directly above mine. "I want to do so much more than make out with you," he murmured, then he pressed his forehead against mine and swore. "I don't have any condoms. Well, I do, but they're old."

"How old?" I asked. Did the age of the condom matter? Do condoms go bad? Honestly, I had no idea, further evidence of my epic dry spell.

"Real old," Sam replied. "Sorry, baby."

"It's all right," I said, leaving off how I hadn't

had sex for so long my hymen might have regrown. Okay, I knew that wasn't possible, but it sure felt possible. As much as I wanted Sam in every way imaginable, I was okay with not going all the way just yet.

"I know how you don't think things counts unless there's penetration," Sam said, stroking his fingertips down my side, his hand coming to rest on my hip. "I just want to make you feel good, baby."

"Well, I'm right here," I said, my fingers dancing across his chest. "Give it your best shot."

He rested his head on one of his hands, while the other stroked down my body, teasing my breasts, my belly, before coming to rest at the apex of my thighs. Sam nudged my legs apart, his fingers tormenting me with long, gentle strokes. Just when I thought I couldn't take it any longer he slid a finger inside me. I gasped, shocked and startled and completely on board with this plan.

"Is that too much?" he asked.

"No," I said, pressing my hips against his hand. "More."

Sam obliged and slipped a second finger inside, strumming me like I was a guitar. Did Sam even know how to play guitar? I bet he was a master at it. If I'd thought masturbating while Sam jerked off above me was hot, having Sam's fingers inside me was nuclear. His free arm snaked around my shoulder, my breasts pressing against his chest as his hand moved faster. Then the room spun and I came hard, biting down on Sam's shoulder as I moaned his name.

"Was that good, darlin'?" Sam asked.

"It was fucking awesome," I breathed. "Sorry about your shoulder."

He shrugged. "It was worth it." Sam withdrew his fingers and squeezed my hip. "So, did that count?"

"You know it did." I pushed him onto his back. "Time for you to have something that counts."

I threw a leg over his hips and kissed my way down his body, ignoring his protests as I took his cock in my mouth. His skin was hot and smooth, like superheated silk that I couldn't get enough of. I sucked it just like Sam had sucked on my tongue, massaging him with my mouth as he writhed and clutched the sheets beneath me. He came even faster than I had, filling my mouth with salty liquid.

When Sam came it was everything and yet nothing, as if I'd somehow transcended the physical and only wished for his happiness. I remembered how happy Sam had just made me and grinned. I know, it made even less sense than a straight girl going to bed with a gay man, but Sam made me feel good; no, I felt better than good. With him, I felt like I belonged.

I kissed my way up Sam's body, across his belly and his smooth chest, the return trip just as wonderful as the first. When I was at eye level with him, I propped myself up on an elbow and asked, "Did that count?"

"God, did it ever." Sam rolled me onto my back and kissed me hard. "I don't ever want to let you out of this bed."

"I'm not going anywhere."

***

The sound of running water woke me, and I realized I was alone in Sam's bed. I deduced that the noise was the shower. I know, I'm like Sherlock. Remembering the fun we'd had the last time we showered together, I slipped out of bed and went into the bathroom. What I saw made my heart fall to the floor.

Sam was standing under the spray with his back to me, shoulders hunched and shaking. He was crying.

A hot tear slipped down my cheek; in my quest to prove that Sam was bi rather than gay, had I forced him to do something with a woman he never would have done otherwise? Was I a sick fuck like Ben?

No, going to bed had been Sam's idea, just like he'd been the one to crawl in bed with me back at my apartment. Whatever had upset him, it wasn't me. I hoped.

I stepped into the shower and wrapped my arms around Sam's waist. "What's wrong?" When he didn't respond, I asked, "Is it what we did?"

"No, baby, no," he said, turning around and taking me in his arms. "Being with you was wonderful. Perfect." He tightened his hold on me, and added, "I meant what I said. I never want to let you go."

My heart did a little somersault at that. "But you're crying."

"I have these dreams sometimes. Nightmares really," he admitted.

"Do you have them often?"

"Ever since I was a kid." He pressed his face against my hair. "No matter how many times I have them, they always wreck me. I'm sorry I woke you, baby; I came in here so I wouldn't disturb you."

"If you're upset, I want you to disturb me." I pressed my cheek against Sam's chest, hot water streaming down my face as I felt his heart hammering away. "You had one last night, didn't you? That was why you went running." When he nodded, I backed up and placed a hand on either side of his face. "If this happens again, I don't want you away running from me. I want you to roll over and wake me up. We can face these demons together."

Sam smiled, but it didn't reach his eyes. "What if you're not there?"

I smiled tightly, happy that he needed me but sad over the reason. "I told you, I'm not going anywhere."

Chapter Twelve

Sam

Thursday morning found me waking up with the most beautiful girl I'd ever seen lying next to me, and me grinning like a fool. Had I been smiling in my sleep? I supposed I had.

A fella could get used to this.

Since Britt was still asleep, I took the time to study her features. She looked younger without her makeup, more like a sweet, innocent angel than the woman who'd posed topless on my kitchen table. I glided my thumb across her cheek, then I rubbed it across her bottom lip, remembering the sight of those pink lips wrapped around my cock.

On second thought, I don't think I'd ever get used to life being this good.

I tugged down the blanket, baring Britt to her waist. Britt's breasts were just about the best looking things I'd ever seen, and I could easily while away the hours staring at them. However, the lack of coverings on Britt's torso chilled her, and she stirred.

"Sam?" she mumbled. "Why so cold?"

"Sorry, baby," I said, tucking the blanket up under her chin. "That better?"

"Mm hm."

I took that as a yes, and pulled her flush against me. "What's on your agenda today?"

"Agenda?" she repeated, cracking an eyelid. "You make all the running around I do sound so formal."

"So you are awake," I said, nuzzling her neck.

"I was enjoying snuggles. Sue me." She stretched her neck for more nuzzling, her long legs tangling with mine.

"You know what I love about you?" I asked, rubbing my foot up and down her calf.

"Only one thing?" she countered.

"Maybe two or three things." We laughed, then I said, "Your height. You're so damn tall, with these legs that go on for miles."

"You wouldn't love me if I was short?" she asked.

"I'd love you if you were a midget," I replied, then I kissed her to stop all that crazy talk. As if Britt was going to shrink or something. When we parted, I said, "You didn't answer me. You working today?"

"Yeah, I have to finish up that catalog shoot. You?"

"I'm scheduled to be at the studio at twelve." I glanced at the clock, and saw that it was just past nine. "Up and at 'em, darlin', I'd best be getting you home."

We got ourselves together, and somehow Britt made catching a cab before ten in the morning in a party dress casually elegant rather than a walk of shame. It didn't hurt that she looked fantastic.

When the cab pulled up in front of Britt's building, I squeezed her hand. I hadn't let go of her since we'd gotten in the cab. "I'll call you when we finish up tonight," I promised.

"Same here," Britt said, then she kissed me on the mouth. "Promise me you'll miss me today."

"Miss you already, baby."

Britt smiled and exited the cab. As I watched her enter her building, I realized that after we'd gone to bed the second time, I hadn't had the nightmares. Maybe Britt really was an angel. Scratch that, she was *my* angel. I just needed to figure out how to keep her.

***

I stopped for some coffee, which didn't taste half as good as Britt's, and an egg sandwich, and got to Nash's studio with thirty minutes to spare. I found the genius himself sitting behind his desk, going over some shots from the last session.

"Morning," I greeted. I sat at my own desk and pulled out my laptop. "What's the good word, Nash?"

"Many good words, my friend, many indeed," he replied. "Have you heard back from the Sullivan girl about those test shots for the harem series?"

"You know, I haven't," I said, thinking about the nude images of Britt sitting in my camera at home. I drank some more coffee, all the while hoping the cup camouflaged my grin.

"That so," Nash said. "Have you checked out *If The Shoe Fits* yet today?"

"You know I don't follow that trash," I said. *If The Shoe Fits* was a website that purported to follow the fashion and arts community, but really served as a who's dating whom site and to pick apart people's wardrobe choices. I had so many better things to do with my time than worry about who wore what designer to which event.

"When you have a second, have a look at today's headlines," Nash said. "I think you'll find them interesting."

"Will do," I said, calling up *The New York Times* instead. I skimmed the actual news, my gaze catching on a picture of two sisters who had been missing for almost a week. They'd been found in a motel room, high out of their minds on so many different drugs it was a miracle they hadn't overdosed themselves. When questioned as to their whereabouts for the past few days, the girls had rambled on about a man who'd spirited them away, fed them all kinds of candy, and transformed them into princesses.

"I'll have what they're having," I muttered. I studied the image of the rescued girls for a moment; they seemed familiar, but I couldn't place them. After deciding that I recognized them from other news reports, I checked Saturday's weather forecast; looked like Britt's cousin would have sunshine and rainbows for her wedding, which was what every bride deserved.

I checked my email, then I got to wondering what Nash had found so all fired interesting on that lame gossip site. Figuring that it might be a piece about Michael's opening, I called up *If The Shoe Fits*. Then I swore.

"Great angle, huh?" Nash called over.

"Yeah." There sure was a piece about Michael's opening, and the top picture was of me punching Ben square in the nose, and Britt standing behind us looking horrified. The headline was even worse:

Man Gets Nose Re-Sculpted At Sculpture Showing.

"Who writes this crap?" I mumbled, skimming through the article. It went so far as to mention Britt and I by name, information probably gleaned from the creep from *Soho Arts Weekly* who'd asked us for quotes. Basically, the article said that Ben had been attempting to have a polite conversation with Britt, and that I flew into a jealous rage and decked him. At least they were right about the rage and decking parts.

"Did you see the last picture?" Nash asked.

"It can't be any worse than the first," I muttered. I scrolled down past the article, and saw an image of me kissing Britt in the back of the gallery, our profiles in full view so there was no doubt about our identities. Her hands were thrust into my hair, and my hand was on her butt, pushing up her dress and exposing those little white shorts she'd worn underneath it.

I leaned back in my chair, scrubbing my face

with my hands. "Britt is going to fucking shit when she sees this."

"Probably," Nash said unhelpfully. "I always thought you were straight up gay, Sam. Although, if you're going to sample the ladies, Britt's a good one to start with."

"She is pretty amazing," I said, taking another look at the image of us kissing.

"You never asked her about the harem shoot, did you?"

I glanced at Nash. "No, I didn't."

Nash clapped my shoulder. "I wouldn't share her either."

I let out a breath I hadn't known I was holding, relieved he wasn't angry with me. "I guess there is something to the opposite sex, after all."

Nash laughed. "There certainly is," he said, then he looked at the images of myself and Britt again. "You two look pretty good together. Now, let's get working."

"Yes, sir." I nodded, scrolling over the images of Britt and I one final time before closing my laptop. We did look good together, dammit, and I was going to do everything in my power to keep us together. Britannica Lynn was my angel, and I wasn't going to give her up for any reason. I only hoped she felt the same way about me.

***

Due to a series of catastrophes ranging from late models to missing wardrobe items, we didn't wrap up the shoot until after ten. Did I say we? I meant I;

Nash took off at five sharp, leaving me to clean up the messes he'd made. Owning my own studio couldn't come fast enough.

I sent Britt a few texts during the evening, letting her know we were running late. She assured me she was fine, and so beat after her own shoot that she was just going to curl up in her apartment for some shut eye. That didn't stop me from calling her the moment I entered my own place.

"Hey cowboy," she greeted. "How did everything work out?"

"It worked out damn exhausting," I replied. "How was your day?"

"The same," she yawned.

I looked at the garment bag hanging off the back of my door, and said, "Got some good news, baby. Your dress was delivered today."

Britt squealed, then she fired off, "Did you open it? What does it look like? Do you think it will fit?"

"No, I'm sure it's beautiful, and everything Jorge makes is a perfect fit," I replied in order. "It's really not hard to dress a beautiful girl well. You'll look great."

She was silent for a moment, and I imagined I'd made her blush. "We'll need to leave early on Saturday," she said. "The wedding's in Westchester, so if we take the train—"

"I can drive us."

"You have a car?"

"Be hard to drive us without one." I smirked.

"Then why are you always taking cabs everywhere?"

"I usually leave the car in the garage beneath my

building. For getting around the city, cabs are easier than finding parking. And most often cheaper," I added, remembering that ticket I'd gotten in Queens and had forgotten to pay. With late fees that astronomical, it's a wonder meter maids weren't writing tickets on gilded pads.

"Okay, then let me see how long it will take to *drive* there." I heard her typing away on her laptop, then she announced, "It's about two hours from my place."

"Your place?" I repeated. "The Dress of Much Magnificence is at my place."

"But all my stuff is here, at *my* apartment."

"Pack a bag and haul your stuff on over," I said. "We can have a sleepover."

Britt giggled. "I like sleepovers."

"Me too. You working tomorrow?"

"I just need to stop by the endless catalog shoot, and hopefully finish up all that nonsense."

Britt's beauty was wasted on something as banal as a mere catalog shoot, but I didn't bother pointing that out. I knew she was only doing them to pay the bills. "Can you meet me at Nash's by five?"

"I can do that."

"Wonderful." I unbuttoned my jeans and asked, "What are you wearing?"

"Panties."

"And?" My phone beeped, indicating that I had a message.

"You should check that," Britt said, her voice husky.

"All right." I checked my messages, and found a picture of Britt that captured her from her shoulders to her knees, clad in nothing but a scrap of blue lace that could hardly be called a garment of any sort.

"You are never going to believe this," I said, resuming our conversation. "Some woman just sent me a picture of her lady bits. She must have had the wrong number."

"Sam!"

"Nice panties, though." Teasing aside, I said, "I wish I was there with you."

"Me too," Britt said, then she yawned.

"I should let you rest," I said. "See you at five?"

"At five," she affirmed. "Sam, wait."

"I'm right here, darlin'."

"What you said." She paused, and I waited for her to speak again. "You said you'd still love me even if I was a midget."

"I do recall that."

"Did you mean that?"

"I absolutely did," I replied, "but don't you go shrinking on me. I love those legs of yours too."

She laughed. "I promise I won't shrink."

"Good. Get some rest."

"I will. Night, cowboy."

"Night, darlin'."

Chapter Thirteen

Britt

I hardly slept on Thursday night, and my tossing and turning was all Sam's fault. If I wasn't lying awake pining for him, I was having these incredibly vivid dreams about him making a surprise visit to my apartment and crawling into bed with me. Around seven I declared sleep a lost cause and took a cold shower.

After the shower, I made a bowl of oatmeal and sat at my drawing table. My sketch of naked Sam was lying on top of the heap of supplies, and I found myself wondering if he'd like it. I also wondered if he'd pose for me sometime; given that I'd posed for him—it would only be fair. Since he liked Central Park so much, maybe we could pick a sunny afternoon and set up on the Sheep Meadow, him with a camera and me with some pencils and a sketchpad.

My phone trilled, and I saw three unread text messages. Fearing they were from Ben, I opened them, then breathed a sigh of relief since two were from Astrid, and one was from my mother. The two from Astrid read:

Astrid: Holy shit, you are a hottie!

Astrid: Damn girl, was that for real or just for the camera?

Since I had no idea what Astrid was talking about, I opened the message from my mother.

Mom: He's furious. Did you have to do this the day before Melody's wedding?

The 'he' in question was probably my stepfather, and I honestly had no idea what I'd done to infuriate him this time. In the past, my transgressions had ranged from coming home a minute past curfew—what eighteen-year-old has to be home by nine, anyway?—to my overall disdain of corporate America, to my mere existence. Complicating the situation was the fact that stepdaddy was infertile or impotent or something, which meant that he'd never have children of his own to carry on his legacy of evil. Mind you, he hadn't told my mom about his little condition until after they'd gotten married, but she got him back but good. Thanks to yours truly, Patrick was saddled with an unruly stepdaughter that preferred art over law as his only heir. As if I'd ever wanted to be an heiress.

I called my mom and she picked up on the first ring. "There you are."

"What have I done to upset Patrick this time?"

Mom sighed. "It's Melody that's really upset."

"Oh, well, who cares about her?"

"Britt," Mom admonished. "You know how Patrick cares for her."

I sure did, being that Patrick had doted on Melody for as long as I could remember, going so far as to pay for the monstrosity that was her wedding. Maybe he could adopt Melody and set me loose. I'd much preferred being Britt Cavanaugh, anyway. "Okay. Why is Melody upset?"

Mom sighed again. "It seems that there are pictures of you on a website."

"Mom, I'm a model. There are pictures of me all over the place."

"These aren't modeling shots. They are of you and a man, and the man is hitting another man, and then you kiss him."

"Omigod." I powered up my laptop, and asked, "Have you seen them?"

"Yes. Melody emailed them to Patrick this morning."

"What website are they on?"

"Something about a shoe."

I banged my head against the table; she meant *If The Shoe Fits*—she had to. Of all the places for pictures of me and Sam to wind up on…

"What was that noise?" Mom asked.

"Oh, just knocking some sense into myself. Hang on, I'm bringing up the website."

One by one the images populated, and yes, they were exactly as Mom described. Sam hitting Ben, me trying to pull Sam away, and…

"Oh, crap."

"Saw the kissing one?"

"Yeah." Not only did the image feature what was perhaps one of the most passionate kisses I'd ever experienced, thanks to Sam's hands pushing up my skirt to get at my butt, the world was treated to an unobstructed view of my undergarments. Thank God I'd worn those hot pants.

"So," I drawled, "damage control?"

"Honestly, sweetie, she's really on the warpath," Mom said.

"Does that mean I get to skip the wedding?" I asked brightly.

"Not hardly. We've put the word out not to mention the pictures during the rehearsal dinner, and you can lay low during the reception. While Melody's in the midst of her princess fantasy she probably won't notice you."

"We can only hope." I wiggled my mouse, moving the picture of Sam and me kissing up and down the screen.

"What's his name?" Mom asked.

"Sam. Sam MacKellar."

Mom sighed, or maybe her brain was developing a slow leak. I sure felt like mine was. "At least he's Irish."

"He's my date for Melody's wedding."

Mom laughed, a bit hysterically if you asked me. "Well, this will certainly be interesting."

***

After I got myself dressed and sent Astrid a text

telling her I'd explain everything later, I packed my overnight bag and headed over to the catalog shoot's location. Since Sam wasn't footing the bill, and I needed the exercise anyway, I opted to walk over instead of cabbing it. Really, walking around the city was the only exercise I got; I'd never been a runner like Sam, and I couldn't afford a gym membership.

Maybe I'd ask Sam if we could go running together. Well, it would have to be just walking at first; at my current level of fitness, I doubted I could run a block without collapsing.

As I daydreamed about Sam in exercise gear, I got a text from the man himself:

Sam: Ever hear of that trash site If The Shoe Fits?

Britt: I saw them.

Sam: Sorry, baby, meant to tell you last night but I forgot. Your ass looks great, tho.

Britt: Play your cards right, maybe we can try that again.

Sam: LOL. See you at the studio at five?

Britt: You bet, cowboy.

Once I got to the catalog shoot's studio, I signed in and made my way over to the set manager. "Hey, Bill," I greeted.

"Britt," he said, his gaze sweeping from my head to my feet. "Looking good, hottie. You here for the final shots?"

"Yeah," I said, taking a step back. "Is the stuff in my usual room?"

"No, you were upgraded to B2."

"Okay. Thanks."

I entered the dressing room and put on the clothes I'd be modeling for the session. Since we were shooting a winter catalog for a national department store chain, my outfit consisted of elegant fawn tweed pants topped with a cream colored sweater. Since I had legs for miles, as Sam had so eloquently put it, all the pants for the shoot had been too short for me, and these were no exception. Today, however, knee high chocolate brown leather boots completed the look, and hid my bare ankles.

When I stepped onto the sound stage, Bill descended upon me again. "So, Britt, we were wondering if you're available for more work."

"Um, sure," I said. "Will it be more catalog work?"

"This will be a Valentine's Day spread," Bill replied. "You're cool with partial nudity, right?" he asked with a wink.

I was cool with nudity, but not his creepy wink. "Is it a lingerie catalog?" My phone trilled; I glanced at the display, and saw it was a call from my agent. "Excuse me."

I stepped away from Bill, and answered, "Hey, Marlys."

"Hey, hottie," Marlys replied. She was the third

person to call me that before noon. "My inbox is exploding with jobs for you."

"Really? Awesome." For a moment I imagined making enough money to get a larger apartment, maybe invest in some new art supplies. "But why now? I've been doing hardly anything but catalog work for months."

"It's all because of your appearance on *If The Shoe Fits*," Marlys replied. "The shot of you kissing that man after he knocked out some creep out is going viral. You're the hottest girl in New York right now."

I pinched the bridge of my nose, suddenly wishing I'd never kissed Sam at the gallery. "Actually, the kiss happened before he hit Ben," I mumbled.

"Even better," Marlys said. "I'll compile a list of the best offers, and email them over to you as soon as I can. Will you get back to me by Tuesday morning?"

"Sure thing," I said, then I asked, "Um, Marlys, why is everyone calling me hottie?"

A pause. "You really don't know?"

"No, I don't."

"When you get a chance, Google yourself. You're being called the hottest of the hotties, worth getting knocked out for."

"Oh, God," I said. "I'm going to need an aspirin."

"Think of all the free publicity you're getting," Marlys said. "This is a good thing, Britt, honey."

"Yeah, a wicked good thing," I mumbled, then I ended the call. I looked around the set; most everyone was looking from their phone or tablet to me, then whispering to each other. So, this was what being famous felt like, everyone staring at you and gossiping behind your back. If this was the sort of life those fame-mongers wanted, they could have it.

And if I ever saw Ben again, I'd punch him myself.

***

The catalog shoot wrapped early, and the production manager had been so impressed with my work he let me keep the clothes I'd worn that day, and had let me pick out some other items from the wardrobe; I guess that was their way of showing me that they really *really* wanted me for that lingerie shoot. I accepted a few sweaters and those chocolate brown boots, but left all the too-short pants behind.

I arrived at Nash's studio just before five and let myself into the studio proper, taking a seat alongside the sound stage. Sam was doing something across the room; I caught his gaze and he flashed me a quick smile. Maybe being infamous wouldn't be so bad as long as Sam could be infamous with me.

"Hey, Britt," came a voice from behind me. I turned and saw my friend Jillene. We had met a few weeks ago at the museum, where she also sat for the occasional art class.

"Hey, Jill," I said, wondering if I should warn her about Ben. I'd never seen her sitting for any of his classes, but the guy was a creep, you know? "You have a gig here?"

"I know, can you believe it?" she gushed. "Out of nowhere, Nash Williams called me for a shoot. I said yes before I even knew what it was about."

"But you know now, right?" I demanded.

"Miss Sullivan," came a voice from my left. I turned and saw Nash Williams himself striding toward me. "Jillene, they need you in makeup."

"Of course," Jillene replied, scuttling away toward the dressing rooms. Nash watched her leave, then he said, "Nice to see you again, Miss Sullivan. Are you here to meet Sam?"

"I am," I replied. "I hope that's all right?"

"Of course it is," Nash replied with a genial smile. "Actually, I was hoping to speak with you again soon. Sands Romance, the publisher for the cover shoot we did last week, loved the images. Since that book is the first in a series, they were hoping you'd be available for the rest of the covers."

"I suppose I am," I said, remembering the three hundred dollar fee. "How many covers are there?"

"Ten altogether, and they want to have the next nine wrapped up within the month."

Wow. That was a lot of work I could add to my portfolio, and a lot of money for me. And I'd have the added benefit of working with Sam. "Sounds good," I said. "Can you get the contracts over to my agent, Marlys Eaton?"

"I'll have them there by the beginning of next week," Nash said.

"Have what where?" Sam asked, as he came up

beside me. "Hey, darlin'."

"Hey, cowboy." I wanted to kiss him hello, but since I didn't know how Sam's coworkers would react to that I settled for slipping my hand inside his. "Nash told me that the romance publisher wants me on more of their covers."

He gave me that lopsided smile that always melted my heart. "Ironic, since you hate romances so much."

"Shh. That's our secret."

Nash cleared his throat, and said, "Sam, we're about done here. Why don't you two take off?" Nash glanced pointedly from our entwined hands to my bag. I guess we were being a bit obvious.

"Thanks, boss," Sam said. "See you bright and early on Wednesday."

With that, Sam grabbed his jacket and we headed toward the elevator, with every single one of his coworkers watching us. No, make that staring; seriously, it was only a picture of a single kiss on the website, and they were acting like our nonexistent sex tape had been leaked. "I take it they've all seen the website," I said.

"Web*sites*," Sam corrected. "Your cute butt is plastered all over the Internet, baby."

"Great. Even my mom's seen them." I glanced at him. "Has yours?"

"She hasn't mentioned it, so I'm going with no," he replied. He hit the elevator call button, and we stood there waiting for the ancient machine while at least a dozen sets of eyes bored into the back of our skulls.

"It's like they're waiting for us to do a trick or

something," I muttered.

Sam rubbed his thumb across my knuckles. "Want to?"

That and his lopsided smile were all I needed. I tilted my face up toward Sam's, but he had more than a quick peck in mind. In the spirit of our kiss at the gallery, Sam grabbed me under my thighs and lifted me against him while I wrapped my legs around his waist. When the elevator arrived he walked us inside, never breaking the kiss. I peeked around Sam's head at his coworkers; to call then slack-jawed would have been an understatement.

"Satisfied?" Sam called over his shoulder. The elevator door wobbled shut as we burst into laughter.

"They looked like they were having a collective stroke," I wheezed.

"It was pretty awesome," he said. "Want to grab dinner?"

"Can I drop my bag off first?" I asked. "With me dragging this around it looks like we're having a booty call."

Sam raised an eyebrow at my phrasing, then he hefted my bag onto his shoulder. "Good lord, woman, did you pack your entire apartment?"

"Just a few essentials," I said. "Change of clothes, some shoes, hair straightener, hot rollers, makeup, art supplies—"

"Art supplies?" he repeated. "Are you going to paint the bride's portrait?"

"No," I mumbled, suddenly shy. The elevator door creaked open, and I plunged out of the building and into the late afternoon light. "I thought maybe you'd let me draw you."

Sam touched my chin, raising my face toward his. "You'd like to draw me?"

"Yeah." I met those blue eyes of his. "I would."

"I'd be honored," Sam said, then he touched his mouth to mine in one of those butterfly-light kisses of his that somehow got me more worked up than when I had his tongue halfway down my throat. Just like with his photography, in real life Sam did sensual exceptionally well.

"So, are we going out or ordering in tonight?" Sam asked.

"Depends. Are you ordering Thai?"

He smiled ruefully. "You really didn't like the Thai food, did you?"

"I really did not." He opened his mouth, and I just knew he was going to make another comment about how I'd eaten all that seafood, except that creepy octopus, and his stupid roast duck, but turned my nose up at all those weird spices. "I also don't care for beets or coconut, just so you know."

"Very well, then no piña coladas or rustic salads tonight," Sam said with a smile. "What would my Britannica Lynn like for dinner?"

I thought for a moment. "What about pizza?"

"Pizza?"

"It's got all the food groups," I explained. "Cheese, bread, and beer."

"I did not know you could put beer on pizza," Sam said. "And aren't you watching your weight? That was your original excuse for not eating the Thai food."

"You can't have pizza without beer," I said,

ignoring his comment about watching my weight. I'd been blessed with a high metabolism that let me indulge in bread and cheese whenever I wanted, but I wasn't telling him that. I did *not* need to give Sam reasons to spring more weird food on me. "And I thought I might start running with you. If that's okay," I added in a rush.

"I'd like that," Sam said as he draped an arm around my shoulders. We picked up some beer along the way to his apartment, and Sam ordered two pizzas—one with extra cheese, and one with everything—from his favorite local delivery place. The pizzas were delivered a few minutes after we got to the apartment, and we spent our Friday night sitting on the leather couch, stuffing our faces and watching bad horror movies. It was the best date I'd had in longer than I cared to think about.

"Well, that one was terrible," I said after the third movie. "Could killer bees even invade a sewer system?"

"I have no idea, darlin', but I sure hope not." He gathered up our empty beer bottles and brought them into the kitchen. "Up for one more?" he called.

"Sure," I replied. Sam appeared a moment later with fresh beers. We clinked bottles, and I asked, "Want to watch another movie?"

"Honestly, I don't know if I can handle another of those," Sam said as he turned off the television. "We should probably go to bed soon. Don't want to be late to your favorite cousin's wedding."

I snorted. "Melody isn't anyone's favorite anything."

"Not even to her soon-to-be-husband?"

I snorted again. Beer definitely brought out the lady in me. "Let me tell you about…" I searched my memory for his name. "Darryl. Let me tell you about Darryl. He's a junior member of my stepfather's firm, and he's almost ten years older than Melody. She's marrying him for his money, nothing else."

"Been happening for years," Sam said, tipping back his bottle. "Money's important. A body needs to feel secure, that the roof over its head won't be going anywhere."

"Then she should get a job," I declared. "Marrying someone for nothing but their paycheck is just wrong."

Sam leaned over and stroked my cheek with his knuckles. "Why do you think people should get married?"

"Love, what other reason is there?" I paused to drink more beer, then added, "I wouldn't even consider marrying someone unless I was head over heels in love with him."

Sam moved closer, his knuckles gliding down the side of my neck. "Ever feel that way about anyone?"

"I think so, once." I glanced at him, and asked, "You?"

"Like you, once."

"How did it work out with her? Him?"

"It's still working out." Sam took the beer from my hand and set it on the coffee table. "Come on, darlin', it's past time for you to be in bed."

"But I'm not tired," I whined.

"Yeah, but you are a bit inebriated, aren't you?" I giggled, thus proving him correct. When my giggling became rampant laughter, Sam hoisted me in his arms.

"I like it when you carry me to bed," I said, kissing his neck. "You have a nice neck. And you smell good. I don't think the average neck smells this good."

"Why, that's the nicest thing anyone's ever said about my neck," Sam said, then he set me on his bed. "Want help with your skirt?"

I batted my eyelashes. "Undress me, cowboy."

"Fresh," he admonished. He fumbled at my waist, so I reached back and unzipped my skirt. Once Sam had it off me, he folded it and placed it on the top of his dresser.

"Do your bra out the sleeve thing," he said.

"My what?"

"You know," he said, gesturing toward my chest. "It's a known fact that all girls can take their bra off while keeping their shirt on."

"Thought you liked me better with my shirt off," I said as I removed the undergarment in question.

"You're keeping yourself covered tonight," Sam said, dropping my bra on top of my skirt before he pulled off his tee shirt—today's was yellow, in case you were wondering—and jeans. "How did you get so drunk off four beers?"

"Just lucky?"

Sam smiled at that, then he turned off the light and got into bed beside me. He tried spooning me, but I wasn't having any of that. I rolled over and put my cheek just where I wanted it, right in the middle of his chest.

"I can hear your heart," I said against his skin.

"Glad to know it's still working."

"And you call me fresh." Suddenly sober, I propped myself up on an elbow and looked down at Sam. "If you have the nightmare, I want you to wake me up."

"I will, angel," he said, smoothing back my hair, "I promise you I will."

Chapter Fourteen

Britt

I woke up with a pounding headache and the feeling that I'd said some profoundly embarrassing things the night before. I debated sticking my head under the pillow and hiding, but the scent of coffee drew me out of bed and into the kitchen.

"Morning, darlin'," Sam greeted, shoving a cup of coffee under my nose.

"Morning," I croaked, then I took a sip of coffee and scowled. "I never taught you the coffee trick, did I?"

"You did not." He pulled out a chair for me, and I wondered if it was the one I'd posed with a few nights ago. "What would you like for breakfast? I make a mean bowl of cereal."

"I'll cook," I said. Even though the coffee was mediocre at best, it was working overtime to restore my wits. "What have you got?"

Sam listed the contents of his fridge and cabinets, and in less than fifteen minutes we were eating grilled bagels topped with eggs and cheese, with some sliced melon on the side. Sadly, Sam hadn't replenished his bacon supply after the other morning, and the melon was a poor substitute for the porky goodness. After we'd finished breakfast, I looked at Sam across the table.

"Do we really have to go?" I whined.

"I believe we do, darlin'," Sam replied. "If I aid and abet you missing this wedding, how will I ever make a good impression on your mother?"

"She's very forgiving," I grumbled.

"Of that, I have no doubt. Now, let's get showered."

We only spent the bare minimum of time messing around in the shower; we were on a schedule, after all, and my hair was so long it took forever to blow-dry. Once my hair had finally gone from dripping to hardly damp, I wound it up in hot rollers, slipped on Sam's bathrobe, went into the kitchen, and made more coffee. Thanks to the many models Sam had worked with over the years he didn't bat an eye at my alien headgear.

"You didn't wake me last night," I said, watching the coffee drip into the pot.

"Was I supposed to?" Sam asked.

"You promised you'd wake me when you had a nightmare."

I heard Sam's chair move, then he was standing behind me. "I didn't have one last night," he said, his hands on my shoulders.

I turned around, and looked up into his bright blue eyes. "I thought you had them every night."

"I didn't last night, or that first night in your

apartment, and I didn't that time we slept on the couch after your four a.m. breakfast," he replied. "I'm beginning to wonder if you're an angel, keeping the bad things at bay."

"You really didn't have one?"

"I really did not have one."

I slid my arms around his waist and pressed my cheek against his chest. "I wonder what it would be like to have wings."

"Probably get a lot of backaches." He rubbed my back, then he tilted up my chin and bestowed one of those butterfly kisses on my lips. "Best get those rollers out, darlin'. We need to leave in an hour or so."

I smiled at him, then I poured myself a cup of coffee and returned to the bathroom. I was still removing rollers when Sam appeared in the doorway behind me.

"Darlin', I need to know how you make coffee this good," he said.

"Then you should have been paying better attention while I was making it."

Sam moved closer and helped me with the rollers. "Come on, tell me."

"I'm telling that secret to the man I marry, no one else."

I'd meant it as a glib comment, but Sam's blue eyes looked pained. "This man you marry, he'll be the one you're head over heels in love with?"

"That's my one criteria for marriage," I said softly. "Unconditional love."

"You and your criteria, Britannica Lynn." Sam withdrew the last roller from my hair and finger combed my curls. "You really don't need to do anything else, maybe just clip it back. Your hair is beautiful."

"Thank you."

Sam stepped out of the bathroom, and I went to work on my makeup. I swept on some eye shadow and mascara, but stashed my lip gloss in my purse so I could apply it once we arrived. Despite Sam's assurances that my hair was fine the way it was, I wound it into a low chignon, leaving a few tendrils free to curl around my cheekbones, and secured the knot at the back of my head with a jeweled barrette. Since I was done from the neck up, I left the bathroom in search of my dress.

"Time to get some clothes on," I called as I stepped into Sam's bedroom, only to find him fully dressed and reclining on the rumpled bed. He was wearing black trousers and a pale gray button down shirt that was open at the collar. A navy blue tie, currently untied, was draped around his neck, and instead of his usual Doc Martins Sam was wearing shiny black cowboy boots. He looked so good it took every ounce of my willpower not to jump him right then and there.

"Did Jorge make your clothes too?" I blurted out.

Sam chuckled. "No, he did not. I've owned this suit for a while. Told you I clean up well."

"I guess you do." My gaze flicked to the garment bag hanging on the closet door. "Is that my dress?"

"The one and only," Sam said. He got off the bed and unzipped the bag. "Ready?"

I shook out my hands, inordinately nervous about seeing a stitched up piece of fabric for the first time. "I am."

Sam unzipped the bag and I gasped. The dress was floor length, with a simple halter back and plunging neckline, nipped in at the waist with a slight A-line to the skirt. The base fabric of the dress was navy blue silk, and Jorge had overlaid it with yards of that tulle that shifted from blue to gold, a technique that added depth but not bulk to the garment. An antique-looking gold and rhinestone brooch was pinned to the lowest point of the neckline.

"It's gorgeous," I breathed. "How did he manage this in just a few days?"

"That's Jorge," Sam said, taking the dress down from its hanger. "Give him a bolt of fabric and he can save the world."

Sam looked at me expectantly; right, time to take off the robe. I suddenly went all bashful, which was absurd. I mean, I'd slept with Sam, showered with Sam…was there anything left for him to learn about me?

I tamped down my embarrassment and took off the robe, and heard Sam suck in his breath at the sight of me in nothing but a tiny black thong. I smiled, my confidence boosted, and stepped into the dress. Sam moved those loose tendrils over my shoulder, then he fastened the single button at the back of my neck. He stroked his fingers down my spine before zipping me up.

"Sit," he ordered. "I'll help you with the shoes."

The shoes turned out to be strappy gold sandals, so delicate they were like more like jewelry than footwear. "I'm perfectly capable of putting on my shoes," I said as Sam buckled on the first.

"Just let me have my fun," he said. Once the shoes were on Sam pulled me upright and turned me toward the mirror over his dresser. "You're beautiful, Britt. And," he added, "the dress has nothing to do with it."

I smiled at his reflection, then I reached up to his cheek and stroked his beard; he'd let it grow in, just like I'd suggested. "We look good together," I said, because it was true. My light brown hair and eyes were a perfect complement to Sam's dark hair and beard, not to mention those pale blue eyes of his.

"Nash said that too," Sam said. He stroked his hands up and down my arms, then he said, "Almost forgot. I have something for you."

"You do?" I couldn't imagine what was left, what with the dress, shoes, and the fact that he'd agreed to be my date to what was sure to be a wedding filled with Sullivan hijinks. I watched Sam rummage in a box atop his dresser, eventually retrieving a gold bracelet.

"I thought this would look nice with your dress," Sam said, as he slid the bracelet onto my left wrist. Once it was on I saw that it was a rose gold Art Deco style cuff.

"It's beautiful," I said. "Where did you get it?"

"I inherited it," he replied. "I was my gran's favorite, and she left me nearly everything, including her jewelry."

"Oh, Sam, I couldn't." I tried removing it, but he closed his hand over mine.

"You can," he said. "Later, I'll tell you what she told me when she gave me that bracelet."

“Later? Why not now?”

“Because right now we have a wedding to get to.”

I smiled and ducked my head, then I gathered my shawl and clutch while Sam retrieved his suit jacket. When he turned around I spied his open collar.

“Your tie,” I said, setting my clutch down on the dresser. “Let me.” I buttoned up his shirt, then I grabbed the ends of the navy silk and knotted them together.

“You’ve done this before,” Sam observed.

“Only on myself,” I replied. “I went through a brief tie-wearing phase during my teens.”

“Did you,” Sam said, then he placed a hand on each side of my face and kissed me hard. It wasn’t one of his butterfly touches; no, that kiss was so hot it seared my soul.

“What was that for?” I asked when we parted.

“I’ll tell you later, right around when I tell you about the bracelet,” he said. “For now, let’s get to the least anticipated social gathering of the year.”

I grabbed my clutch and gave my reflection a once over. “All right,” I said, “let’s get this over with.”

Chapter Fifteen

Britt

"Okay, buddy, you've got some explaining to do."

Sam glanced at me, then he returned his gaze to the road. "Explaining about what, might I ask?"

"This car, for one." When we'd gone down to Sam's building's garage, I'd been expecting the attendant to bring out a regular old two- or four-door vehicle of the Honda or Toyota variety. Instead, the attendant presented us with a shiny black BMW 325I. Once I was a passenger in said vehicle I discovered that the butter soft leather seats were also heated, which made me wonder if there were BMWs in heaven.

"Hey now, I love my car," Sam said, patting the dashboard.

"Yes, it's very nice," I said. "As is your apartment, which comes with a doorman *and* a garage, and that suit you're wearing could feed a family of four for a month." I watched him not look at me; okay, maybe he was watching the traffic. "Spill. Are you the highest paid photographer's assistant in the world, or do you have a goose that lays golden eggs stashed in your pantry?"

Sam chuckled. "Neither, I'm afraid. I mentioned my gran earlier, the one who left me your bracelet?"

"You did."

"I never knew my grandfather; he died long before I was born. However, he worked in the stock market, and he taught my gran everything he knew. She, in turn, taught me."

"Are you saying you're rich?"

"Not by a long shot. I'm comfortable, and I have a nice cushion against emergencies, but I still need to work. Hell, if I lost my job that apartment would be nothing but a memory."

"But not the car?" I teased.

"I rent the apartment. Car's paid for." We stopped for a red light, and Sam glanced at me. "Are you saying you wouldn't love me if I was rich? I said I'd love you if you were a midget."

"I would," I said. "It would just take some getting used to. I am step-related to a bunch of rich jerks, you know."

The light turned green and Sam shifted into gear; once he was in third he took his hand from the gearshift and squeezed my knee. "Glad to hear you wouldn't want me only for my small amount of money."

"You heard my criteria," I said. All this skirting about the topic of love had me intrigued, so I asked, "What's your criteria?"

"For what? Marriage?"

"Yeah. What are the deal breakers?"

Sam was silent for a time. "It would have to be someone I was crazy about," he said at length. "Someone I thought about all the time, who I couldn't get out of my mind. Someone I could be proud of. Someone I couldn't imagine living without."

"Sounds just like my terms and conditions."

The corner of Sam's mouth curled up. "Sure does, darlin'."

Eventually, the road brought us to the country club in Westchester that was hosting Melody's wedding. I knew the place well, since my stepfather's family held all of their important functions there: weddings, anniversaries, the occasional meeting to plot world domination. My sixteenth birthday party had been held there as well, which was my stepfather's last-ditch attempt to transform me into a society girl. As you can probably guess, that hadn't quite worked out for him.

Sam pulled up to the carport at the country club, where we disembarked and he handed over the Beemer's keys to an overdressed valet. I put my hand inside Sam's elbow, squared my shoulders, and stepped through the double doors toward the sort of life I'd avoided at all costs.

Gilt signs directed us to where the Vindale-Moore ceremony would take place. As we followed the pink-carpeted hallway, Sam murmured close to my ear, "No fancy church wedding for Melody?"

"No, Darryl refused one," I replied. "Stepdaddy was so furious, he nearly called the whole thing off;

he's a devout Catholic. Well, as devout as a slimy lawyer can be. Having the ceremony here is the compromise between Darryl and stepdaddy."

"Melody didn't have a say in where she gets married?"

"When you sponge off the men in your life, you get what you get."

The hallway led us to a garden room bordered on three sides by evergreen hedges. A vine-covered gazebo took pride of place, and carefully tended flowering shrubs were scattered around its base. White folding chairs surrounded the gazebo in orderly rows, and fairy lights glinted in the trees.

"This is…pretty," I said. I'd planned on hating everything about the wedding. The nice scenery was a pleasant surprise.

An usher stepped forward, and inquired, "Moore or Vindale?"

"Moore," I replied, though I seriously considered joining Darryl's side. The usher indicated that we should sit on the right of the aisle, then he offered to place our gift on the proper table. I handed over the envelope, then Sam and I found some seats neat the back.

"Is your mother here?" Sam asked.

I craned my neck and found her smack dab in the front row, right where Patrick would have wanted her. "Front row, fourth seat from the aisle," I said. "She has blonde hair, and she's wearing a green dress."

Sam leaned to the side, nodding when he saw her. "That stepdaddy on her left?"

"Yeah," I said. "His name is Patrick Sullivan,

just so you know. Though I'd love to see the look on his face if you call him stepdaddy."

"Behave," Sam warned. "Who else are you related to around here?"

I spent the next half hour pointing out various relations to Sam, sharing anecdotes about my days in New Rochelle, and my grand escape to New York City. After I'd named every Sullivan in attendance, Sam glanced at his watch.

"A quarter past three," Sam said. "What bride arrives late to her own wedding?"

"She's probably trying for a dramatic entrance." I glanced at the gazebo, where the groom paced back and forth. "Or maybe she wants to make Darryl stress a bit."

"That's evil," Sam said, shaking his head. "Man's probably nervous as hell, waiting on his bride."

"Well, that's Melody."

Sam laced his fingers with mine. "You wouldn't make your groom sweat it out?"

"I would never do anything like this." I toyed with the floral swag perched on the seat back in front of me. "I wouldn't want anything this garish. I mean, the gazebo and all the flowers are nice, but I would never get married at a country club."

"Then where?" Sam pressed. "Family church?"

"I'm not exactly a regular churchgoer," I replied. "Still, a church wedding might be pretty. Not that this isn't pretty, but it all seems so fake."

Sam squeezed my hand. "As long as you love who you're marrying, I suppose any wedding can be perfect."

I squeezed back. “I suppose so.”

The generic background music increased in volume and became “The Wedding March,” and all eyes turned toward the end of the aisle. Melody appeared on cue, to the *oohs* and *aahs* of the assembled guests. She wore a form-fitting white satin sheath overlaid with white lace, her dark hair piled atop her head and her veil pinned just below the profusion of curls. She carried a small bouquet of pink calla lilies, the stems bound with white ribbon and pearl topped pins. As much as Melody got on my nerves, I had to admit that she looked stunning.

“Jorge would hate her dress,” Sam whispered in my ear.

“I think it’s nice.”

“Too boring, too safe,” Sam said. “She isn’t doing anything that hasn’t already been done a thousand times.” Melody passed us and we faced forward. “Don’t worry, darlin’, when it’s your turn to be a bride, Jorge will make you something spectacular. He lives for dressing brides.”

“Who knows if I’ll ever even get married?” I said.

Sam squeezed my hand again. “I have a feeling you will.”

The ceremony went exactly as it was supposed to, with rings and vows and Melody tearing up at just the right moment. Once Melody and Darryl were legal, they stood in their receiving line of two and Sam and I queued up to offer our congratulations.

“You look beautiful, Melody,” I said once we

reached the happy couple. “Congratulations.”

“Thank you, that means so much coming from my beautiful model cousin,” Melody gushed, then she leaned close to me and indicated Sam with her eyes. “Is that him?”

“Melody, this is Sam MacKellar,” I introduced.

“So he *is* the one from the website you were whoring around on,” she accused.

“Um, yeah.” Being that zero percent of my self-esteem was derived from Melody’s opinion of me, the whoring comment didn’t even faze me. “Is that a problem?”

“I can’t believe you brought him here,” she hissed. “This is *my wedding*!”

“I know, that’s why the card’s addressed to you.”

Melody frowned but remained silent, so I took that as my opportunity to move on. While Sam offered his congratulations to the bride, I stepped forward to the groom. “Darryl.”

“Britt.”

And we were out of the receiving line. Sam and I retreated to the reception hall, and he swiped a few *hors d’oeuvres* from a passing waiter. “Man, I’m starved,” he said, handing me a tiny spring roll nestled on a cocktail napkin.

“Me too,” I agreed. We hadn’t eaten since breakfast, and my stomach was none too happy about that. I spied a woman in a stunning green gown watching us from across the room, and formulated a plan. “Want to grab some drinks? Open bar.”

“Surely.” Sam wolfed down his spring roll, then he placed his hand on my back and escorted me to the bar. "Why the sudden desire for alcohol?"

"I think my mother wants to meet you," I replied. "You're familiar with the phrase liquid courage?"

Sam grinned. "Mothers love me. Bring on the parents, baby."

Sam ordered us two glasses of Merlot, then we downed them and ordered two more before heading toward my mother. She was standing with a gaggle of Sullivan harpies, but excused herself when she saw us. I didn't miss the look of relief she bore.

"Britt, baby, thank God you're here," Mom said in a rush, then she plastered her patented Mrs. Sullivan smile across her face. "Wasn't the ceremony nice? And Melody was such a beautiful bride."

"It was, and she was," I agreed. "Mom, this is Sam MacKellar. Sam, this is my mother, Cynthia Sullivan."

"A pleasure," Sam said. "I must say, Mrs. Sullivan, you don't look nearly old enough to have a daughter Britt's age."

"Good to meet you, Sam. I notice that you started right away with the flattery." Mom smirked. "Is that because you're worried I saw those pictures online, the ones of you with my daughter?"

Sam's cheeks darkened, but he didn't miss a beat. "I assure you, I only speak the truth. And now I know that Britt came by her beauty honestly."

At that, Mom blushed a bit. "Mmm hmm. Britt, you and Sam will be sitting at our table." I opened my mouth to whine, but Mom held up her hand. "No, I can't change the seating arrangements, and yes, Patrick will be sitting with us. I'm certain that you can deal with your stepfather for a few hours."

"Okay," I mumbled, leaning against Sam. Confident in her victory, Mom looked at Sam.

"So, Sam, tell me about yourself," Mom said. "Where did you two meet?"

"Yes, Sam, tell us where you met our Britt," said my stepfather, appearing out of nowhere like a frickin' evil ninja. "Patrick Sullivan, Britt's stepfather," he said, extending his hand toward Sam.

"Sam MacKellar," Sam replied, shaking Patrick's hand. "Britt and I met at a photo shoot."

"Are you a photographer?" Patrick asked.

"I am," Sam replied, omitting that he'd been the photographer's assistant on that particular shoot.

"And what were *those* pictures used for?" Patrick pressed. "They didn't end up on any websites, did they?"

"Patrick," I hissed.

"Surely not, sir," Sam said, ignoring my outburst. "Britt is the new face of Sands Romance novels."

"Sands Romance?" Mom asked, clapping her hands together. "I love those books! Maybe you can do a cover with Giovanni!"

"Um, I already did," I said.

At that, my mother squealed like a pig, then she ran off to tell the harpies that I was famous; it seemed that Giovanni had his own little Sullivan-based fan club. I'd never felt so vindicated in my hatred of romance novels. While Mom spread the word of my newfound glory, Patrick continued his interrogation of Sam.

"Interesting that you're so settled in a career at such a young age," Patrick continued. "When I was your age, I was in the Marines."

"I do come from a military family," Sam replied. "I'm named for my grandfather, who was a general in World War Two, and he was named for his father, who served in World War One. Both of my parents are Air Force officers."

"And you didn't enlist, because?" Patrick pressed.

"Patrick," I snapped. "Sam is *not* one of your witnesses."

"It's all right," Sam soothed, then he replied to Patrick. "I could not enlist due to a medical condition. It was a great disappointment, to both myself and my family. Since then I've done my best to support our military as a civilian."

Patrick eyed him for a moment, then he clapped Sam on the shoulder. "We all serve where we can, son."

"That we do, sir," Sam agreed.

Before I could properly appreciate that Sam and my stepfather were getting along, Mom returned with the harpies. Instead of the harpies' usual behavior, which involved sneering and looking down their noses at me, they were thrilled to death to be in the presence of someone who'd not only spoken to, but touched Giovanni. I wonder how they'd react if I told them how he'd oiled up his chest. Knowing them, they'd probably like it.

Chapter Sixteen

Britt

The harpies—I mean, my lovely relations who hoped to the dickens I'd get them Giovanni's autograph—stayed close to Sam and I during the cocktail hour, but once dinner was served they let us eat in peace. My salmon was delicious, and Sam claimed that his gray-tinged chicken entrée was as well. After seeing the prime rib that Mom and Patrick had been served, I wished I'd selected the beef for my plus one.

While we ate, Sam regaled my mother and stepfather with stories of his youth in Iowa, and Patrick attempted to impress Sam with tales of his tour of duty in the Marines, though those stories quickly gave way to his work at the law firm. Yeah, because twisting legal loopholes around to suit your clients always made for riveting dinner conversation.

Once the dinner plates had been cleared, and Melody got all those required dances out of the way, Sam stood and extended his hand to me. "Dance with me, darlin'?" he asked.

"Of course," I said, and I let him lead me to the dance floor. Sam was a good dancer, but that didn't surprise me. Wherever anything romantic was involved, Sam proved to be a master of the art.

"Earlier at my apartment," he began, "after you saw to my tie, I told you I'd tell you later on why I kissed you like that."

"I remember," I said, the memory of that kiss warming me to my toes. "Later is now?"

"I think it is." We swayed to the music for a moment, then he continued, "I love sleeping next to you. I love waking up with you, having breakfast with you. And your coffee is amazing."

"Thank you," I said. "I really enjoy being with you too." I didn't add how much I missed him when we were apart, or how I thought about him constantly. I had a feeling he knew that.

"Britt, I have to be honest with you. When we first met, I thought I was just infatuated with a pretty girl. I mean, it would make no sense for someone like me to fall for you. I thought that for a few days, but…"

"But?" I prompted, slightly terrified that Sam was about to break up with me in the middle of the dance floor at my cousin's wedding. Wait—could he even break up with me when we weren't even technically dating?

"But I've realized that mere infatuation can't account for everything that's between us." Sam gathered me closer, and asked, "You feel it too, baby?"

"Yeah. I do."

"Then, when you took care of my tie earlier at my place, I had this vision of us together. Together for so long you tied my ties out of habit, because you'd done it so many times before."

I placed my hand on his chest. "Stop."

Sam straightened his back. "I'm sorry, baby. I didn't mean to offend you."

"You didn't," I whispered. "But if you continue down that road, I'm either going to cry or kiss you like I mean it, and I can't do either of those right here."

He smiled, and gathered me against his chest. "Fair enough."

"Tell me more later?" I asked, moving my hand so it was above his heart.

Sam smiled down at me, and covered my hand with his. "I surely will, my Britannica Lynn."

The song ended, and the DJ announced it was time to cut the cake. Sam and I made our way back to our table, then he offered to fetch drinks for myself and my mother. Since Sam was at the bar, and Patrick was elsewhere, Mom and I took a moment to gossip.

"That boy has it bad for you," Mom said, nodding toward Sam as if I hadn't known who she meant. "You two look more in love than Melody and Darryl."

"Sam's just so perfect," I said, ignoring the comparison between us and Bridezilla and her sugar daddy. "Sometimes, I can't even believe he's real."

"Is that why you let him feel you up in public?" Mom asked.

"We were just dancing," I said.

"I meant those pictures of you and him at the gallery," Mom explained. "And why did he hit that other man?"

"That other man had been a jerk to me for weeks," I said, giving my mother the edited down version of what had happened with Ben. "I'm thinking about getting a restraining order against him."

Mom's eyebrows shot halfway up her head. "Did he hurt you?" she demanded. "We can always sic Patrick on him. Being a legal nuisance is the one thing he's good at."

"He didn't hurt me," I replied, wondering just how much I disliked Ben. He was definitely a jerk, but sending Patrick after him would just be mean. "He just followed me around, wouldn't stop trying to talk to me."

"Sam hit him because he was bothering you?" Mom asked, and I nodded. "How gallant. No wonder you let him push your dress halfway up your back."

I covered my face with my hands. "Are those pictures going to haunt me forever?"

"Welcome to the digital age," Mom said, then she looked past me and donned her Mrs. Sullivan face. "Patrick."

"Miss me?" Patrick asked, taking his seat next to my mother. "Britt, did you and Sam take the train up from the city? I'm sure one of the valets can bring you to the station so you can save cab fare."

What a nice jab at my low income level. "Actually, Sam drove us here. In his *own* car."

"Sure did," Sam said, having returned with our drinks. "I love driving, but I don't really get to do it much in Manhattan. Too much congestion."

Patrick nodded, swirling the amber liquid in his glass; idly, I wondered what the liquid was. Patrick never drank alcohol outside of his home, preferring to pretend he was inebriated and therefore lull others into a false sense of security while they spilled their secrets. Really, being a slimy lawyer was his ideal occupation.

The waiters moved among the tables and tiny perfect plates of wedding cake were delivered, little slices of dark chocolate decadence with raspberry filling, along with cups of coffee that were almost as good as mine. While the guests ate their dessert, Melody and Darryl made their way from table to table, thanking everyone for coming. I excused myself to the bathroom before they made it to our table.

After taking care of business, I stood in the bathroom's vanity area fixing my hair. The chignon had held up well, even if the loose curls around my face were looking a little wilted. As I reapplied my lip gloss, the bride herself entered the bathroom.

"Hey, Melly," I greeted, using her nickname from when we were kids. "Need help with your dress?"

"No, I just came in here to get away from it all." She eyed my lip gloss, and asked, "Got any red in there?"

I rummaged in my purse, and pulled out a deep mauve. "This is the closest I have."

"It'll do." I tossed her the tube, and returned my

attention to my own lips.

"You look really happy with Sam," she said.

"I am," I affirmed. "Are you happy with Darryl?"

"Yeah. I guess." She put down the tube and looked in the mirror. "I mean, it's what's expected of me, to marry someone like him."

"You mean what Patrick expects," I said. "Always with his plans for our futures, never caring about what we might want."

"Is that so bad?" Melody countered. "I have a secure future, and a pre-nup that means I'll never want for anything. Maybe you shouldn't have run screaming from Patrick's plans."

"See, that's the difference between me and you," I said, rounding on my cousin. "What I want is happiness, and the freedom to be myself. All you want to do with your life is stay home and eat bonbons all day."

"That's not true," she insisted. "You think I don't want to be happy? To be in love? We're not all like you, Britt."

"What the hell is that supposed to mean?" I demanded.

"You just ran off, didn't tell anyone what you were doing, and started living your dreams," Melody shouted. "Instead of going through with college—college that Patrick paid for—you dropped out, grabbed your trust fund, and became some kind of avant-garde."

"Avant-garde?" I repeated. "What does that even mean?"

"You know, those art types that don't vote or

bathe." She gave me a once over, and amended, "Well, I suppose you still bathe. Good for you."

"First of all, Patrick was not paying for my education," I snapped, ignoring the insult to my hygiene. "I had a full academic scholarship. Second of all, I told my mother exactly what I was doing, every step of the way. She helped me get away from Patrick and his stupid plans."

Melody's eyes widened. "You had a scholarship?"

"I did, for NYU's anthropology program," I replied. "No way was I taking more of Patrick's money than I had to."

"But…you had a trust fund. I know you did."

I laughed through my nose. "That wasn't Patrick's money, either. My father—my real father—won the lottery when I was ten, and he put the money aside for me."

Melody leaned her hip against the counter. "You planned your escape from us for years."

"I did," I admitted. "I made my own plans instead of following Patrick's."

Melody nodded, then she looked in the mirror. "And I ended up with Darryl." She glanced at me, and said, "Honestly, Britt, he is so gross. I can hardly stand kissing him."

"He doesn't seem that bad," I said.

She shuddered. "You know how you're always touching Sam, leaning on him or holding his hand?" I nodded. "I try to stay as far away from Darryl as possible. He sweats constantly, but his skin is always ice cold."

It was my turn to shudder. "Sounds like a fish."

"Great. I'm Mrs. Fish." Melody made fish lips in the mirror, and we laughed.

"If he's so cold and icky, how do you two, um…?" I asked.

She grimaced. "We haven't. I've been telling him I'm saving myself for our wedding night, but that excuse won't work any longer."

"Maybe you can get an annulment on the grounds of no consummation?" I suggested. I guess some of my stepfather's law knowledge had seeped into my brain. Ick. "Check your pre-nup, though, there might be a clause about that."

Melody's eyes lit up. "That would be perfect! Then I wouldn't have to sleep with Darryl, and I could sleep with men like Sam instead!" My back stiffened, and Melody amended, "Hey, I wouldn't sleep with *your* Sam. Just someone like him."

I smiled tightly. "I know. I just want to keep him all to myself." Mel and I stood there grinning like fools for a moment, just like when we were kids, then I took her hands. "Listen, if you need ever need anything, call me. We were friends once."

"Yeah, before you left me," she grumbled.

"I wasn't leaving *you*," I clarified. "Come on, let's get out of here before they send a search party in after you."

Melody checked her reflection one last time. "All right. New mission: not fucking Darryl."

We were laughing as we returned to the reception hall, which made both Patrick and Darryl eye us suspiciously. Melody ignored her husband in favor of talking to more guests. I looked around the hall and saw Sam leaning against the bar, drink in hand, and made a beeline toward him.

"You two looked like you were having fun," Sam murmured once I reached him, draping his arm around my shoulder. "I thought you and Melody didn't get along."

"We were really close when we were younger," I said, wondering if the rift between Mel and I really had come about by me fleeing Patrick's carefully constructed plans. "I guess she's not so bad."

"What were you two talking about that was so funny?" Sam asked, brushing his lips against my temple.

I stood on my toes, and whispered in his ear, "Fucking you."

Sam choked on his drink, and turned an impressive shade of red. After I pounded on his back he said, "You ladies couldn't find anything else to discuss?"

"Nope." I grabbed his now empty glass, and signaled the bartender. "Let's get you another drink."

"Just water," Sam replied. "I need my wits about me if I'm to drive my beautiful Britannica Lynn home tonight."

"Am I staying at your place again?" I asked, even though I had no intention of going to my own apartment.

"As if I'm letting you out of my sight," Sam declared. "I still need to tell you the story behind the bracelet."

"That's right. You do."

The reception wound down shortly afterward. Melody threw the bouquet, and one of the silver-haired harpies caught it; great, the harpies were also cougars. After Sam and I said our farewells to Mom and Patrick, we made our way to the bride. To my surprise, Melody wrapped her arms around me in a bear hug.

"Thank you for coming," Melody said. "I'm going to call you."

"Remember, no fucking your husband," I whispered in her ear.

"Only if you promise to fuck Sam," she whispered back.

"Deal."

Sam raised an eyebrow at our whispered exchange, but didn't ask what it was about. We stopped by the coat check for my shawl, then we went to the car port so the valet could bring up Sam's Beemer. The night was chilly, and the first thing I did when we were in the car was activate the heated seat.

"God," I moaned, wiggling against the warm leather, "this heat is frickin' heaven."

Sam gave me a sidelong glance. "That good, huh?"

"Oh, yeah."

He was silent for a moment, then asked, "Would you love me more if I wasn't rich, or if I was a heated leather seat?"

"Does the heated seat come with massage?"

"For you, anything."

I thought for a moment. "That's a tough one. How not rich are you? Do you have any income, or are you wicked poor?"

"Wicked? Like a witch?"

"Sorry. Old New England saying." I turned sideways in my seat, and studied his profile. "I think I'd love you either way."

Sam grabbed my hand and kissed my knuckles, never taking his eyes from the road. "I'd love you too."

The trifecta of heated seat, wine, and too much dancing took their toll, and those coupled with the motions of the car lulled me to sleep. I woke briefly as Sam wrestled me out of the passenger seat and carried me up to his apartment, then again when I felt something cold and wet on my face.

"Shh," Sam soothed when I jerked away. "It's just a washcloth."

"Why do I need washing?" I mumbled.

Sam chuckled. "Don't want to sleep in your makeup, do you?"

"No, that would be tragic," I replied, then sleep claimed me again.

When next I woke the bedroom was dark, and Sam was sleeping beside me. He'd gotten me out of my dress and shoes, but my underwear was still present and accounted for. After a brief inspection I found that Sam was totally naked. I propped myself up on an elbow and looked down at his face, his features limned in moonlight. The pale light gave Sam's skin a bluish tinge, and made his dark beard and eyebrows black as night. I smoothed his hair back from his forehead, and thought about what he'd said earlier.

When we had talked on the dance floor, had Sam been telling me he loved me? All that talk about him loving me if I was a midget made it seem likely. God, I hoped that was the case, because I sure didn't think I could live without him.

I stroked my hand down his chest, feeling the crisp hairs scattered across it, and followed those hairs down to his naval. After the barest hesitation, I slipped my hand underneath the blankets, and found him hard as a rock. I wrapped my fingers around his cock, enjoying his smooth hardness. I'd meant what I said the first time we were in bed together about his cock being just about the most perfect male appendage I'd ever encountered. I loved holding it, taking him in my mouth, even just feeling him press against me.

Since I had just enough of a buzz left to be daring, I wiggled out of my thong and climbed onto Sam's hips. I kissed his mouth, his neck, my kisses traveling lower in my quest to wake him in the best way possible. When he finally stirred and stroked my hip, I raised myself up and fit him between my thighs.

Sam's eyes snapped open. "What are you doing?" he demanded.

"Waking you up," I replied, bending to kiss his chest. "You know you like it."

"Never touch me again!" Sam screamed as he threw me off the bed. I hit the wall with a thud, and my world went black.

Chapter Seventeen

Sam

"What are you doing?" I demanded.

"Waking you up." She grabbed my cock, stroking her hand up and down my shaft. "You looked ready for me."

"I-I don't want this," I pleaded. "Please, stop it. Stop touching me."

"You know you like it."

I turned my head and cried into my pillow; I didn't like this, I hated this. Night after night it kept happening, and I had no idea how to stop it.

"You know you like it," she said again, squeezing my cock harder. "If you didn't want it you wouldn't be able to get it up."

No, I didn't want it, I never wanted anything less than this.

"You know you like it."

That was the last straw. I sat up and threw her off me and off the bed, and hopefully out of my life. "Never touch me again!"

***

I blinked myself awake, relieved beyond words to be in my own bed, in my own apartment in New York, far, far away from where those things had happened. Even though I was shaking so bad I could hardly move, sweat pouring off me, I smiled. I'd had that nightmare a thousand, maybe a million times since I'd moved out of my aunt's place, but never once had I fought back. No, my dreams had always been the same as the reality, with me being just a scared boy unable to stop her.

This time I stopped her, threw her right off me. That had to mean something.

I heard whimpering coming from the floor by my bed, and as my senses dribbled back I recognized Britt's voice. Remembering our conversations earlier in the day, and that we'd gone to bed nearly naked, I figured out what had happened and wanted to kick myself. I hadn't fought back against my aunt so much as I'd thrown the woman I love against a wall.

I slid out of bed and found Britt huddled against the wall, her arms wrapped around her waist. "Baby," I said as I knelt before her, "Are you okay?"

"I get that I shouldn't have climbed onto you like that," she choked out around her sobs. "But did you have to push me off the bed?"

"I'm so sorry, baby," I said, pulling her into my arms. "I was having one of my nightmares, and when I woke up I thought you were part of it. Are you hurt?" I probed her shoulders and the back of her head, feeling for bruises. God, please don't let her be bruised.

"A nightmare made you freak out like that?" Britt asked.

"Yeah. They always do."

"God, Sam," she murmured, tracing her fingertips down the side of my face. "What the hell do you dream about?"

"Terrible things." I touched her cheek, my fingers coming away wet. "Don't cry, baby."

She frowned and ducked her head. "Sorry. Hurts."

I placed a hand on either side of her face and forced her to look at me. "Please, baby, don't cry. This is all my fault. I'm so sorry, baby." She smiled, but her tears didn't slow. She was so beautiful, her honey brown eyes shining in the dim light, and I couldn't help but kiss her. Her mouth was sweet, sweeter than the wine we'd had at the wedding, sweeter than anything I'd ever tasted. I stood, lifting Britt under her thighs as I turned and deposited her on my bed.

"What are you doing?" Britt gasped.

"I think it's kind of obvious," I said, kissing a path down her neck.

"Sam," Britt said. "Sam, I know you don't really want to—"

I kissed her between her breasts, then I slid up her body so my face was directly above hers. "Oh, you know what I want, do you?"

"Like you said after you pushed me off the bed, I think it's kind of obvious."

"Wrong, baby," I said, raining kisses onto her

face. "God, I want you so much."

"After you pushed me, I thought you hated me," she whispered.

"Hate you?" I said, gazing down into her brown eyes. "I could never hate you. Said I'd love you even if you were a midget, remember?"

Britt laughed as she wrapped her arms around my neck, sinking her fingers into my hair. "And I'd love you if you were rich. Or poor. Or somewhere in between."

"Would you, now?" I asked, grazing my thumb across her cheek.

She smiled the sweetest smile I'd ever seen. "I would."

I kissed her lips, her cheeks, then I nudged her thighs apart with my knee, but I hesitated with my cock poised at her entrance. Should I go get a condom? That would be smart. Wait, I still hadn't bought any new condoms, and the ones in my bathroom cabinet were more than two years old. How could I have forgotten condoms? I'm a guy, I should be on top of these things.

I looked down at the woman in my bed, and decided that condoms didn't matter. Well, I hoped they didn't matter, but that would be up to Britt. I knew I was clean, and Britt had mentioned on more than one occasion that she'd been single for over a year. Of course, there was still the threat of unintended pregnancy, but I pushed that out of my mind. If that happened, I'd let Britt make the decisions and support her all the way.

Still, my biggest fears loomed over me: what if I couldn't do it? What if I disappointed Britt?

"What's wrong?" Britt asked.

"I, um, forgot to buy condoms," I admitted. "I still only have the old ones. And, um, I don't want to get you—you know."

Britt smiled tightly. "It's okay, I have that birth control implant," she said. Well, that was one less thing to worry about. "There's one in my bag, inside pocket."

I got off the bed and located the pocket, and the little foil wrapped package inside. Once I'd rolled it on, I climbed back on top of Britt. Her honey brown eyes were gazing up at me, so full of trust and love I froze in place. Of all the times to have stage fright.

"All set?" she asked.

"All set."

When I still didn't move, she said, "Sam, we don't have to—"

I rubbed my cock against her, and her words dissolved into moans. "I think we do, baby," I murmured. "I need you so much I fear I might burst. Is this okay?"

Britt tensed for a moment, then she relaxed underneath my body. "It's okay."

Thank fucking God for that. I worked my way inside her, inch by inch, until I had no idea of where I ended and she began. Finally I was where I needed to be and I held her close, my forehead pressed against hers, feeling our hearts beating in time.

"I had no idea it could be like this," I said. I felt at one with the universe and bigger than the universe, complete unto myself and part of something amazing; I felt like my life's sole purpose was making Britt every bit as happy as she made me.

Britt moved her hips beneath mine, sending electric shocks of pleasure throughout my body. "It can be even better," she said.

"Show me, cowgirl."

Show me she did.

Afterward, I laid on my back with Britt's head resting on my chest, feeling like the king of the world. For the first time in thirteen years I'd let myself be who I really was, Real Sam, as Britt had put it. And Real Sam wasn't plagued with nightmares from the past, or terrified his aunt would burst through the door and ruin his life some more. Real Sam was happy.

Real Sam was completely in love with Britt, and he had no idea how to tell her.

Out of the blue, Britt pinched my nipple. Hard. "Hey," I said, swatting her hand away.

"If you hadn't been all about my nipples at Nash's, we probably wouldn't be here now," she said.

I smoothed back her hair, then I kissed her forehead. "Do you like being here now?" I asked.

"Yeah. I do." Britt arranged herself so she was propped up on an elbow, her soft brown waves falling onto my chest. "Have you ever been with a woman? Before me, I mean."

"Not like I was with you," I said, squeezing her bottom. "And before you ask, I've never been with a man like that, either."

"What?" Britt clambered on top of me and planted her hands on my shoulders, staring me in the eye. "I thought you'd been gay all these years."

"Oh, so being gay means you're promiscuous too?" I demanded.

"No, of course it doesn't," she said, ducking her head. "But if you've never been with any boys…"

"I've messed around a bit," I said. "Me and Michael dated for over a year, you know. We were hot and heavy for a while, but I never wanted him that way. You know, he's the only guy I've dated since I came to New York.

"Really?" Britt asked. "I thought all the boys liked you."

"Of course they do," I replied, Britt laughing as she buried her face in my neck. "Anyway, since you think it only counts when there's penetration, then I guess none of what I did before tonight counted."

Britt laid her body flat atop mine with her arms crossed on my chest, her chin resting on her wrists. "Sam MacKellar, are you saying I popped your cherry?"

"Britannica Lynn…" I almost said "you surely did," but that would have been a lie. I'd already lied so much, and I just couldn't do it any longer, especially not to her. "Britannica Lynn, I wish you had."

She frowned. "What does that mean?"

"If you really want to know, I'll tell you," I replied, working my fingers into that silky hair of hers. I would never disparage drugstore conditioner ever again. "I'll warn you, it's a hard story to hear."

Her brow creased. "Did someone hurt you?"

"Yeah. Someone did."

"Is this what started the nightmares?" When I nodded, Britt relocated again, this time pressing herself against my side and wrapping herself around me in one of those octopus moves I loved. Once she was settled, she said, "Okay, I've got you. Tell me."

"When I was ten, both of my parents were deployed to Afghanistan. I was sent to stay with my Aunt Sophia, but she's not really my aunt. She's more like a third or fourth cousin. Anyway, there was no one else who could take me without me having to change schools, so to Aunt Sophia's I went."

"I take it all was not well with auntie," Britt said.

"Sure wasn't." I held Britt for a moment, burying my face in her hair. "I assume you know, darlin', that a man's body checks its circulation every morning? With a most embarrassing side effect?"

"As evidenced by this morning's wood," Britt mumbled into my shoulder.

"Well, Aunt Sophia saw it as an opportunity." I squeezed my eyes shut, remembering the worst days of my life. "The second morning I was in her house, I woke up with her on top of me."

Britt gasped. "Oh my God."

"God had nothing to do with it," I snapped. "I tried hiding from her, locking my door, but she always found me. Or she used a screwdriver and took the doorknob right off."

"Did you tell anyone? Call the cops?"

"No. If she'd been taken away, there would have been no place for me to stay. That's pretty scary to a ten-year-old." I snuggled Britt closer, and warned, "This might be the worst part."

She squeezed me. "I'm here. Tell me."

I sighed. "It got to the point where she'd walk in

on me in the shower, in my room while I was changing, putting her hands all over me. Since I didn't want anything to do with her—"

"And you were frickin' ten," Britt snapped.

"—my cock didn't react. One time, she was real mad that I wasn't getting hard, and yelled what's wrong, are you gay or something? So I said yeah, I am."

Britt reached up and loosened my fingers; while recounting my aunt's misdeeds I'd clutched her hair so tightly I nearly pulled it from her scalp. "Sorry, baby," I murmured, kissing her forehead.

"It's okay," she said. "But I don't understand. Your aunt thought you were gay, so you decided you were?"

"Not exactly. When my mother returned from overseas, Aunt Sophia gave her an earful about her nasty, deviant son. You see, my aunt was so disgusted by the thought of a homosexual nephew, she never touched me again."

Britt snorted. "Homosexuality is bad, but it's okay to rape a kid."

I shuddered; for so many reasons, I hated that word. "She was sick, but my parents were awesome. Instead of being disgusted, they supported me and my gayness. They found groups of other gay youths for me to hang out with, campaigned against bullying, and made sure no one ever talked down to me because of my sexual preference. By the time I figured out that being gay meant kissing boys, I'd been out for years."

"But you were never gay."

I brought her hand to my mouth and kissed her

fingertips. "No. I never was."

"When we met at Nash's studio, and you were making a big deal about my cleavage, you weren't gay."

Hadn't we already established that? "No, Britt, I wasn't. When I first saw you in that orange dress—"

"You lied."

My blood turned to ice in my veins. "I was lying to myself," I said. "I went from being a scared kid to someone with an identity he never wanted to—"

"To someone who lies." Britt got out of bed and threw on the skirt and blouse she'd worn the day before yesterday. "At any time, you could have said hey, maybe this gay thing isn't for me. Maybe I'll give the chicks a try. But you didn't do that. You kept right on lying."

"Every time I thought about a woman I saw my aunt coming at me in the dark," I shot back. "You think I didn't try to be with women? That I didn't want women? I did, but I couldn't."

"We got on pretty well," Britt snapped.

"Sorry my childhood trauma didn't manifest while we were kissing," I sneered.

"What happened to you was terrible," she said as she pulled on her boots, "but you're pretty terrible too."

I jumped out of bed and grabbed Britt's arms. "Baby, I'm sorry," I said. "I never wanted to lie to you. I've never told anyone what happened with my aunt, not even my parents."

"So I can't verify any of it." She smirked, and added, "Convenient."

"What, you think I'm lying?" I demanded. "What kind of psychopath would make that shit up? I shared the worst moments of my life with you!"

"You want to hear about some of my worst moments?" she countered. "Imagine being a single girl in the city, sick to death of being alone, then all of a sudden you meet this perfect guy. Perfect as in, too good to be true perfect." Britt tossed back her hair and speared me with her gaze. "Then you find out that he really is too good to be true—because he's a fake."

I staggered back as if she'd knifed me in the heart. "You think I made all that up?" I rasped. "Britt, I swear to you on my life I've never been with anyone romantically before tonight. Ask around, try to find someone who fucked me. You won't."

A tear slipped down Britt's cheek. "You're right, I won't, because I won't be asking. Stay away from me, Sam MacKellar, if that's your real name."

She turned her back on me and grabbed her bag, then she headed toward the door. I got there before her, putting myself between her and her escape. "Samuel Milton MacKellar," I said. "I'm named for my grandfather, who was a general in World War Two. He was named for his father, a lieutenant in World War One. Remember, I mentioned them to your stepfather?"

"Great, your name's real," she said. "I'm still leaving."

"What about all the times we've been together?" I pleaded. "The times we hung out, holding hands? The time on the ferry, or watching movies, or when we had oysters? That was all me and you, Britt. Just me and you."

"Sam." Britt raised her head, revealing more tears. "Let me leave."

I placed my hand on the nape of her neck. "Britt, baby, I don't know if I can. You're the best thing that's ever happened to me."

"Yeah, well, you might be the stupidest thing I've ever done." She reached behind me, and grabbed the doorknob. "Sam, please, let me leave. If I really mean something to you, let me leave."

I did the only thing I could do, and stepped aside. Britt was out of my apartment in a hot second, leaving me more alone than I'd ever been. I leaned my forehead against the closed door, and said, "I love you, Britannica Lynn."

Chapter Eighteen

Britt

"I love you, Britannica Lynn."

After I'd stormed out of Sam's apartment I leaned back on his door, my emotions flying around my head like those winged monkeys from Oz. God, making love with Sam had been perfect, and I'd hoped that my fantasy about him really being bisexual instead of gay had come true. But it turned out that nothing about him was true.

Then I heard him say he loved me, and I almost ran back into his arms. Was he lying when he said he loved me? Yeah, probably. From his own admission he'd lied about everything for most of his life. I did not need that in my life; the fact that I wanted Sam more than anything was just something I'd have to learn to deal with.

And there was no way last night was his first time. No one is born knowing moves like that.

I burst out of Sam's building into the chill morning air; being that it was early on Sunday morning, the streets were still rather empty. I searched my purse for my phone so I could see what time it was, then I remembered leaving it on Sam's kitchen table before we'd left for the wedding. Crap.

Well, I sure as hell wasn't going back up to his apartment, and filed my phone situation away to deal with at a later date. I resolved to hail a cab, but swore when I looked inside my wallet. Since the wedding had been open bar, I'd left all my cash at home.

Whatever, I'll just walk. I looked left and right, mentally calculating how many blocks it was to my apartment, when I heard the door behind me. I looked over my shoulder and saw Sam standing there, clad only in a pair of jeans.

"You forgot your phone," he said, holding the device toward me.

"Thank you," I said. I grabbed my phone from his hand, then I started down the street.

"You're walking home?" Sam called after me. "Britt, at least take a cab."

"No cash," I replied without stopping. Sam jogged in front of me, blocking my way.

"I'll pay," he said.

"I don't want your money," I said, trying to slip around him. Not that that worked.

"Then let me drive you," he implored. He grabbed my elbow and said, "Please."

"Don't touch me," I snapped, stepping out of his reach. "Can't you just leave me alone?"

"I will, as soon as I know you're home safe."

I stared at him, the most stubborn, most

infuriating man I'd ever encountered. However, it was cold, and I didn't relish the thought of walking all the way to my place. I weighed my options, and decided that Sam driving me would put me less in his debt than owing him cab fare.

"Fine. Drive. Just keep your hands off me."

Sam winced, but he nodded. After he went up to his apartment for a shirt and some shoes, he had the garage attendant bring out the Beemer. Once the car had been brought up Sam put my bag in the backseat, and we got in. We made it an entire block before he started talking.

"Britt, baby, I'm so sorry," he began. "You were right. My whole life, I've been a fake. The only person I've ever been myself with was you."

I stared out the window, refusing to acknowledge him. After a full minute of silence, he sighed.

"I wish I could say what it is about you that made me not want to hide," he continued. "When I first saw you at the studio, I thought you were beautiful, but I see beautiful people all the time. Then we hung out that night at Catalonia, and I found out that you're smart, and funny, and…" We stopped at a red light, and Sam fell silent. I looked at his reflection in the window, and saw him rubbing his eyes.

"God, Britt, you want to know why I got so drunk at Astrid's party? I was trying to get up the nerve to talk to you. I was surrounded by Michael and the rest of the guys I always hang around with, but then I saw you and I knew I wanted to spend that night with you. I want to be with you, each and every night."

I glanced forward. “Light’s green.”

“Thanks.” Sam slammed the car into gear, and we jerked away from the intersection. He didn’t speak again until the next red light.

“I meant everything I said to you yesterday,” Sam said. “About wanting a life with you. I can’t get you out of my mind, Britannica Lynn.”

“Don’t call me that,” I said, sinking down in my seat. I hadn’t activated the heat, and the leather was cold. “It’s not my name.”

“Fine, I won’t call you that. Instead I’ll call you baby, darlin’, woman I’ll love until the day I die.”

I slid down a bit further. “Don’t call me any of those, either.”

Sam pulled into an empty parking spot that was nowhere near my building. “What are you doing?” I demanded.

“We’re going to sit here until you talk to me,” he replied.

“I’ve said everything that I need to say.”

Sam dragged a fingertip across the back of my hand, and said, “Help me, Britt. I need to know how to make this right.”

I caved and flipped on the heat; if I was being forced to do this, at least I could be warm. “It’s not just that you lied to me,” I began. “You lied to everyone in your life. Your parents, your friends…everyone. How can I ever know if you’re being honest with me?”

“I didn’t mean to lie,” Sam said. “Once I got older and understood how wrong it was, I didn’t know how to end it. Since I couldn’t be with women anyway, I figured it didn’t matter.”

"It matters."

"I know that now. I'm sorry."

"I know you are." I looked at him then, his mournful face nearly breaking my heart. "But I don't know if I'm in love with the real you or the fake you. I can't be with a man that doesn't exist."

"Only you know the real me," Sam said, putting his hand on the back of my neck and drawing me close. "When my gran gave me that bracelet, she said—"

"It's on your dresser."

Sam blinked. "Pardon?"

"The bracelet. I left it on your dresser." When his brows peaked, I added, "Obviously, you're supposed to bestow it to your one true love, or something like that. Well, you shouldn't waste it on me. Give it to someone who's sure she—or he—is in love with the real you."

As soon as the words were out of my mouth, I wanted to take them back. Sam's face fell, then his blue eyes went hard. He checked the road, then he put the car into gear and pulled away from the curb. We didn't speak for the rest of the journey.

When we got to my building I leapt out of the Beemer, but Sam was there in an instant retrieving my bag from the back seat. When he handed it to me, he grabbed my hand.

"Britt, I will fix this," he said.

"I really don't see how you can," I said.

I entered my building without another word. Once I was inside my apartment I looked out the front window, and saw Sam standing there on the sidewalk, staring up at me. Then I threw myself on my bed and cried.

Chapter Nineteen

Sam

My Sunday morning was rather craptastic. After dropping off Britt at her building, I returned to my apartment and sat on my couch in a near catatonic state, wondering how I'd handled myself so badly. I mean, who gets punished when they decide to improve themselves and tell the truth, leaving all their lies behind? Me, that's who.

Of course, Britt had a point; being that I'd lied to everyone for over half my life, how could she know whether or not I spoke the truth? Well, I'd just have to prove it to her, wouldn't I?

Not that I had the slightest idea how to do that.

A little after ten a.m. on Monday morning the icon jumped in the bottom right corner of my laptop's screen; someone wanted to video chat with me. My heart leapt, hoping it was Britt. I opened the window, and saw my mother staring back at me.

"Hey, Momma," I greeted, trying to hide the disappointment in my voice. "What's the good word?"

"You okay, Sammy?" Momma asked. "You look tired."

"Been working a lot." I didn't add that I'd been up since Britt walked out, intermittently crying and raging. Momma didn't need to know that.

"You've got to take care of yourself, Sammy."

"I know, Momma." I picked up my camera, and scrolled through the pictures I'd taken of Britt for the millionth time. "Can I ask you something?"

"Of course."

I scrolled to my favorite shot of Britt, the one of her topless straddling the kitchen chair, her hair tossed to the side. "If someone you loved lied to you, how could they fix it?"

"I guess that would depend on the lie," Momma replied.

"It was a whopper." I scrolled ahead to one of the last pictures, the one of Britt naked in my bed. "A real whopper."

"Hm." Momma sat back in her chair, considering. "In that case, I suppose it would depend on why they lied in the first place." I nodded, and went back through the images of Britt, all I had left of my angel. "So, who'd you lie to?"

"Everyone," I whispered. "Everyone, except one person, and she doesn't believe that I told her the truth."

"Her, huh?" Momma said. Trust my mother to catch all the pronouns.

"Yeah, her." I scrolled to an image of Britt where she was fully clothed, the one I snapped right before we left for her cousin's wedding. Man, Jorge knew how to make a dress. "This would be the her in question," I said, holding my camera's display up to the laptop's video camera.

"She's beautiful," Momma said. "So, what was the lie?"

I shook my head. "If it's all right with you, I need to fix things with her before I can fix them with anyone else."

"All right, then."

I stared at the image of Britt, then it dawned on me that Momma had called me. "Listen to me with my sob story," I said as I set the camera aside. "What's happening in Iowa these days?" I grabbed my coffee mug, filled to the brim with crappy coffee to match my crappy life.

"Well, I'm sorry to be the bearer of bad news," Momma began. "Your Aunt Sophia died yesterday."

The mug crashed to the floor. "What?"

Chapter Twenty

Britt

After Sam dropped me off on Sunday morning, I stayed in bed for the rest of the day, alternating between crying, fuming, and beating my pillow and wishing it was Sam's heart. What's that they say about being careful what you wish for? I had wished and wished and *wished* for Sam to not be gay, and presto, he wasn't. My perfect gay man was gone, and a liar had been left in his place.

It was late afternoon on Sunday before I dragged myself out of bed and into the shower. The tears started up again when I saw my cheap conditioner, so I threw the bottle against the tiled wall. "You're a bastard, Sam MacKellar," I sobbed as the pink liquid dripped down the wall and into the drain. "Nothing but a fucking bastard."

After I finished showering, I put on my ratty old robe and raided my cabinets and refrigerator for alcohol. All I could find was a half empty bottle of Chardonnay I'd used for a sauce a few weeks back;

being that I don't care for white wine it had been minding its own business in the fridge door rack, but broken hearts have the tendency to make all alcohol look delicious. While Chardonnay wasn't my favorite poison, it sure did the trick. The fact that I hadn't eaten since the wedding helped the booze go straight to my head, and I was passed out before nine.

So my heart has splintered into a thousand pieces and I'm embarking on a new career as an alcoholic. Awesome.

Monday morning dawned bright and sunny and gorgeous, and I hated everything about it. I was hung over, starving to the point I was digesting my own stomach, and my heart hurt so much I thought it might kill me.

I found a box of crackers and shoved them into my face while I thought back over my few past relationships. I realized that I'd never been heartbroken before. Oh, sure, guys had broken up with me, and I'd dated my fair share of losers, but no break up had ever hurt this much. Even when my one long-term boyfriend and I had parted ways, I hadn't felt this gutted.

God, Sam MacKellar, I don't know if I can live without you—but I'm equally certain that I can't live with a liar.

Around noon I stumbled across my phone, dead battery and all. I plugged in the charger, then I powered up my laptop and checked my email. Nothing yet from Marlys about all those jobs I'd supposedly been offered, but it was only Monday morning. I guess even agents needed weekends off.

There was an email from my mother, with a subject line that read "Patrick has really lost it this time." I pretended not to see that one. I had plenty of my own drama going on, and no time to worry about his nonsense.

My phone buzzed, then buzzed again. I shut my laptop and went to investigate, and saw more pending text messages than I'd ever gotten in one sitting. There were three from Ben, which meant that I'd forgotten to block his number. I deleted those without opening them, then I saw two from Astrid, five from my mother, one from Melody, and a whopping seven from Sam—and that wasn't counting the voice mails.

Against my better judgment, I opened the text messages from Sam first. The first three, all sent the night before, read thusly:

Sam: I love you, baby. Talk to me.

Sam: I can't stand the thought of you sad. I'm going to fix this, baby.

Sam: Britt, baby, I need you. Please, talk to me.

Seems like I hadn't been the only one drinking on a Sunday night.

The next four were all from Monday morning, and all of them had been sent within the last hour.

Sam: I need to talk to you.

Sam: Something has happened.

Sam: Come on, baby, write back.

Sam: If you don't reply I'm coming over.

"No, you're not," I muttered. I pushed the shattered bits of my heart aside and called Astrid.

"Hey," she greeted. "How was the cousin's wedding?"

"Horrible," was all I got out before the waterworks came back on. Somehow, I choked out that Sam and I had gone together as planned, that I was head over heels in love with him, and that I never wanted to see the rat bastard again.

"Hold up," Astrid said. "You mean to tell me you fell in love with a gay man?"

"He's not gay," I snuffled.

Astrid was silent for a moment. "Exactly how do you know that?"

"Trust me, I'm pretty positive."

"I'm coming over," Astrid declared. "Want me to pick anything up?"

"Lobotomy in a box?" I suggested.

"Ha. Be there in an hour."

I spent that hour making my apartment presentable, if not my person. I splashed some cool water on my eyes, but it did little to help the puffiness. Eventually I made some tea, then I stuck the waterlogged bags on my eyes. At least the warmth was nice.

I fell asleep on the couch with the tea bags plastered to my eyes; thus, they were as cold as my cold dead heart when I woke to a knock at my door. I tossed the bags in the trash, looked through the peephole and did a double take.

"Melody," I said as I opened my door. My newly married cousin was standing in the hallway, surrounded by stacks of matching hot pink luggage. "Shouldn't you be on a honeymoon or something?"

"I'm not having one," she said, jumping up and down and clapping her hands. "I did just like we planned!"

"Uh, what plan was that?"

"I didn't sleep with Darryl! He's furious, and he wants an annulment!"

I stared at my cousin, wondering if all the Sullivans and Moores shared a brain, and if my stepfather had been hogging it for the past few years. "You *what*?"

"Remember? My part of the plan was for me to not fuck Darryl, get an annulment, and live out my dreams just like you do." Melody tilted her head to the side, and asked, "You did keep up your end of the plan, right?"

"What end would that be?" Astrid asked as she strode into my apartment; in my shock over seeing Melody I'd forgotten to shut the door.

"Britt was supposed to fuck Sam," Melody said.

Astrid froze in place. "Sam MacKellar? You *fucked* Sam MacKellar?"

Melody's eyes narrowed. "You did fuck him, didn't you?"

"Will everyone please stop saying fuck," I shrieked as I slammed the door. "Astrid, meet my cousin, Melody. Melody, meet my friend, Astrid. I'm going to go sit in the corner and die."

I flopped onto the couch and hugged one of the

throw pillows to my chest. Astrid sat down beside me. "I brought wine," she said. "Merlot, your favorite."

"Won't help."

"Want to talk about it?"

"That won't help either."

"Maybe not, but I'm dying to know what happened," Astrid said.

Since I'm not one to disappoint my best friend or sort of best cousin, I talked. I gave Astrid and Melody the annotated version of my relationship with Sam, leaving out his nightmares and whatever had happened with his aunt; just because I was furious with him didn't give me the right to spill his darkest secrets. After all, I was *not* the jerk in this scenario. When I was finished, they both stared at me, slack-jawed.

"So all this time he's just been pretending to be gay?" Astrid asked. "That doesn't make any sense."

"He claims that something happened to him when he was younger," I said. When they both looked at me expectantly, I added, "It's not the sort of thing I should out him on."

"Yeah, I suppose being outed as a heterosexual is more than enough," Astrid muttered.

My phone rang, the name on the screen making my heart beat a mile a minute, happy and terrified all at once. "It's Sam."

"How many times has he called?" Melody asked.

"A few."

"And how many times have you called him?" Melody pressed.

"None," I admitted. "Not once, but maybe I

should—"

"Let me," Astrid said, taking the phone from me. "Sammy baby, it's Astrid," she greeted. "Britt's right here. She's…yeah, she's pretty upset. Hang on, I'll ask." Astrid put down the phone and asked, "Would you like to talk to Sam?"

"No."

Astrid put the phone back to her ear. "I'm sorry, Sam, Britt doesn't want to talk right now. Um, okay, I'll tell her." Astrid ended the call and set my phone on the coffee table.

"What are you supposed to tell me?" I asked.

"He wanted me to tell you this: I love you, Britannica Lynn."

I shoved my face into the throw pillow, while Melody asked, "Britannica Lynn? Why is he calling you an encyclopedia? Oh, is that his way of saying you're smart?"

"My name is Britannica," I said. "Britt is a nickname."

"You're named after an encyclopedia?" Melody asked. "No offense, but that's a little weird, even for you."

"I thought you two were related," Astrid said.

"We're step-cousins," I explained. Desperate to change the subject, I asked, "So, Mel, what happened with you and Darryl?"

"Oh, well," Melody began, "I never really wanted to marry Darryl." She turned toward Astrid. "I have this uncle—he's Britt's stepfather, that's how she and I are related—and he arranges things for the family. When he arranged a marriage for me, I just figured it was time."

"Wait," Astrid said, holding up a hand. "In twenty-first century America, this man is arranging marriages?"

"That's Patrick," I said. "Why do you think I stay here in the city, far away from him?"

"It wasn't a bad arrangement," Melody said. "The pre-nuptial agreement provided very well for me. I'd never want for anything for the rest of my life, so long as I followed the stipulations in the agreement."

"But," Astrid prompted.

"But she'd have to be married to Darryl," I supplied. "How did you describe him, Mel? Cold and clammy like a fish?"

Melody shuddered. "The thought of having sex with him was revolting. However, I'd just accepted that it would be my life, at least until Darryl and I divorced in a few years. Then I saw Britt and her date, Sam. At first, I couldn't believe Britt brought that man from those horrible internet pictures to my wedding."

"Hey, those pictures are hot," Astrid said.

"Sure are," I chimed in.

"Then I saw how Sam looked at Britt," Melody continued, "and I realized that Darryl had never once looked at me like that."

"How was Sam looking at Britt?" Astrid asked.

"Oh, like this." Melody retrieved her tablet from her bag, and called up a folder. "The photographers have already sent me all of the wedding pictures. They took numerous shots of those two lovebirds. Really, you'd think it was Britt and Sam's wedding."

Astrid moved to sit on the arm of the couch, looking at the tablet's screen over Melody's shoulder. "Britt, that dress is stunning," Astrid murmured.

"Thanks," I mumbled. "It's the one Jorge made." Since I'd left it at Sam's, I figured I'd never see it again.

"Here's a good one," Melody announced. Astrid took the tablet from Melody, and whistled.

"Damn, girl," Astrid said. "Could he be any more in love with you?"

I frowned and grabbed the tablet from Astrid. The image was of Sam and I on the dance floor; he had one of his hands on the small of my back, while his other hand held mine over his heart. My face wasn't visible, being that the photographer had been behind and to the left of me, but Sam was looking down at me as if I was the center of his world. "I remember this exact moment," I said, a hot tear slipping down my cheek.

"What were you talking about?" Astrid asked.

"His tie," I said. "I'd tied it for him back at his apartment, and he said he wanted us to be together for so long I'd always tie his ties. Out of habit."

"Britt, baby," Astrid said, "maybe you should talk to him."

"But he lied," I said, flailing my arms and almost flinging the tablet across the room. "He lied to everyone!"

"So?" Melody asked. "*Jane Eyre,* which is the greatest romance in the history of romances, is basically about Mr. Rochester lying. Then he came clean and he got the girl."

"Didn't he lose a hand?" Astrid countered. "And go blind?"

"Romance novels suck," I muttered. "I'd rather read something worthwhile, like a comic book or the classifieds."

"Be that as it may," Melody said, "don't you want your own happily ever after?"

When had my vapid cousin become the smart one in the family? I swiped through the images from Melody's wedding; she was right, the photographers had followed Sam and I like hawks. I paused, my finger hovering over an image taken just before we had left the reception; Sam was standing behind me as he settled my shawl onto my shoulders, and I was looking up at him. I remembered kissing him in gratitude.

"You look like you love him just as much as he loves you," Astrid said.

"Maybe." I swiped to the next image; there was our kiss, immortalized in pixels. "I guess."

Melody took my hand. "Want to know why I'm here with you and not on my honeymoon? I want someone to look at me the way Sam looks at you. He did a bad thing, yes, but if you love him this much isn't he worthy of forgiveness?"

I looked from Melody's earnest face to images on the tablet. "If he calls again, maybe I'll talk to him."

Melody patted my hand. "That's a start."

Chapter Twenty-One

Sam

My phone vibrated, so I grabbed it from my back pocket and read the display. Turned out it was a text from Astrid.

Astrid: Sammy baby, Britt's still upset. Her cousin talked some sense into her, and she admitted she has a thing for you. Maybe even a love thing.

"Yes," I said, and actually did one of those lame fist pumps. In the midst of my victory dance my phone vibrated with another text from Astrid.

Astrid: If you call, she'll talk to you, but wait on it a while. She's dealing with a family thing right now, so give her some space to handle that. Hang in there, baby.

Sam: Thank you, Astrid. Thank you so much.

I clutched the phone to my chest, and silently declared Astrid the best friend I'd ever had. Britt loved me. As long as I knew she loved me, I could give her all the time she needed.

Chapter Twenty-Two

Britt

I had two separate, yet equally important, missions on Tuesday morning: review the jobs my agent had sent over, and pretend that I had no idea where Melody was.

"No, Mom, I can honestly tell you that I don't know where Melody is," I said into my phone, and that was the truth. Melody had gone out to pick up lunch, and being that she could be anywhere in a five block radius, I really didn't know where she was at that moment. For all I knew, she could be as far away as Brooklyn. As long as my mother kept asking me these suitably vague questions, this phone call would be a piece of cake.

"If you see her, tell her we're all very worried," Mom said. "Darryl is beside himself."

"Yeah, not getting any on my wedding night would irk me too," I muttered.

"What was that?" Mom asked. "What do you know about Melody and Darryl's wedding night?"

"Melody sent me this weird text," I said, which was another truth. She had also sent me a weird email that had included details of her wedding night that I'd deliberately purged from my memory. A girl could only take so much, you know. "Apparently, she refused him. Told him to his face that he was more like a fish than a man."

Mom burst out laughing. "That he is, but we all knew Melody wasn't marrying Darryl for his good looks."

"Well, it seems that she's decided she needs true love or no love," I continued. "Really, money's only worth so much."

Mom was quiet for a time, then she said, "I'm sorry."

Where the heck had that come from? "Sorry for what?"

"For marrying Patrick, for dragging you down to New Rochelle," she replied. "For a lot of things. I-I really thought marrying Patrick was the best way to help your future."

"I know you did," I said; it was no secret that my mother hadn't married for love either. "You can always leave the creep."

Mom laughed through her nose. "Patrick has a mountain of paperwork to keep that from happening."

"Mom—"

"It's okay," Mom said over me. "I'm okay. I mean, I have a good life here, all the shoes I could ever want, and Aggie's cookies. It's not so bad."

I smiled. "Yeah, Aggie's cookies make everything better. I just wish you had a better man to eat cookies with."

"Maybe you'll be a good daughter and share some details about Sam so I can live vicariously through you," Mom suggested. When I was quiet for too long, she asked, "Aww, honey, did something happen?"

"Yeah, something did. We're working on it, though." At least, I hoped we were still working on things. Sam hadn't called or texted me after Astrid talked to him, but she had told him to give me some time. Maybe he was erring on the side of caution.

"Good. I think that boy might be good for you, Britty."

I winced; Britty was so much worse than Britannica. Melody picked that moment to reenter my apartment, so I waved my arms about in the universally acknowledged gesture for keeping quiet. "So, Mom, I really need to read this email from my agent."

I could just hear her eyes narrowing. "You'll tell me if you learn anything new about Melody?"

"Yep, I'll report on all the new developments." I paused, and added, "Of course, you don't *have* to share those developments with my evil stepfather."

I kid you not, Mom giggled. "You're right. I don't."

Mom and I said our goodbyes, and I had a look at what Melody had gotten for lunch. She must have hit up the Middle Eastern place a block over, because falafel was what was on the menu.

"Eastern Star had the shortest line," Melody

explained.

"Good choice," I said, but before I could eat, my phone rang again. Normally I didn't answer unknown numbers, but in light of the many offers Marlys had sent me, I hoped it would be a potential gig. "Britt Sullivan," I said in my best professional voice.

"Sugar, I need to know what you did to this boy."

"Who is this?"

"Michael DuFresne," he replied. "You must remember me. We met at my cousin Astrid's party, then you attended my gallery opening with Sam, and somehow the spectacle of Sam punching another boy in the nose and then touching your bottom got more media coverage than my artwork."

"Sorry. Hi, Michael." My brain processed what he'd said, and I demanded, "What makes you think I did something to Sam?"

"I don't think, I know. Check your text messages."

I did, and opened the picture Michael had sent me. It was of Sam sprawled on his back, his arm draped across his eyes. At least Sam was lying on a couch and not passed out on the side of the road somewhere.

"He looks tired," I said, resuming the conversation. "People get tired all the time. Biology and such. I haven't seen him in days, therefore I did not make him tired."

"He's not tired, he wasted," Michael clarified. "He went on a bender last night, mourning the love he may have lost."

"That's not my fault, either," I squeaked.

"Are you not the recipient of the love in question?" Michael demanded.

"Yeah, well, that's debatable. Did you know that Sam's not gay? He's been pretending to be gay for like his entire life."

Michael laughed. "Please, the only person who ever thought Sam was gay was Sam. And you, apparently. Really, sugar, I thought you were one of us smart girls."

I sat there, my mouth hanging open. *Michael had known all along?* "But Sam said you two dated for more than a year," I said. "Why did you date him if you knew he wasn't gay?"

"Have you seen Sam's ass?" Michael countered, and I laughed. "With an ass like that I had to give it my best effort. But even I couldn't get him to change teams."

Because I couldn't resist, I said, "I saw the pictures Sam took of you and Starla. You are one beautiful man, Michael."

"Don't you forget it, sugar. Now, about our boy here, what do you want me to do with him?"

"Can he sleep it off at your place?"

Michael sighed. "Lord knows he's done it before."

"Okay, then have him call me when he wakes up."

"Will do. You know, he's been saying all sorts of interesting things in his sleep."

"Interesting?" I asked. "Interesting like what?"

"All sorts of things," Michael said. "Mostly about how he can't wait to get back on his cowgirl and ride her into the sunset."

"He did not say that! Or call me that!"

"Oh, he's been sharing lots more juicy tidbits," Michael said. "Been talking all about his Britannica Lynn, her sweet little bottom, and about the time he—"

"That's enough," I said. "Just have him call me."

"Will do, sugar."

"And Michael?"

"Yeah?"

"Thank you. Really, thank you."

"Any time, sugar. We both want our Sam happy."

I smiled. "Yeah, we do."

I ended the call and grabbed my falafel wrap. "You know, the first time I ordered falafel I thought it was some kind of salad," I said as I took a bite.

"Are you getting back together with Sam?" Melody demanded.

"I just said I'd talk to him," I hedged. "What happens next depends on what he says."

"And what you say," Melody pointed out. "If you keep shooting him down, eventually he'll just stop trying."

My bite of falafel turned to lead in the pit of my stomach. I put down my lunch, grabbed my phone, and sent Michael a text.

Britt: Can you tell Sam that I really want to talk to him? Like, super really?

Michael: I will, sugar.

***Britt:* ☺**

"Okay, Michael's on it," I said.

"He's going to get the two of you back together?" Melody asked.

"Um." As much as I wanted to be with Sam, I felt like I should hear him out before I made any final decisions. "Michael's going to have him call me."

"And then?" Melody asked.

"And then, I don't know." I put down my yummy falafel that I was apparently never going to eat and held my head in my hands. "Seriously, Mel, I just don't know."

My phone trilled with yet another unknown number. I accepted the call, and said, "Britt Sullivan."

"Miss Sullivan," said a male voice. "This is Nash Williams, photographer for the Sands Romance novels."

"Yes, of course. Hi, Nash." While I spoke, I wandered over to my laptop; nope, still no contract for those nine covers I'd been promised by the very man on the other end of the call. "What can I do for you?"

"It's what I can do for you, actually," Nash replied. "Sands Romance, they're being a bit, shall we say, difficult. Before they send over the contracts for the remaining nine covers, they'd like to see a few more test shots. Would you be up for a quick session?"

"Today?" I asked. I didn't have anything else booked, but I didn't want Nash to know that. I had an image as a highly sought-after model to preserve.

"Sure. If we can get the shots done today, with any luck Sands will have the contracts drawn up by Friday."

I did some quick math; contracts by Friday meant possible shooting by Monday, and Britt making her next month's rent *sans* life drawing classes or other disreputable pursuits. Not that I was really going to rob that bank I'd thought about robbing a million times. That was just a backup plan. "Okay, I can do them today. What time?"

"Five sound good?"

"I'll be there."

I ended the call, and took another bite of my falafel. "Well, looks like I have a gig tonight," I said to Melody.

"Gig? A gig as in a modeling gig? Can I come?" she fired off.

"These are test shots, so no, you can't come," I replied. Melody frowned, so I added, "I can take you to an actual shoot, though. Just not this one."

Melody brightened. "I'd like that."

Once Melody and I had finished our lunches, we spent a few hours watching bad daytime television. I wondered if the dearth of decent programming was what drove people to spend their days in cubicle farms. When four o'clock rolled around I threw a few things in my bag, then I texted Michael.

Britt: I'm headed over to Nash's for some test shots. Tell Sam?

Michael: Anything to get this lunk off my

couch.

Britt: Love you, Michael.

Michael: Whatevs.

Britt: XOXO

I slid my phone into my bag, and faced Melody. "Okay, I'm off to my shoot. I should be back in a few hours."

"Break a leg," Mel said. With that, I headed out the door. I'd pose for the test shots, and before long Sam would call. For the first time in days, thinks were looking up.

Chapter Twenty-Three

Britt

I rode the elevator up to Nash's studio, more nervous that I'd been when I'd been booked for the cover shoot. It felt weird going there without Sam; if I was honest with myself, I'd admit that Sam was part of the reason I'd agreed to do the test shots today. Okay, Sam was most of the reason. Working on those nine covers would mean lots of sessions at Nash's studio, and therefore lots of working with Sam. Then Sam and I could spend time together, and I could get to know the real man, the one behind the lies. I hoped I'd love the real Sam just as much as the Sam that was a figment of my imagination.

The elevator door creaked open, revealing nothing but darkness. I checked the buttons to make sure I'd selected the correct floor. Yep, I was on the floor fourth, but the normally bustling studio was deserted. "Nash?" I called.

"Britt, hello there," Nash greeted, walking toward the elevator. "So glad you could make it today."

"Of course," I murmured. "Where is everyone?"

"I'm afraid this shoot will just be you and I," Nash said. "I wasn't scheduled to shoot anything today, but when Sands called earlier and asked for the test shots I didn't want to wait. Are you okay with it being just the two of us?"

I wasn't, especially after what had happened with Ben, but my empty wallet and I decided to just power through the awkwardness. "I'm sure everything will be fine. Are there costumes?"

"The only costume we have on hand is the dress you wore for the last shoot," Nash replied. "What Sands is interested in is how you work with the camera, not the outfits, and if your look is strong enough to carry a cover without Giovanni."

Of course my image can stand up to that oily, muscle bound freak's. "Well, then, I guess I'll go change."

As I made my way to the dressing room, Nash called after me, "Will Sam be meeting you here, later on perhaps?"

I thought of the picture Michael had sent earlier, of Sam passed out drunk on his couch. That man wouldn't be going anywhere for days. "I don't believe so."

I got myself into the ochre gown, no mean feat without someone to help with the laces, and scowled at the grease stains, courtesy of Giovanni. I also kept my bodice at a respectable level, as opposed to Sam's nipple-baring tactics; really, I'm an idiot for not seeing through his façade after that incident. What gay man cares about a woman's breasts that much? When I stepped out of the dressing room, I saw Nash setting up a few props.

"Auditioning for Sam's job?" I smirked.

"I'd never make the cut," Nash said. "People like Sam are one in a million."

Truer words were never spoken. I smelled coffee and glanced at the full pot. "Is that fresh?" I asked.

"I just brewed it," Nash replied. "Help yourself."

I did, only to frown when I tasted it. "This is really bitter," I said. "What kind of coffee is this?" I asked, looking for the package.

"Some swill one of the gophers picked up. I'll get you a Starbucks later." Nash made a final adjustment to the set, then he grabbed his camera. "I thought we'd start with some profile shots."

"Sounds good," I said, setting down my horrendous coffee. "Just tell me what you need me to do."

Chapter Twenty-Four

Sam

When I woke, the ills of my body momentarily overcame the ills of my heart, being that my eyes were sore, my head pounded, and there was a crick in my neck. All in all, I felt the same I always did when I woke up on Michael's couch. I rolled to the side and grabbed my phone from my back pocket, only to frown when I checked the display. Britt still hadn't called or texted me.

"Maybe she's right, maybe I can't fix this mess," I muttered. I opened the gallery app on my phone, and scrolled through the pictures of Britt I'd uploaded. God, but she had looked like an angel in that blue and gold dress. My angel, that's what she was—emphasis on the was. "Maybe it really is over."

"You're really going to give up on her that easily?" Michael asked. He sat in the chair across from me and offered me a glass of water and some aspirin. "That's not like you."

"If she doesn't want me, she doesn't want me," I said. I'd scrolled to the image of her topless in my bed, her pink panties just visible above her shorts. "The least I can do is respect her wishes."

"Well, I happen to know that she does want you." Michael sipped from his own glass, and added, "Fool girl that she is."

I looked at Michael. "When did you and Britt start sharing secrets?"

"While there was a passed out pseudo-homo on my couch," Michael snapped. I opened my mouth to explain, but Michael held up a hand. "You can give me all the dirty details later. Britt wants you to call her after her shoot."

"She does?" I was shocked, for once in a good way. "Where's her shoot? When does it end?"

"She said they were test shots at Nash's," Michael replied. "And no, I have no idea when they'll be over with."

"Nash has a shoot scheduled for today?" I rubbed my eyes; man, had I gotten so drunk I'd forgotten about a shoot? No, it was after five, and one of Nash's many quirks was that he refused to work after five. Amazing that man ever got anything accomplished.

"Well?" Michael asked.

"Well, what?" I countered as I lowered my hand.

"Are you going to call her, or what?"

"You think I should?"

"I think all the bourbon in New York can't drown what you feel for her," Michael said. "And if you insist on being with a woman, Britt's a good one to be with."

I looked at my phone, then I shoved it in my back pocket. "I'll do her one better," I said as I pulled on my Doc Martins. "I'll head on over to Nash's and talk to her in person." Once my boots were on, I stood and grabbed my leather jacket.

"Thanks, Michael," I said, then I clapped him on the shoulder. "For everything."

"I know, I know," Michael said, waving away my gratitude. "Go on, get your girl, cowboy."

I grinned. "I sure will."

***

It took me about half an hour to get from Michael's place in Soho to Nash's studio. As I rode up the elevator I was nearly jumping out of my skin; I had no idea what I was going to say to Britt, or how she was going to react to my being there. All I knew was that she wanted to talk to me, and that made things a whole lot better than they had been yesterday.

The elevator door wobbled open, and I stepped into the studio. Instead of the usual bustle that accompanied most shoots, the place was dark and empty. "Britt? Nash?"

When there was no answer, I made my way to one of the rear soundstages, the one Nash favored for smaller shoots. After I'd navigated around some equipment and got an unobstructed view of the stage, my heart jumped into my throat. Britt was lying stock still on a couch, her skin pale as death.

"Britt! Baby," I said as I rushed forward, brushing her hair away from her face. Her skin was cold, and there was a bluish tinge to her lips. As I grabbed her icy fingers I saw that she was wearing the orange gown from the romance novel shoot. The bodice was unfastened and her breasts were fully exposed.

"Britt," I said, chafing her hands, "Britannica! Britt, baby, talk to me." She was breathing, so that was something. I took off my jacket and laid it across her torso, then I stood and looked around the studio. "Nash," I called. "Nash, are you here? What the hell happened to Britt?"

Pain exploded across the back of my head, and I slumped across Britt's prone form.

***

I don't think I was out for that long, just long enough for whomever had hit me to high tail it out of the studio. I checked on Britt, relieved to find her still breathing, then I grabbed my phone and dialed 911.

"911, what is your emergency?"

"My girlfriend, she won't wake up."

"Is she breathing?"

"Yeah. Her skin's real cold, clammy even."

"Address?"

I rattled off the studio's address, then I sat on the couch and pulled Britt's head onto my lap. "Stay with me, baby," I pleaded. "Please, baby, stay with me."

***

By the time the EMTs arrived I was in tears, begging Britt to open her eyes.

"Let us do our work," one of the EMTs said, dragging me away from Britt. "How long has she been out?"

"Since I got here," I replied, watching as they shone a light in Britt's eyes, and flung aside my coat so they could check her heart. "I…I'm not really sure how long ago that was."

"Do you know what she took?"

I paused. "Took?"

"Looks like an overdose," he replied. When I just stared at him, he demanded, "You take something too?"

"No, I think someone hit me." I rubbed the sore spot on the back of my head, and felt wetness. "Yeah, I was hit," I mumbled, looking at my bloody fingers." The EMT started toward me, but I backed away. "I'm fine. Britt needs you more than I do."

The EMT frowned, but he returned his focus to Britt. "She do drugs often?"

"Never."

"Drink?"

"Only socially," I replied. "Can't hold her liquor worth a damn."

The second EMT looked up at her partner, and said something full of medical jargon. The first nodded, then he and asked me, "What is this place? How would she have gotten drugs?"

"This is a photography studio," I began, then I realized I hadn't seen Nash once since I arrived.

"Nash? Nash, are you here?" I called. When there was no response I turned around, and saw the nearly full pot of coffee. Odd, since Nash hates coffee nearly as much as he hates Mondays. "Can you put drugs in coffee?" I asked.

The second EMT followed my gaze to the coffee pot. "You think she's been roofied?" she asked.

A few facts clinked into place in my head: the young girls in the harem costumes, Nash's lack of a presence in his own studio, the fact that somebody had almost brained me. "Yeah, and I think I know who did it."

Chapter Twenty-Five

Britt

I didn't want to open my eyes, but the bright light streaming down on me had other ideas. I blinked, then I coughed; when I raised my hand to cover my mouth, I saw a white plastic band around my wrist, my name printed on it in neat little letters. For some unknown reason, I was wearing a hospital bracelet.

I looked around, and saw that I was lying on a cot surrounded by blue curtains. While I was wondering what the hell had happened, my gaze fell on Sam. He was sleeping in a chair next to my cot.

"Sam," I rasped. His eyes snapped open, then he staggered to his feet and sat beside me on the cot.

"Hey, baby," he murmured, smoothing my hair back from my forehead. "You're gonna be all right."

"What's wrong with me?" I slurred. *Who'd*

packed all that cotton into my mouth?

"You were drugged."

"Drugged? Who the hell would drug me?"

Sam frowned, his dark brows nearly touching. "Do you remember anything?"

I thought for a moment, which was pretty difficult since my head pounded as if a marching band was tromping across it. "I got a call from Nash to do some test shots for the romance covers," I said. "I…I remember getting to the studio, but then there's nothing. Nothing until now." I looked down at the once-blue hospital gown, and asked, "Where are my clothes?"

"I have the ones you wore over to Nash's," Sam said, jerking his chin toward my backpack sitting on the floor next to the chair. "The EMTs had to cut your gown off."

"EMTs? Gown?" I sat up, searching my memory but finding nothing but blackness. "Why were there EMTs? And what gown?"

"When I found you, you were unconscious, wearing that gown Jorge made," Sam replied. He dragged his thumb across my cheekbone, then he shook his head. "I've never been so scared in my life as when you wouldn't open your eyes."

I reached out to ruffle my fingers through Sam's dark hair, pausing when I felt the edge of adhesive tape on the back of his head. "Are you hurt?" I asked, feeling the bandage.

"Someone smacked me from behind," Sam said. "It was right after I found you."

My hand fell into my lap; in my wildest dreams—make that nightmares—I never thought something like this would happen to me. "Sam, what happened to me back there?"

He gathered me against him, his warm arms doing nothing to chase the coldness from the pit of my stomach. "I don't know, baby," he murmured, pressing his face against my hair. "I really don't know."

***

Once the ER doctor gave me the all clear, I excused myself to the bathroom and got dressed. Earlier, the doctor had advised me in his cold, clinical tone that they'd performed a complete examination of me, including a rape kit. When I asked about the results of the exam, he dropped his gaze to the chart in his hands.

"It takes a few days for results," he'd said, while writing me a prescription for sedatives. "We will be in touch."

Yeah, can't wait to hear about the results of my rape kit. "Anything else I should know?"

"Yes. You will feel the aftereffects of the drugging for a day or so, including headaches, dry mouth, and nausea."

"Sounds like a hangover."

The doctor met my gaze, his mouth pressed into a thin line. "In essence, that's what it is."

For a moment I wondered what he was implying, that maybe I was some party girl who often got drunk and let herself be…well, let whatever had happened to me happen. Instead of defending my honor, I just went into the bathroom and got myself dressed. When I left the bathroom, the doctor was gone and Sam was waiting for me. After we stared at each other for a few moments, he spoke.

"The police want to talk to us," he said. "It can wait until tomorrow."

I shook my head. "Let's just get this over with."

Sam laced his fingers with mine, and we went hand in hand as we rode the elevator and then walked down the hall. When we stepped out into the bright light of day I sighed aloud. "What time is it?" I asked, shielding my eyes with my hand.

"About eleven in the morning," Sam replied. "Thursday morning, that is. You were out for around thirty hours, near as I can tell."

I stopped walking. "What?"

Sam wrapped his arms around me, but I didn't reciprocate. I was so shocked I could hardly move. "Never been so scared in my life, baby," he murmured against my hair. "I didn't quit holding my breath until you opened your eyes up there."

"How long…" I swallowed, and began again. "How long was I there before you found me?"

"That's something else I don't know," Sam said. "I got there about an hour and a half after the last text you sent to Michael."

Wow. Ninety minutes. An awful lot can happen in ninety minutes. "And you've been with me ever since?" I asked, looking up at him.

"I have." He frowned, and stepped away from me. "I can go, if you don't want—"

"No." I grabbed his hands. "Please stay."

Sam smiled tightly. "I'm not going anywhere, baby."

After an all too short cab ride, we arrived at the police station. Sam and I were shown to a waiting room; it had plain walls and a plain wooden table with a few chairs scattered around it, pretty much what you would see on any given episode of *Law and Order*. In the corner sat a television on a rolling cart. We sat in silence until two detectives entered.

"Detective Salter, Detective Fillion," the man said, indicating first himself and then his female companion. They sat opposite Sam and me, then Officer Fillion set a manila folder on the table. "Miss Sullivan, we understand that you remember very little of what happened?"

"I don't really remember anything," I said. "Nash called me, and asked me to do some test shots. I'd been hired as a cover model for some books. I got to the studio, then Nash offered me a cup of coffee…" I shook my head. "Everything after the coffee is just empty."

The detectives glanced at each other, then Detective Fillion withdrew a disc from the folder. "Miss Sullivan, during our investigation we learned that Mr. Williams has been videotaping the events that transpired within the studio. We would like you to watch it, and see if it jogs your memory." Detective Fillion paused, then added, "I will warn you, it contains difficult subject matter."

I laced my fingers with Sam's, then I nodded. As long as Sam was with me, I could handle anything. "I'll watch it," I said.

Detective Fillion rose and slid the disc into the slot, then she turned on the television and rolled the cart closer. "There's no sound," she said, as the screen flickered to life. The video began with Nash moving around the studio, arranging the set pieces.

"That's Nash Williams?" asked Salter.

"Yes," Sam and I replied in unison, then another man moved into view and I gasped.

"Do you recognize that man?" Fillion demanded.

"Yeah," I said. "His name is Ben. He teaches an art class at the museum near my apartment. I used to model for the classes, and he paid me fifty dollars per session." I shuddered. "He started acting weird, so I called the museum and asked about him. They told me that they don't pay models. Ben had been paying me out of his own pocket to go there."

Salter frowned. "Our investigation revealed that Mr. MacKellar here struck and injured Benjamin Williams at a gallery opening, and that Mr. MacKellar is also Nash Williams' assistant," he said.

"Sam had nothing to do with what happened at the studio," I snapped, then my brain processed what else Office Salter had revealed. "Ben's last name is Williams?"

"Yes. Benjamin and Nash are brothers. You didn't know?"

"I did not." I flopped back in my chair, my thoughts spinning. While I searched my memory for any indication that the two had known each other, Detective Salter asked Sam, "Were you aware that they were related?"

"Stop questioning Sam," I said, but Sam squeezed my hand.

"It's all right, they're just doing their jobs," Sam murmured. "I've worked for Nash for over a year, and I never once heard him mention a brother, or any other relation, for that matter. I've only seen Ben three times, twice at the art class at the museum, and once at the gallery when I decked him good."

Salter said something else, but I didn't hear him. Ben was gone and I had appeared on the screen, and I watched as Nash greeted me, then he sent me off to change. I emerged a few minutes later wearing Jorge's gown, its swan song before the EMTs had cut it to shreds, and then video me poured a cup of coffee. Nash and I stood together for a few moments, then he posed me and took a few shots. After the third pose, Nash put down his camera and brought me my coffee. When I finished the first cup he promptly poured me a second.

"That coffee was terrible," I said. Oh good, the video had jogged my memory. "Bitter."

Detective Fillion glanced at me. "We're still waiting for the final analysis, but we believe that the coffee was how they drugged you."

"What kind of bastard drugs coffee?" I wondered, then the king of bastards strode into the frame: Ben. Britt on the television laughed when she saw him, and kept laughing as he unlaced her bodice and started playing with her breasts.

"I-I don't remember any of this," I said, unable to tear my gaze from the screen. To my horror, Ben unzipped his pants, and I went down on my knees before him.

"Oh, my God," I whimpered, tears streaming down my cheeks. Sam scooted his chair closer and put his arm around me, but I hardly noticed him. On the screen Nash dropped his pants, and for a moment they crowded so close to me I was hidden from the camera's view. Thank God for that. Then, the me onscreen toppled over.

"What happened?" I asked the detectives. "Did one of them push me?"

"We think they put too much of the drug in the coffee," Salter said. "You passed out."

"Oh." I bit my fist, watching the screen as Nash and Ben slapped my face for a while, then they dragged me to the couch and set me on it. They stood over me for a minute, gesturing in a way that made me think they were arguing. All of a sudden they stopped, both of them looking toward the elevator, then they retreated behind the set. A moment later Sam rushed to my side, dropping to his knees as he tried to rouse me. When I wouldn't wake up, he covered me with his leather jacket, then he stood and looked around the studio. While Sam's back was turned, Ben crept up behind him.

"Behind you," I whispered, but it didn't matter since video Sam couldn't hear me. Ben hit Sam with some metal object, and Sam fell across my body. Sam was only down for a moment, then he was trying to rouse me again, shaking my shoulders as his tears streamed down his face and onto my cheeks. He grabbed his phone and spoke into it for a moment, then he pressed his forehead to mine as he held my hands.

The EMTs burst into the studio, and Detective Fillion paused the video. "Do you remember any of that?" she asked.

"No," I replied. "I'm sorry, but I don't."

"There's no need to apologize, Miss Sullivan," Salter said in his gruff voice. "If you're up for it, there are some other videos we'd like you to watch."

"Videos of me?" I asked, my voice panicked.

"No, videos of other victims." Officer Salter scrubbed his face; I wondered how long he'd been working on cases like this. "We would like to know if you recognize any of those involved."

As much as I wanted to run away and hide, the thought of there being additional victims turned my stomach. I had to help those girls or boys any way I could. "All right."

The detectives glanced at each other, then Fillion ejected the disc documenting my humiliation, and proceeded to insert disc after disc featuring different girls, though all of the encounters followed the same basic theme. Nash and Ben gave the girls something to drink, then they started giggling and taking their clothes off. Even though Fillion ejected the discs before anything too unseemly was captured, I knew that all of those girls had been raped. Just like I had been raped.

"Those are the girls from the news," Sam said, when we saw a video of two blonde girls who looked no more than fifteen. They were topless, wearing only see through pink pants. "The sisters that were found in the motel room. I walked in on Nash and them, and he sent me home with pay."

Fillion nodded. "Luckily, they survived." Before I could ask what the hell that meant, she ejected that disc and popped in a different video. "This is the last one taken before the events involving you, Miss

Sullivan."

I turned toward the screen, and saw yet another topless girl stumbling around Nash's studio. Then she turned toward the camera, and I gasped. "That's Jillene," I said. "She was another model at the art museum."

"Do you know her surname?" Fillion asked.

I shook my head. "I don't really know anything about her. We were just acquaintances, never said much more than hi to each other. She was always so nice." I tore my gaze from the screen to Fillion; the detective was frowning. "Is Jillene okay?"

"She is not." Fillion looked at Salter; when he nodded, his walrus mustache flapping, she continued, "We found her body last week, behind a motel in the Bronx. Until we reviewed this footage, she was listed as a Jane Doe."

I shivered. "What happened to the other girls?"

"Most were found in a similar manner," she replied. "Found dead of apparent overdoses, their bodies dumped like so much garbage. In fact, out of all the girls you've seen here today only you and those young sisters survived. If it hadn't been for Mr. MacKellar walking in on the Williams brothers when he did, who knows what would have happened to you."

And those were the words that killed me. "Can I go now?" I asked. "I…I don't think I can do this any longer."

Fillion nodded while Salter frowned, making him look even more walrus-like than before. "We do still need an official statement from both of you."

"Can we provide one at another time?" Sam asked, rising to his feet. "I'd really like to get Britt home for some rest, if that's all right."

Salter eyed us, as if we were the ones in the wrong. "You two live together?"

"No, but I stay at Sam's often," I said. "Please, can I go now?"

Salter stared at us for a moment, then he shrugged and shuffled a few papers. "We'll be in touch."

Wow, those were the same words I'd heard from the ER doctor. Thus dismissed, Sam and I left the police station. I stood on the sidewalk with my arms wrapped around my stomach while Sam hailed a cab, then I let him bundle me into the back seat. I remained silent during the ride, while Sam paid the cabbie, when his doorman greeted us, and as we rode the elevator up to his floor.

"Are you hungry?" Sam asked as he shut the apartment door behind us. Instead of answering, I flung myself into Sam's arms and bawled. I let loose the tears I'd held back at the hospital, and at the police station, crying for myself and the sisters and Jillene, and the rest of the poor girls that hadn't made it out of Nash's studio alive. Throughout my breakdown, Sam held me, speaking softly against my ear while he stroked my hair.

"Let it out, baby," he said. "I've got you. I'm never letting go of you."

Chapter Twenty-Six

Sam

"Is she going to be okay?" Melody asked. She had been kind enough to bring over some clothes and a few other essentials for Britt, and pick up the sedatives prescribed by the ER doctor. After assuring her cousin she was all right, Britt downed one of the sedatives, took a shower, and went to bed. As such, Melody and I were standing in the bedroom doorway, watching Britt toss and turn among the blankets.

"She will," I said with a confidence I didn't feel. I watched Britt sleep, my angel nestled among the pillows. "You need anything? Groceries?" I asked, remembering that Melody had walked out on her new husband with nothing more than a few suitcases.

"I'm good," Melody replied. "For a model, Britt has a rather large amount of food in her apartment."

"Britt's a great cook," I said, remembering the breakfasts she'd made for me, not to mention that killer coffee. Realizing I was grinning like a lovesick fool, I coughed and steered Melody toward the door.

"Here," I said, emptying out my wallet and shoving the bills at Melody.

"What's this for?" Melody asked.

"Cab fare," I replied. "You know when Britt's rent is due?" Melody shook her head, so I added, "Find out, and let me know. I'll make sure it's paid."

"Why are you doing all this?" Melody asked.

"Seems like Britt's not going to be working for a while," I said. "Until she's on her feet, I'll take care of her bills."

Melody nodded. "I wonder if Britt realizes how lucky she is to have you," she commented. "If Darryl was in your situation, he'd let us both get evicted."

"Well, that's one of the reasons why you left Darryl, now, isn't it?"

Melody smiled; turned out that Britt's cousin wasn't half bad. "True. Aunt Cynthia's been asking about Britt. What should I tell her?"

I sighed, and rubbed the back of my neck. No mother should ever have to hear about what had happened to Britt. No mother should have to hear about what had happened to me, either. "Tell her the truth," I said at last. "Tell her Britt's been staying here and give her my number. It won't be easy to talk about, but the truth will be better than a lie."

Melody's smile became a grimace. "Britt knew what she was doing when she hooked up with you."

With a grimace of my own, I replied, "No, Mel, she didn't."

Melody left, and I flopped down onto the couch. Except for a few minutes at the hospital, I hadn't slept a wink since I'd come to over an unresponsive Britt at the studio, and the last forty-eight hours of wakefulness finally took their toll. I was asleep before I realized my eyes were closed.

***

When I woke on my couch, the sky outside the windows was dark, but that wasn't the only difference from earlier. Britt had thrown a blanket over me, and was curled up against my side with her head resting on my chest. I laughed softly; either she had forgiven me for all of my untruths, or she was too shaken up to sleep alone. Either way, I wanted to stretch out this moment until the end of time.

But if we stayed on the couch we'd both end up with a crick in our necks. "Come on, darlin'," I said, getting to my feet as I hoisted Britt in my arms and carried her back to the bedroom. "No reason we can't both be comfortable."

I laid a sleeping Britt down on my bed, then I took a moment to look at her. After her shower she'd put on one of my old long sleeved shirts, and her honey brown hair was mussed with sleep. The combination of Britt wearing my clothes and lying in my bed was placing heretofore unknown stress on my chivalrous aspects.

I shook my head, then I shucked off my own clothes and laid down beside Britt, drawing her back against my chest as I pulled the blankets up to our chins. Since she was asleep, I thought it was a great time to tell her how I felt.

"I love you so much, baby," I murmured against her hair. "I'm so glad you're safe. I'm sorry for what I did, all the lies I told, but I swear to you that I'll spend the rest of my life making it up to you."

Britt rolled over and mumbled something into my chest. "What was that, baby?" I asked.

"Eggs and salt."

I frowned. "What exactly do eggs and salt have to do with the price of tea in China?"

"It's how I make coffee." Britt cracked an eyelid, and damn it all if she wasn't smiling at me. "It's what I add to the grounds."

I kissed Britt's hair, and tucked her head underneath my chin. "Thank you, angel," I said. "Thank you so much for sharing that with me."

Chapter Twenty-Seven

Britt

Since it was dark outside, I figured it was Thursday night. Or maybe it was really early on Friday morning, who knew? What I did know was that I'd been hired by not one, but two psychopaths, and was lucky to have gotten away as unscathed as I did—and it was all because of Sam.

I vaguely remembered Melody coming by earlier in the day, dropping off some of my things and mentioning that Mom wanted me to call her. While I knew that my cousin and my mother were both concerned for me, I couldn't focus my thoughts on anyone but Sam. I'd been so mad at him, said such horrible things, and still he'd been there for me. He was, without a doubt, the best man I'd ever met.

That wonderful man was holding me, his arms wrapped tight around me as if he'd never let anything hurt me ever again. After what Sam had been through as a child I couldn't imagine how he'd felt when he found me, not to mention when he'd watched all those videos the police had insisted I see; really, watching all those girls was more like government sanctioned torture than providing information for the case against Nash and Ben.

But Sam had watched them with me, just like he had been there for me when he found me passed out in the studio. Despite the terrible things that had happened to him, Sam had pushed all of his demons aside and been my rock.

I pressed my bottom against Sam's hips and felt his cock move against me. Was I really the only person he'd ever made love to? The idea was so unreal to me, that I could have reached beneath all the layers of hurt he'd accumulated over the years and touched the real Sam. Just as unreal was the fact that someone like Sam loved me.

Of course, there was still the fact that he'd lied. Although, after my talks with Melody and Michael, I understood forgiveness a bit more.

Sam's hand snaked around my hips toward my thighs, and I flinched. After everything that had happened, both at the studio and otherwise, I didn't know if I could make love to Sam again, now or ever.

"Sam," I breathed, and he withdrew his hand.

"I'm sorry," he said, moving away from me. "I was afraid that you weren't really here, and I was dreaming."

I moved onto my back, looking up at Sam. "I thought you only had nightmares."

"I did, then I met an angel." Sam smoothed my

hair back from my brow. "My angel, she chased the nightmares away."

I reached up and petted his beard; now that it had grown in it was irresistibly soft. "I'm glad."

Sam stroked my cheek. "How are you feeling?"

"Better," I said; now that I'd had some real sleep my headache was gone, and I no longer felt hung over. "How do you feel?"

"Me?" Sam countered.

"Yeah, you. All of that couldn't have been easy for you." I scooted closer, so close the tips of my breasts brushed his chest. "Thank you for staying with me."

"Of course I stayed," he murmured. "Sorry I got a little handsy with you. I know that's probably the last thing you want right now."

"It's okay. I've been known to get a little handsy with you too." I traced little circles on his chest. "Sam, you really hurt me when you lied."

"I know," he said, pressing his forehead against mine. "I regret nothing in my life so much as lying to you. I'm so sorry, baby."

"I don't want you to be sorry. I want you to be honest." I moved back and looked up at Sam; he was frowning. "Why are you looking at me like that?"

"Are you leaving me?"

"Sam, it's the middle of the night and I'm not wearing pants," I replied. "Where would I go?"

His frown lightened, but it didn't reach his eyes. "Meant what I said in the car. I'll do anything to fix this. Just tell me what you need."

"I need your honesty," I said. I laced my fingers

with his, and pressed our hands over Sam's heart. "I mean it. Promise me that there will be nothing but the truth between us from now on. Even if it's an ugly, nasty truth, I want the truth."

"I swear it, baby," Sam declared. "Nothing but the truth, now and forever." His brows lowered, then he moved away from me and propped himself up on his elbow. I did the same.

"What is it?" I asked.

Sam dropped his gaze, busying himself with rubbing an invisible spot on the sheet. "I…" He shook his head. "No. It's stupid."

"Hey." I ducked my head under his, forcing him to look at me. "Tell me."

"About forever." His gaze met mine. "I want forever. If I give you honesty, you give me forever."

"Okay."

Sam blinked. "What?"

I grinned and sank my fingers into his thick dark hair. "Okay. Yes. I agree."

He blinked again, then he laughed. "I…God, Britt, I just want you so much."

I wiggled closer. "I'm right here. Have me."

Sam placed his hand on the nape of my neck, bringing my face so close to his our lips were a hair's breadth apart. "Are you sure?"

"Do you still want me? Like that?" I asked, suddenly terrified that Sam thought I was ruined.

"Are you kidding?" he countered, then he kissed me hard. I pulled Sam on top of me, my leg snaking around his waist. Sam's hands slid under my shirt and grasped my thighs, lifting my hips as he fit us together. He rubbed his cock against me, nothing but his thin boxers separating us as he pushed my shirt up under my arms. As Sam kissed his way toward my breasts I freed his cock, the hot, heavy weight of it feeling like it belonged in my hand.

"Missed you so much," Sam said between kisses. "Thought I'd die if I never got to kiss you again." Then his face was directly above mine, his cock pressing against me. "You're sure, baby?"

I hesitated; was I sure? I didn't even want to be sure, I just wanted to be okay, and go back to before I knew Sam had lied, before I'd gone to the studio, and stretch out those halcyon days until the end of time. But I couldn't go back. I could only go forward.

I wanted to go forward with Sam.

I pulled off my shirt and tossed it aside. "I'm sure."

Sam nodded, frowning when I tensed beneath him. "Don't stop," I warned. God, if he stopped I'd probably just give up. Then Sam slid inside me and everything was right again. My body knew Sam, knew he wouldn't hurt me. Deep in my bones, I knew I was safe with him.

Sam was careful as he made love to me, rocking me slow and gentle like the ocean's tides, and I fell in love with him all over again. You see, I've never been one of those girls that had always wanted a bad boy with a room filled with toys. All I'd ever wanted was a man that loved me. Sam loved me, and he was proving it with every tender movement. I bit his shoulder when I came, stifling my cries against his flesh. Sam came a moment after me, the cords in his neck straining as he filled me.

Thus spent, Sam pressed his forehead against mine and kissed me. "Are you okay?" he asked against my lips. "Be honest, angel."

"I'm okay," I replied, and truer words were never spoken. "As long as I'm with you, I'll be okay."

***

A few hours later, I rolled over and found myself alone in bed. I rose and put my shirt back on, then I wove my hair into a loose braid and made my way to the kitchen. I found a pot of coffee waiting for me. If this was what moving forward looked like, sign me up.

"Try it," Sam said, wrapping his arms around me from behind. "I made it according to your exacting preferences."

I leaned back and kissed him. "Did you, now?"

"I surely did."

I rested in Sam's arms for a moment, reveling in the feel of him. He was shirtless, clad only in a pair of sweats, and I was wearing nothing but Sam's shirt. All that warm skin against me relaxed me as much as a hot bath. As for me, I knew I should probably look into wearing something other than Sam's old shirts, but I was putting that off for as long as possible.

I slid free from his arms and poured myself a cup of coffee. "Not bad," I said after I took a sip, then I peeked inside the basket and frowned. There were some shell fragments and a sort of cooked egg floating amidst the grounds. "You put an *entire* egg in there?"

"And salt, just like you said."

I put down my mug, then I stood on my toes and kissed Sam's nose. "Next time, try using just the egg *shell*," I suggested.

He responded with that lopsided grin of his. "I'm afraid I'm not the gourmet chef you are."

"If you ever have the misfortune of visiting the house in New Rochelle, I'll introduce you to Chef Aggie," I promised. "She'll teach you every cooking hack there is." My gaze settled on Sam's shoulder, which was mottled with purple and green bruises. "What happened here?" I asked, worried it was yet another injury from the studio.

To my surprise, Sam's smile widened. "That angel I was telling you about earlier?" he replied. When I nodded, he added, "Sometimes, when we're together, she bites."

I flushed to the roots of my hair; I knew that I'd bitten Sam when I came, but I never intended to leave a mark. Before I could apologize for gnawing the crap out of him, Sam's laptop chimed from the living room. "Hold that thought, darlin'," Sam said as he followed the noise. "There's a call I have to take."

"Call?" I repeated, following him into the living room. Since Sam had brought me to his place, I'd done a pretty good job of pretending the outside world no longer existed. "Is it about work?"

"No, it's my mother," he said as he pulled on a shirt.

"Oh, I can wait in the bedroom—"

Sam silenced me with a kiss. "I'd rather you

stayed," he said against my lips. "Do me a favor, and stay out of the camera's view at first? I need to tell her a few things, then I'll introduce the two of you."

I nodded, then I sat on the couch and pulled the blanket up to my waist while Sam sat at his desk. He typed away on his keyboard, then greeted, "Hey, Momma."

"Sam," said a woman's voice, "what's so important you have to talk to me right away? Are you all right?"

"I am, Momma," Sam replied, glancing toward me. "I'm better than I have been in quite a while."

"Then what is this all about?" she asked.

"Remember the last time we talked, and I told you about a lie I was responsible for?"

"I do."

"It seems that it's time for me to come clean." Sam looked down and picked at the edge of his desk. "Dad around?"

"No, but he'll be back soon," his mother replied. "Would you like to wait for him?"

"No, no, if I don't start now I'll never do it." Sam pursed his lips, then he blew out a breath. "I'd better start at the beginning. Momma, do you remember when you and Dad both went overseas when I was ten, and I had to stay with Aunt Sophia?"

Sam's mother affirmed that she remembered that particular deployment, and Sam launched into the tale of what had really happened to him at his aunt's hands. He stated nothing but the facts of what happened, his spine rigid and eyes downcast as he recounted his aunt's misdeeds, and how she had threatened to hurt him if he ever told anyone what had gone on in her house for those terrifying six months.

"Oh my God, Sammy," his mother said. "Why didn't you ever say anything?"

"At first, I didn't think I could," he replied. "Sophia convinced me that no one would believe me, and I'd be sent so far away I'd never see you or Dad again. Then you came home, and…well, you know that part."

"Was it really six months?" I asked.

Sam looked at me for the first time since he began the story. "Yeah. They let my mother come home after I'd been with Aunt Sophia for six months, and that's when I became Iowa's most eligible gay youth." He laughed mirthlessly. "I'd never been so happy in my life as when I saw Momma standing in the doorway, telling me she was there to take me home."

"Sam, who is that?" his mother asked. I'd forgotten that she didn't know I was there.

"I'll introduce you to her, Momma." Sam held out his hand and I went to him, my own emotions so ragged I didn't concern myself with the fact that the first time Sam's mother saw me I was wearing nothing but one of her son's shirts. I settled myself on Sam's lap, fitting myself against his chest. "Momma, this is Britannica Lynn Sullivan, the very same lady I showed you a picture of the other day."

"You showed your mother a picture of me?" I asked, startled.

Sam kissed my temple. "I did."

Sam's mother cleared her throat, then said, "Yes, Sam, I do recall that. Britannica, is it?"

"Yes, Mrs. MacKellar," I replied. "My friends call me Britt."

"Captain," Sam whispered.

"Captain?" I repeated.

"Captain MacKellar," Sam clarified. "Momma is an officer."

"Oh!" My hand flew to my mouth, and I turned toward the screen. "I'm sorry, Captain MacKellar. Sam told me that both of his parents are officers, but I didn't make the connection."

"That's quite all right," she replied. Now that I was looking at her, I saw that she had the same dark hair and icy blue eyes as her son. Not surprisingly after what Sam had just shared with her, her eyes were rimmed in red.

"Sam, am I to understand that this is the young lady you first needed to repair things with?" Captain MacKellar asked.

"The one and only," Sam replied. "I told Britt everything about Aunt Sophia. She was the first person I felt I could be myself around since all of that happened."

"Britt?"

I tore my gaze away from Sam and faced his mother. "Yes, ma'am?"

"Based on your position, am I to assume that you found Sam's apology satisfactory?" she asked in her best military officer voice.

"Yes." I laid my head on Sam's shoulder, and laced my fingers with his. "I feel very, very lucky to have Sam in my life."

Captain MacKellar smiled. "That makes me happy. Very happy." She glanced at her watch, and continued, "I'm sorry, Sam, but I have a meeting I need to get to. Can we talk again later?"

"Sure thing, Momma," he replied. "Name the time and I'll be here."

"Good. I'll make sure your father can join us." She gathered up some paperwork, and added, "We both have some leave time coming up. Why don't you plan a visit to Sioux City? You can bring Britt. I know I would love to meet her face to face, and I'm sure your father would as well."

"Bring this city girl out to the country?" Sam countered with that devilish smile. "She wouldn't last a day."

"I'd be fine," I said. "I'd have you to protect me."

Sam kissed my temple again. "That you would."

"Then it's settled," Captain MacKellar said as she stood. "I'll arrange for our time off here. How does early November sound? We can have an early Thanksgiving, just the four of us."

"What do you think, angel?" Sam asked. "Wanna carve a turkey with me?"

I grinned, unable to think of anything I'd rather do. "Fight you for the wishbone."

***

After Sam's mom had signed off, Sam and I whiled away the morning watching talk shows, game shows, and other examples of bad daytime television. When Sam insisted on watching one of those sensational news channels for more than an hour, I expressed my displeasure at being forced to watch such garbage by engaging in my new favorite pastime: I fell asleep.

Ha. That'll show him.

When I woke up, Sam was at his desk again, talking on his cell and making notes. "All right, then, Monday at one," he said into the receiver. "See you then."

He ended the call just as I snuck up behind him and slid my arms around his shoulders. "Miss me?" I asked.

"You were right there on the couch," he replied, but leaned back for a kiss anyway. "What are your plans for Monday?"

"Um, I have no idea." Since it was Friday, I'd been planning on putting off real life at least until the weekend was over. "I suppose I should call my agent at some point."

"Oh, Marlys emailed me your contracts. You'll be happy to know that Sands Romance still wants you as their cover queen."

"They do?" I asked, then I realized that if Sam has spoken with Marlys, she, and therefore others, might know about what happened at the studio. "Why did Marlys email you?"

"I called her, let her know that Nash would be out of commission for a time." He swiveled around in his chair and cupped my face with his hands. "And no, I didn't tell her why."

"Marlys didn't interrogate you?" Whenever I refused a job she practically demanded a doctor's note.

"She tried. I told her that Nash was not one to share his plans with me, and that I really had no idea of when he'd be working again. All true statements," he added.

I draped my arms around Sam's neck, and he settled his hands on my waist. "Getting good with this truth thing, aren't you?" I teased.

"More than you realize." He paused, his thumbs tracing little circles against my ribs. "Did you hear me make that appointment?"

"I did," I replied. "Is it for a shoot?"

"No, I made myself a therapy appointment."

"Therapy? For what?" My brain caught up with my mouth, and I added, "But you're already fixing things. Do you really need to go to therapy too?"

"I think I do." Sam sighed, and leaned back in his chair. "It's not just about telling the truth. You don't know what it's like growing up gay, even just pretending to be gay. There are great people out there, and great support groups, but some people just hate for the sake of hating…"

Sam cleared his throat, then he rubbed his eyes. "If I suddenly become not-gay, what's to stop all those anti-gay groups from saying that I'm cured? What's to stop them from using me as an example of how being gay is wrong, something that can be fixed?"

"You really think that would happen?" I asked.

"I don't know," he replied, "but I mean to do everything in my power to be the other sort of example."

"Other sort?"

"Yeah, an example of how being gay is a good

thing." He straightened his back and took my hands in his. "I want the world to know that it was a heterosexual woman that hurt me, and how the gay community took me in. They loved me, accepted me, and never asked me for anything except to be myself. Well, I guess I didn't really live up to that condition," he smirked.

"You did the best you could," I said. "You must have felt so scared and alone."

Sam shook his head. "I wasn't ever scared or alone, not even once, because the entire gay community had my back. Now that I'm outed as a straight guy, they need to know that I still have theirs."

I raked my fingers through his dark hair, pushing his just barely too long bangs off his face. "You're pretty fucking awesome, you know that?"

Sam brought my hand to his mouth and kissed my knuckles. "I'm just a man that loves a woman, is all," he murmured.

"Really? Do you?" I asked. I know we had that forever talk and all, but I'd only heard Sam say that me he loved me through a closed door, or while he thought I was sleeping. Or worse, a text message. "Because I love you an awful lot."

"I love you so much, angel," Sam affirmed, keeping me in his arms as he stood and walked us toward the bedroom. "More than anything, I love you."

Chapter Twenty-Eight

Sam

After spending the best three days of my life holed up in my apartment with Britt, our days filled with nothing more strenuous than ordering takeout and making love, Monday rolled around. The beginning of the week ended our little fantasy life in more ways than one.

For one thing, we both needed to see to our employment situations. Since Nash was currently a fugitive from justice, I was officially out of a job. I did have my savings to fall back on, but I'd promised Melody that I'd cover the rent on Britt's apartment, and I still had my own rent to pay. As strong as my financial situation was, I couldn't afford rent on two Manhattan apartments for more than a few months.

As for Britt, her agent had emailed over twenty solid offers, and she needed to pick some of them quick. Britt had already told Marlys that she would accept the Sands Romance contracts, so those were a go as soon as the publisher found a new photographer. As for the rest of the offers, Britt wavered between excitement over her many prospects, and wanting to give up modeling altogether.

"You warned me modeling was dangerous," she said when I asked her why she was throwing in the towel. "I mean, if you hadn't come by…"

"Hush, angel," I said. "I did, and I will never allow you to go to one of those shoots alone again. All those photographers will have to learn to deal with your annoying boyfriend tagging along behind you."

"My annoying boyfriend, huh?" She smirked at me, then she took off her shirt. Well, it was really my shirt; we were getting our laundry together to drop off at the wash and fold, so she dutifully shucked off the shirt she'd slept in. Of course, that meant she was standing before me naked.

"I can't believe you pay people to do your laundry," Britt said as she rummaged through her clothes. I'd surrendered one of my dresser drawers and half of my closet to Britt, and she hadn't wasted any time in filling them up. "Can't you just hit up a Laundromat like a regular person?"

"The wash and fold is more convenient, and it works out to be about the same price," I countered. "They charge by the pound."

"Clean or dirty?"

"Pardon?"

"When they weigh your laundry, do they do it

when you first drop it off, when it's dirty, or after they wash it?"

"Does that really matter?"

"Of course it does. Dirty laundry, what with the dirt still attached, would weigh more." Britt indicated the bags of laundry on the bed. "I'm afraid the wash and fold may be taking advantage of you, my poor, sweet Sam."

"You really think my clothes are so filthy they could cause a weight discrepancy?"

Britt flashed me that grin of hers, then she got on the bed and crawled toward me. "Maybe I don't want other women handling your delicates," she said, rising up on her knees so her face was level with mine. Of course, since she was still naked, I had no idea what her expression was.

"Get some clothes on or we're going to be late," I said, ignoring what was happening in my pants. "Besides, what with your perpetual nudity, this'll be my lightest load yet."

Britt kissed my nose. "Whatever. You like me nude."

"That has never been in question, angel."

Britt glanced meaningfully below my waist, then she returned to the dresser and located some undergarments. "What time is the appointment again?"

"One." I glanced at my watch; it was just after nine. That meant we had plenty of time to drop off the laundry, grab an early lunch, and fill out the million forms I was sure were waiting for us at the therapist's office.

"How did you snag an appointment so quickly,

anyway?" Britt asked. "Have you seen this doctor before?"

"Never met her in my life," I replied. "However, she is Michael's aunt, and he put in a good word for me. Good to have friends in high places, you know?"

"I sure do."

***

"That wasn't nearly as bad as I thought it would be," I said as Britt and I stepped out into the brisk autumn air. I'd been expecting the therapist to rip out my most terrible memories and leave me a weepy mess. Instead, I felt…better. Lighter, even. Maybe there was something to this therapy business after all.

"Dr. Janvier was nice," Britt said, sliding her arm through mine and cuddling close. "I bet she's Michael's favorite aunt."

"I wouldn't be surprised." That initial session had involved the three of us—me, Britt, and Dr. Janvier—talking about what truth meant to each of us, and whether or not truth can be viewed as something fluid. "What do you think about her idea that the truth can change over time?"

"It's an interesting theory," Britt replied. "I suppose the answer really depends on the truth in question."

"I suppose it does."

My phone rang, so I extricated myself from Britt and fished it out of my pocket. I didn't recognize the number, other than the local area code. "Sam

MacKellar."

"Mr. MacKellar, Detective Salter here," came the gruff voice. "Is Miss Sullivan with you?"

"She is," I replied. "Would you like to speak with her?"

"Actually, I'd like both of you to come down to the station," Detective Salter replied. "We may have the Williams' brothers in custody, and we'd like you two to identify them."

I almost pointed out what a foolish waste of time that would be; being that I'd been Nash's assistant for over a year, and that we'd both met each of the brothers on several occasions, of course we could identify them. Then I recalled that I was speaking with a government official, and that whatever was laid down in the procedures manual would trump any bits of common sense I might bestow.

"We can be there in less than an hour," I said.

Detective Salter grunted and hung up, then I pocketed my phone and turned toward Britt. "What is it?" she asked.

"Seems that you and I are needed at the police station."

***

Britt was silent during the cab ride to the station, and I quickly gave up my attempts at small talk. Once we were inside the station, and Detective Fillion came out to collect us, we were ushered into one of those rooms with a two-way mirror, though the viewing area on the other side was dark and empty.

"I thought we were supposed to be identifying people," Britt said, eyeing the empty room. "Where are the people?"

"They will be brought in shortly," Fillion added. She watched Britt's face for a moment, then she added, "I'm sorry we asked you down here for this. It was Salter's idea."

Britt nodded. "So, what do we do here?"

Fillion indicated that we should sit, so we did. "Listen, Britt, the Williams brothers are claiming that you three had something going on. That you weren't assaulted, and that what was recorded in the studio was just a regular night for you."

"What?" Britt rasped. "There is a video of them drugging me, and me passing out!"

"They don't know we have the videos," Fillion said. "We're trying to get them to admit to as much as possible before we reveal that." Fillion paused. "There's also the fact that you admitted to being a nude model for Ben Williams. That's not helping things."

Britt was so mad her face was bright red. I squeezed her hand, and asked, "What about the other girls? The sisters, and the other girls that were found dead?"

Fillion's eyes hardened. "Those cases, and the rest, are helping convict these bastards. Look, I want these guys gone too, and we have a strong case against them. I was just giving you a head's up."

"Much appreciated," I said. "Now, can we please do what we were called here to do?"

Fillion pursed her lips and nodded; apparently

she'd been looking for some sort of appreciation. Little did she know, Britt and I just wanted to get the hell out of that place. Fillion exited the room and returned a minute or so later with Salter in tow. Before either of them spoke, a line of suspects filed into the room beyond the glass.

When the suspects were lined up against the wall, Salter asked, "Miss Sullivan, can you identify Nash Williams?"

"Number four," she replied without hesitation.

"I assume you can identify your former employer," Salter drawled in my direction.

"You assume correctly," I said.

Salter barked a few orders into an intercom, and the suspects filed out and a new set filed in.

"Mr. MacKellar, can you identify the individual that struck you at Nash Williams's studio last Monday?" Salter demanded.

"Actually, I can't," I replied. "Whoever hit me did it from behind. I didn't even know I was injured until after the EMTs arrived to see to Britt. She had been drugged and was unresponsive, as I'm sure you know, and I was far more interested in her well-being than about whoever might be lurking around behind me." I glanced at Salter, and added, "I believe you have a video recording in your possession that corroborates my statement, and that the recording appears to show Ben Williams as my assailant."

Salter grunted. "Miss Sullivan, did you once model for one of these individuals at a museum?"

"Number two," Britt replied, indicating Ben.

"Do you recall seeing him last Monday?" Salter

pressed.

"No, I don't," she replied. "I don't remember anything after I drank that first cup of coffee. All I know of what happened afterward is what I saw on the video."

Salter grunted again, which was evidently his all-purpose response. "Is it still your intent to press charges?"

"It is my intent to do whatever I can to make sure no one else ends up like Jillene," Britt shot back. "Have you at least learned her last name?"

"Leonas," Fillion replied. "Jillene Margaret Leonas."

Salter glared at Fillion, but didn't reprimand her. I wondered what the penalty was for divulging a murder victim's name. "You can both go," Salter said, careful not to look Britt in the eye again. "We'll be in touch."

I nodded toward the detectives, then I placed my hand against Britt's lower back and guided her out of that room, and out of the station. We stepped out into the early afternoon light for the second time that day, our mood much fouler than before.

"I hate them," Britt growled.

"Do you dislike all of the NYPD, or just Salter?" I asked. "Fillion seems all right."

"They're all in it together." A breeze whipped up and Britt turned her face into the wind, letting it blow her long hair off her face. "I'm sorry, I don't want to be a downer. When do we have to pick up the laundry?"

"We can get it tomorrow," I said as I hailed a cab. "Let's get the car."

"Where are we going?"

"Not sure yet," I replied. "You up for an adventure, baby?"

Like the angel she was, Britt grinned. "Always."

Chapter Twenty-Nine

Britt

Sam and I cabbed it back to his place, but instead of getting the car right away we went up to his apartment. I didn't ask him why until he dragged out a suitcase and started flinging clothes into it.

"I take it this will be an overnight adventure?" I asked.

"Yeah, I think an overnight adventure is in order." Sam held up one blue and one maroon hooded sweatshirt, ultimately packing the maroon one. "After everything that's happened, I think we need to get out of the city."

"Today's the first day we've been out of this apartment in almost a week," I said. "We've hardly been in the city, lately. Maybe we can just go to Central Park or something."

Sam flashed me that grin of his. "Never underestimate the power of getting away from it all, darlin'."

Since resistance was futile, I grabbed the bag Melody had brought over for me along with my clothes and laptop, threw it onto the bed, and set about putting together a few outfits. Speaking of my cousin… "How do you think Melody's doing in my apartment?"

"I'm sure she's getting along just fine," Sam replied. "She just needs some time to sort out her place in the world."

I snorted. "I just hope she stays out of my art supplies. Those paints are expensive."

Sam flashed me that lopsided smile of his. "Now, darlin', don't go stifling her artistic talents," he warned. "Didn't your stepfather try that on you?"

I made a face, then I resumed packing. "I guess she can touch the watercolors."

"That's my girl."

Not twenty minutes later we were in the Beemer, mired in traffic while Sam swore at everything in his path. "This is new," I said, marveling as Sam insulted another driver's mother, intelligence, and weight all with one pithy comment.

"What's new?" he demanded.

"All this fury," I replied. "You're normally so calm and collected."

"This nonsense would drive anyone over the edge," Sam said, gesturing at the traffic. "This is why I don't drive in the city. All these morons have no idea—no idea!—what they're doing." Sam swerved to avoid a bus and ended up cutting off a cab. "It's like all the unlicensed drivers on the planet converged on New York."

"You're cute when you're mad."

That earned me a glare. "I'm glad you find this amusing."

Before I could enlighten Sam as to how very, very amusing I found it, my phone trilled. "Hi, Marlys," I greeted.

"My missing client," she said. "I trust your keeper forwarded my emails to you."

"Keeper? Oh, you mean Sam?" I glanced at Sam, wondering exactly what kind of talk he'd had with Marlys. "Yes, he sent them to me. When we hang up I'll email you about the jobs I'm interested in."

"Good, good, very good. In addition to the ones I sent over, you got a very interesting offer this morning."

"Interesting?" I repeated, wishing there was some way I could put Marlys on speaker without her realizing it so Sam could hear her as well. Based on the way he was yelling at the traffic, Marlys would be on to us in a hot second. "Interesting as in good, or interesting as in psycho killer crazy?"

"Interesting as in hot and sexy." She paused for dramatic effect, and asked, "How would you feel about a shoot featuring you and your Sam?"

"My Sam?" I repeated. "Who's interested in that?"

"Everyone," Marlys replied. "If you two hadn't been hiding under your bed for the past week, you'd realize what celebrities you two have become. All the gossip sites are painting Sam MacKellar as your knight in shining armor, rescuing you not once, but twice from certain harm."

I swallowed; I so did not want to talk about that

with Marlys, now or ever. "Are these offers even legitimate, or just from lame sites like *If The Shoe Fits*?"

"Speaking of *If The Shoe Fits*, they have a few more pictures of the two of you up," Marlys said. "You're in a blue dress, and Sam's in a suit. The two of you are dancing, giving each other those love puppy eyes."

I swore, knowing exactly what picture of Sam and I Marlys was referring to. "Melody," I grumbled.

"Something wrong, baby?" Sam asked.

"Melody sent some pictures of you and I that were taken at her wedding to *If The Shoe Fits*," I replied. "Well, I don't *know* if it was Melody, but she's my top suspect."

"Any shots of your bottom?"

"Sam!"

"Well, that has to be an improvement over the last set of pictures," he observed.

I made a face at Sam, then I asked Marlys, "So, which of these awesome offers for the two of us are the best?"

"Well, *Metro Arts* is offering ten thousand."

"Ten thousand?" I squeaked. "Dollars?"

"No, ten thousand MetroCards," Marlys deadpanned. "If you two agree to do a few nudes, the fee goes to ten thousand each."

Holy crap. Ten thousand each was real money, money I could use to pay my bills ahead for a few months and concentrate on my art. Maybe I could even give some of that money to Melody and get her the hell out of my apartment. I said to Marlys,

"Hang on," then I put my hand over my phone and asked Sam, "Have you ever done any modeling?"

"A bit here and there," Sam replied. "Someone want to shoot us?"

"Yeah, *Metro Arts*."

Sam nodded approvingly. "Good publication."

"Ask him about the nudity," Marlys prompted.

"Sam, we get paid double if we agree to nudes," I said.

"What?" he demanded. "*Both* of us? I can't do that! What if my mother sees those pictures?"

"That's a damn double standard, and you know it," I retorted. "You were fine with taking pictures of *me* naked."

"That was different," he countered. "*You* are a professional."

"Yeah, well, maybe your ass is too cute to keep under wraps." I put Marlys on speaker, and asked, "Marlys, what would they pay if only I was nude?"

"Britannica Lynn, you had better not be planning on modeling nude for anyone but me," Sam warned.

"Or what? You'll show up with a bunch of towels and cover me up?"

"Damn straight you'll be covered."

"I'll leave you two to your lovers' spat," Marlys croaked into the phone. "I'll tell *Metro Arts* yes to the shoot, and that the nudes are up for discussion. Let me know if you want to sell those nudes Sam took of you. I bet we can get a pretty penny for those."

"'Kay. Bye, Marlys."

I ended the call, and looked at Sam. "You're blushing."

"Of course I am," he said. "You just asked me to pose nude. And," he added, giving me the sternest gaze he could while keeping his eyes mostly on the road, "those pictures I took of you are *not* for sale. Those are part of my private collection."

"Private collection, huh? Does that collection include the pictures of Michael's cock?"

Sam grinned. "Consider yourself in good company, darlin'.'"

***

Despite the traffic's best efforts to snare us, we eventually escaped the city. Sam headed north and east, and soon enough we were leaving New York State and entering the wilds of Connecticut.

"So, where are we going?" I asked. "Want to hit up one of the seafood places down by New Haven?"

"Nah, I thought we'd visit your hometown."

My jaw dropped. "Okay, I know you're kidding based on two facts."

"And those facts are?"

"For one thing, I never told you what town I'm from. You have no idea where you're going."

"Massachusetts is a tiny state," he replied. "Once we cross the border the town in question can't be all that far away."

That comment made the New Englander in me bristle. So what if we weren't huge like those Midwestern states? We'd earned our street cred a few centuries ago as an original colony. "Still, it takes about four hours to get there from New York. What are we really going to do there on a Monday night anyway?"

"Get a room and wait for Tuesday?" Sam countered. "C'mon, Britt, be spontaneous with me."

I flopped back against the seat. "It's not the spontaneity I'm worried about so much as the inevitable boredom once we get there."

Sam reached over and squeezed my thigh. "I'm sure any location that can breed the likes of you has plenty of excitement."

"Yeah, well, you haven't seen Northampton on a weeknight," I grumbled.

"Northampton," Sam said triumphantly as he updated his GPS. "See, darlin', it's only three hours from here. We'll be there by dinnertime."

I made a face, though I was madder at myself than Sam. "Trickster."

Sam squeezed my thigh again. "I promise you can torture me in a similar fashion when we go out to Iowa. I'll even let my mother show you my baby pictures."

I slid down in the seat and activated the heat. "You bet I'm having a look at those."

***

It ended up taking us a total of five hours to get to Northampton from the city. Despite the fact that Sam had employed all of his masculine wiles to get me there, I enjoyed being in my hometown again. Mom had married Patrick when I was twelve, and we'd moved to the big house in New Rochelle shortly afterward. For a few years after their marriage Mom and I would make a couple trips back per year, but those had ended once Patrick had my grandparents moved to a retirement community in Larchmont, then Dad went and got a girlfriend. Without her parents to visit, Mom just hadn't found the drive worth her while.

Oh, and she was totally avoiding Dad, but I wasn't supposed to notice that.

As Sam navigated the few downtown streets, filled with unique shops and interesting old architecture, I wondered why anyone would want to leave this quirky little town for stupid old New Rochelle. "That's new," I said as we drove by a tattoo parlor.

"Maybe I'll get me some ink on this trip," Sam mused.

"A tattoo?" I demanded, and he nodded. "A tattoo of what exactly?"

"Oh, I've got a design in mind," he drawled. "A heart with an encyclopedia in it, Cupid's arrow shot through the pages."

"You're kidding."

Sam's gaze slid toward mine. "Am I?" When I only gaped at him, Sam chuckled. "Hey, this place looks nice," he said, indicating a massive brick hotel covered in white pillars and elegant balconies. "Let's stay here tonight."

"That's the most expensive hotel in town," I warned.

Sam shrugged. "I bet their best king size room costs less than a single bed in Manhattan."

Turned out Sam wasn't exactly right, but we did get a nice room with a king size bed and *two* balconies for less than three hundred a night. The room itself was bigger than my apartment, and came with a sitting area filled with tastefully arranged furniture and a kitchenette equipped with marble counters and stainless steel appliances. While Sam investigated the bathroom, I picked up the menus for the hotel's two restaurants.

"What do you want for dinner? Restaurant food or tavern food?" I asked, since the hotel had one of each.

"Neither," Sam replied, plucking the menus from my hand and dropping them on the table. "Let's go for a walk and find us a nice local place."

I couldn't agree more. We grabbed our coats and headed out into the fall night, and wandered past the assorted restaurants and store fronts. Since it was a weeknight most places had closed early, but before long we found an Irish pub that kept the kitchen open till eleven.

"This is surreal," I said as we slid into our booth. "This place used to be a video store. You know, back when you had to leave home to rent movies."

"Times change," Sam observed, then the waitress appeared for our drink order. After she'd taken them, Sam reached across the table and took my hands. "I haven't told you the story about Gran's bracelet yet," he said.

"Oh, you mean you're not supposed to put it on your one true love?" I teased.

"You gonna let me tell it, or what?" he countered. I nodded, and Sam continued, "By all accounts, my gran was quite a looker when she was younger. All the boys were courting her, including the son of the local railway owner, the richest man in town."

"Sounds like a nice life," I said.

"I'm sure it was. While Gran never admitted to having chosen one of her suitors, apparently she'd been leaning toward the railway owner's son. Then, he gave her that bracelet, which was worth a small fortune at the time. Everyone figured the deal was done, and that they'd marry come spring."

"I take it that's not what happened."

Sam smiled, then he brought my hand to his mouth and kissed my knuckles. "Not by a long shot. One day, Gran went to the ice cream parlor and saw that there was a new guy behind the counter. He made her a milkshake, and then another, and the two of them talked until closing time. Gran said she'd never before met someone she felt so comfortable with, someone who had the same likes and dislikes as her. That was my grandpa, and they were married inside of a year."

"Aww," I said, since that story was certainly aww-worthy. "I thought your grandfather worked in the stock market."

"He did, but not when he was seventeen," Sam replied.

"I guess that would have been weird," I murmured. "But why did she keep the bracelet? And why did she pass it on to you?"

"I don't rightly know why she kept it," Sam admitted. "Maybe because it was a gift? But I can tell you this: when she passed it on to me, it was accompanied by a few sage words of advice. She said, 'Sammy, you go out and live your life, but know that someday someone is going to waltz into your world and turn it upside down. You won't be able to stop thinking about them, or imagine your life without them. That is the person you're meant to be with. When you meet them, hold on tight and never let them go.'"

The waitress appeared with our beers, so Sam released my hands and we ordered dinner. Once that was done, Sam raised his glass to me. "Britannica Lynn, you've driven me crazy since the first moment I saw you. I can't get you out of my mind, nor do I ever want to. Live your crazy life with me?"

We clinked glasses, and drank. "I'm crazy about you too, Sam MacKellar. Let's do it."

Sam put down his beer and took my hand. "Really, baby? You'll marry me?"

My jaw dropped. "I-I hadn't realized that was what you were asking," I whispered. "Are you sure?"

"More sure than I've ever been," he replied, kissing my knuckles again. "I'm dead serious, Britt. I can't imagine my life without you in it."

I stared at Sam, shocked and speechless and maybe a little bit elated; okay, make that really elated. We'd known each other for such a short time that him proposing already was almost laughable, and certainly not the responsible thing to do. Wasn't the world already full of people who'd gotten married too quickly, and for the wrong reasons? I didn't want to be one of those people.

But I loved Sam, of that I was certain. And since I'd already promised him forever, I guessed making it official was the logical next step. That didn't mean I couldn't play with him a bit.

"Tell me you love me," I said.

"I love you, angel," he replied. "I love you so much I fear my heart might burst."

"Will you take care of me?"

"Always. Forever."

I smiled. "I like these answers."

"That a yes, baby?"

Instead of answering, I shoved our beers aside and climbed up onto the table, wrapping my arms around Sam as I kissed him hard. "It's a yes," I said against his lips. "I love you too, cowboy."

We were still kissing when the waitress appeared with our food, clearing her throat and scowling. "Forgive us," Sam said as I slid back to my seat. "Britt here just agreed to marry me, and we got a little carried away."

The waitress's scowl instantly became a grin. "Ray, get me two glasses of champagne," she called over her shoulder. "Looks like we're gonna have a wedding."

Chapter Thirty

Britt

"Tell me, darlin', does your daddy still live nearby?"

"Yeah, he's a town over. Why?"

Sam and I were nestled in the hotel room's ginormous bed, lazing away the morning. He'd already called the front desk and extended our stay to Wednesday, and advised the wash and fold that we wouldn't be picking up our laundry for a few more days. Yeah, my man was sexy and organized.

"I was thinking we should pay him a visit." Sam propped himself up on his elbow and looked down at me, gliding his fingers along the side of my neck. "After all, I do need to ask his permission to marry you."

I laughed, burying my face in Sam's shoulder. "I don't think people do that anymore," I said. I sure couldn't imagine Patrick asking my grandfather if he could marry my mom. Then again, Grandpa was an excellent judge of character. He probably would have said no.

"What's wrong with being old fashioned?" Sam asked. "Besides, I can't rightly call you my fiancée before I've met your father."

"What about your parents?" I asked. "I still need to meet your father. And your mother, in real life."

"Sioux City will be our next stop," he said. "Promise."

"So, we're not engaged until then?" I pouted. "Maybe I don't want to wait that long."

"Careful, darlin', you'll give me ideas," Sam said with his lopsided grin.

"Ideas?" I pushed him onto his back and climbed onto his chest. "What sort of ideas?"

"Well, we did drive by the town hall," Sam said. "I believe that's where they issue marriage licenses."

"Sam, we can't get married today," I said. "I mean, it's a Tuesday!"

Sam chuckled. "I'll make a mental note, no Tuesday weddings. Besides, Massachusetts has a three day waiting period after the license is issued." When I raised an eyebrow, he explained, "I may have Googled it while you were sleeping."

"Three days, huh?" I laid my cheek over Sam's heart and laced my fingers with his. "So, Friday then?"

Sam kissed my hair. "If you want Friday, angel, then Friday it is."

A small thrill went down my spine; we were really doing this. "Won't we be back in New York by Friday?"

"New York's waiting period is twenty-four

hours," he said. I guess he'd done quite a bit of Googling.

"What about your parents?" I pressed. "Will they be able to come out?"

"What if," Sam began, rolling so I was beneath him, "we get married, and then have a party later on? I'm sure Stepdaddy will want something large and extravagant."

"Do we have to invite him?" I whined.

"Not specifically, but who do you think your mother will invite as her guest?"

"Good point." I pulled Sam in for a kiss that quickly became something more.

"Love you, baby," he murmured, nudging my thighs apart with his knee.

"Love you more."

"Nope."

"I'll prove it."

Sam grinned. "Well, all right."

Afterward, we were snuggled close, and I tugged at the dark hair near Sam's navel. "I don't want to get married on Friday."

Sam tensed against me; I debated teasing him a bit, but that would have been mean. "I want Jorge to make me a dress, and I don't think even he can finish a wedding dress by Friday."

Sam relaxed, and kissed my forehead. "Anything you want, angel. Anything at all."

***

After showering and scarfing down our room service breakfast, we hopped in the Beemer and headed north. About half an hour later we pulled into the parking lot next to Rocket Comics.

"I thought we were going to your father's house," Sam said.

"We are at my father's house." I gestured toward the sprawling Victorian mansion. "The first floor is the store, and the living areas are the upper floors." We got out of the car and entered the shop, the little bell tinkling above the door.

"Your father lives above a comic shop?" Sam asked.

"No, he owns the shop, and the rest of the place." I looked at the shelves of graphic novels and racks of comics, feeling like I'd come home in more ways than one. "Dad? You around?"

"Wait, I thought your father was some kind of an athlete?" Sam asked. "Wasn't he trying for a baseball scholarship and all?"

"Athletes can't be well read?"

I turned around and saw my father exiting the storeroom. "Daddy," I said as he hugged me so tight my feet left the floor. "I hope you don't mind us just dropping in?"

"Mind a visit from my pumpkin? Never." Dad set me down, and asked, "What brings you out to see your old man? Looking for rare Silver Age graphic novels?"

"Always," I grinned. I grabbed Sam's hand, and said, "Dad, this is Sam MacKellar."

"The one from the text messages?" Dad asked.

"The very same," I affirmed.

Dad smiled, and extended his arm. "Good to meet you, Sam," Dad said, shaking Sam's hand.

"Likewise," Sam said. "I must say, Britt is the spitting image of you."

"She sure is," Dad said, rumpling my hair. "All my girls are O'Rourkes, through and through. Come on up, pumpkin, your sisters are just up from their nap."

Dad locked the shop door and flipped the sign to closed, then he beckoned us back through the storeroom. "Is Emily home?" I asked.

"No, but Grandma is," Dad said with a glance over his shoulder.

"Grandma? No way!"

I ran past Dad and up the creaky old steps toward the kitchen; no matter if it was her house or someone else's my grandmother always took command of the kitchen. I burst through the door and found her pouring juice while my sisters toddled around her legs.

"Britt, honey," Grandma said as we hugged, "it's been too long."

"I know," I said. "Grandma, I brought home a boy."

"Did you? Tell me all about him."

***

An hour later found my grandmother, sisters, and I hanging out in the living room, having cookies and juice while my father gave Sam a tour of his shop. I had told Grandma everything about Sam, from how we met to his horrible traumas, to how he promised me nothing but honesty. Grandma's eyes hardened when I told her about Sam's lies, only to soften again when I relayed how he'd rescued me.

"Good Lord, without Sam I might have lost my grand baby," Grandma said, her eyes shining as she clutched my hands. "That man has earned my undying gratitude."

"Mine, too." I looked at Penelope and Veronica, who were busily arranging plastic blocks on the floor. "Grandma, he asked me to marry him."

"I hope you said yes," Grandma said. "Men like him don't come along often."

"I did, Grandma," I said. "Didn't even hesitate."

***

Sam and I spent the rest of the day at Dad's house, my sisters climbing all over Sam while Grandma whipped up the equivalent of a full Sunday dinner. After stuffing our faces with pot roast, mashed potatoes, and caramel cake—okay, the twins just had cake—Dad cleared his throat and made an important announcement.

"So, Sam here asked me for permission to marry Britt," Dad said. "Pumpkin, I want you to know I gave him my blessing…and I have a little gift to help you two out."

Dad placed a little velvet box on the table, and I felt my heart plummet to the floor. Even though I knew what was inside, I reached out and opened it, my hands shaking the entire time. It was a platinum ring, the center stone a three-carat amethyst that was surrounded by no less than fifteen brilliant diamonds. I was certain of these details because I'd been with Dad when he bought it.

"Dad, this is the ring you bought for Mom," I protested, shoving the box away. "We couldn't."

"Why not?" Dad countered. "It will look a lot better sitting on your finger than gathering dust in my sock drawer."

"Why don't you give it to Emily?" I asked.

Dad made a face. "That won't be happening." Well, thank God for that. One unlikable stepparent was more than enough. Dad reached across the table and took my hands. "Listen, pumpkin, I get the impression that Sam here loves you a great deal, easily as much as I loved your mother. If that's the case, I can think of no better recipient of this ring than you."

My eyes welled up, and I smiled. "Well, okay."

Chapter Thirty-One

Sam

Britt and I were at JFK, boarding passes in hand as we waited for our flight to be called. After a transfer in Chicago we'd be in Sioux City, and I would finally get to introduce my parents to the woman I was about to marry. I hoped Britt would get along with my father as well as I'd gotten on with hers.

Speaking of her father…"You really don't think your daddy will be mad when he sees you wearing a different ring?" I asked.

"That ring belongs on my mother, no one else," Britt replied. "Besides, this one is perfect."

Britt spread her fingers and admired her engagement ring, and I admired it with her. While I'd appreciated her father's gesture I just couldn't bear the thought of someone else's ring on my angel's finger, so I cashed in some stock and bought her one on my own. After weeks of surreptitiously hitting up jewelry stores across Manhattan, I settled on a piece of estate jewelry. It was a four carat emerald in an Art Deco setting, with diamond baguettes framing the green stone. And yeah, it happened to match my gran's bracelet to a tee.

"I'm so glad you like it, angel."

Britt smiled. "I don't like it. I love it."

A voice came over the loudspeaker, announcing that our plane was ready to board. "Come on, angel," I said as I hefted our carryon bags. "It's our turn to fly."

"Let's do it," she said, grabbing my hand. "I can't wait to meet your parents."

"The future is ours, angel," I said as we queued up. "And as long as I'm with you, I know my life will be perfect."

Britt stood on her toes and kissed my cheek. "I love you too."

******The End******

Acknowledgements

Those of you that have read my other work might be a bit confused right now. I mean, this is a straight up romance with no elves or swords in sight; heck, there aren't even any zombies. However, if there's one thing any writer will tell you it's that you have to write for the characters screaming the loudest.

In the case of *Changing Teams*, that was Sam. He originally appeared as a bit character in a horror short; even then he was a Midwestern photographer. Sam kept talking long after that piece was done, so I sat down for NaNoWriMo and told his story, beginning to end. I ended up finishing the first draft of *Changing Teams*—which clocked in at sixty-six thousand words—in nineteen days.

Not only was Sam talkative, he was demanding.

Then I, a fantasy and horror writer, had this contemporary romance on my hands and no idea what to do with it. Enter the Three Beta Readers Of Awesome: Cindy Thomas, Kelly Hager, and April Wood. Seriously guys, without you three this story would not be a tenth of what it is now. Thank you.

But they weren't my only helpers. Trisha Wooldridge and Jennifer Carson are two amazing authors, and I'm lucky enough to call them friends. Without them I probably would have jumped off a bridge years ago. Neither Trisha nor Jenn ever let me give up, and they always pushed me to be the best writer possible.

Last but not least I need to thank the Wonder

Twins, Ember and Robby, and my husband Robb for putting up with me writing yet another book, and all the revisions and deadlines and lack of Mom that came with it. Without you guys I really would be lost. Love you!

About the Author

Jennifer Allis Provost is a native New Englander who lives in a sprawling colonial along with her beautiful and precocious twins, a dog that thinks she's a kangaroo, a parrot, a junkyard cat, and a wonderful husband who never forgets to buy ice cream. As a child, she read anything and everything she could get her hands on, including a set of encyclopedias, but fantasy was always her favorite. She spends her days drinking vast amounts of coffee, arguing with her computer, and avoiding any and all domestic behavior.

Facebook:
http://www.facebook.com/jennallishttps://www.facebook.com/copperraven

Twitter:
https://twitter.com/parthalan

Website:
http://authorjenniferallisprovost.com/

Goodreads:
https://www.goodreads.com/author/show/2975887.Jennifer_Allis_Provost